# the Devil's PAWN

CAVALERI BROTHERS #2

## LILIAN HARRIS

Editor/Interior Formatting: CPR Editing

Proofreader: Judy's Proofreading

Cover Design: Covers by Jules

Love can tame even the wildest of
hearts.

# One

# RAQUEL

I wonder if there's an alternate version of ourselves somewhere. Like a mirror reality, but better.

If there is, I'll be the first in line to go. Just drop me in there, no questions asked, because I'll bet it's better than my life on this side of the world.

I've always been a good daughter. There was never a time when I disrespected my parents or caused them grief of any kind. I was obedient and responsible at all times. I got good grades and went to medical school. I made them proud, or at least I hope I did. You'd think they'd give me an ounce of respect back, but they haven't.

I may be twenty-eight, but to them, I'm still a child. Someone whose life they can control. They're always ignoring my input, especially about the man I should marry.

When I thought of marriage as a young girl, I imagined falling in love with an amazing guy. Someone I'd chosen. Instead, they chose for me. And he couldn't be any worse.

Carlito, the man they threw at me, is not someone I'd ever want to end up with. He's vile. Angry. Constantly groping me in private when I ask him to stop. Telling me how much he can't wait to do whatever he wants to me.

No one would stop him, either.

In our circle, women have no voice and men have all the power. Even my own mother expects me to be a dutiful wife and listen to my husband. It's sick, really.

He can hit me or cheat on me, and no one will care. No one will help me.

I'll be alone. Forever.

I can't live that kind of life.

I won't.

Being a Bianchi has its advantages, like money, but no amount of money will get me to settle for a life I want no part of. Growing up, we didn't struggle. I've always lived in a large, expensive home, and I attended a great school and an even better university. But I'd give it all back if I didn't have to be forced to marry.

My father, Salvatore, is a powerful man. He's been a consigliere, the advisor to the don of the Palermo crime family, for as long as I can remember. All the money comes from whatever illegal operations they're a part of. I've done what I can to keep my eyes closed when it came to that side of my dad.

My uncle Faro Bianchi, the don, is as ruthless as they come. He treats my cousin Chiara like absolute shit. She and I are really close. We were born a few weeks apart and are more like sisters than cousins.

I guess I'm lucky that my parents *do* love me. They just have a crappy way of showing it, especially my mother. She's always been tougher than my father. I've tried to make them both understand that I don't want Carlito, and I don't want the kind of life they want for me, but it's as though I'm talking to a wall. They think they know what's best, and Carlito is it.

He's a soldier in the Palermo family, someone they believe will give me the type of life they think I should have. His family comes from old money, and for my mom especially, that's what matters.

Chiara has tried to help me with Carlito by talking to my parents and even her piece-of-shit father, but it hasn't helped.

I'm doomed.

Lately, I've considered dying. The very thought makes me sick, but what else can I do? I spend most nights crying myself to sleep, knowing it's either true death or a lifetime of living death.

I'd rather have the former.

Carlito will ensure that every day I take a breath, I'll regret ever doing it. That's no way to live.

The mere thought of him makes me sick. He's fourteen years older than me, which isn't a deal breaker, but he's just not a good man.

My friends from work have seen him out at clubs making out with random women, touching them, leaving with them. It's humiliating to hear their stories and not know what to say in return. I wish they'd never found out about him, but he loves stopping by my job and making sure every man there knows I'm his.

How do I tell my coworkers that my parents are making me marry him? They probably wouldn't understand how a grown woman can't just say no.

My wedding is supposed to be in six months. I have some time to figure out my options before I pay the ultimate price for my family's intrusion. There's no way I'll allow my parents to ruin my life this way.

There has to be something I can do. Some option I'm not seeing yet.

"We're almost home," Mom says as we drive back home well past midnight, with Carlito at the wheel.

His cousin got married and we were invited, to my absolute displeasure. I had to act like the devoted fiancée all damn night while everyone came up to us, telling me how much they can't wait to attend our wedding. Carlito was practically glued to me the entire night.

If only there was someone to help me run far away from here. I'd leave it all behind—my family, my job, everything—for a chance to escape.

Once the car stops in front of the house, I immediately get out from the passenger side, hoping to finally be away from my future husband. I wait for my mother to join me, but she doesn't.

"Come in for a cup of coffee, Carlito," she says from the back, opening the door.

My eyes widen.

*What the hell is she doing? It's late!*

"You sure?" he asks, grinning like a fool.

"Yeah." She waves a hand. "Come on. I'm not even tired."

"Okay."

Mom shuts the door, allowing him to park in the driveway. I can't believe she's entertaining him at this insane hour. My father would've been at the wedding too, except he's currently at war with someone. He's been in hiding with my uncles for over a week now. I don't ask many questions. I don't want to know any of it. The further I am from that, the better.

Chiara and I both want nothing to do with this lifestyle. She swears she's going to stay single forever, or at least until she can meet someone who can defend her against her father.

Who'd be willing to do that?

My other uncles, Benvolio and Agnelo, are the underbosses in the family, in that order. I do have another cousin, Aida, who's Agnelo's daughter, but we aren't close, though we could be if she was allowed to do anything. Chiara thinks something bad is going on with her, that Uncle Agnelo has her scared. I wouldn't put it past him. He's got a frightening way about him, like the devil is constantly on his shoulder, leading him into hell.

Once the car is parked, Carlito gets out.

"What a beautiful wedding that was, wasn't it, Raquel?" My mom's voice goes all chirpy. "I bet it made you want to have your day too, right?"

"Right," I grumble in response, waiting a few feet ahead.

I'm not sure what she's trying to pull, bringing this up when she knows my feelings. But I guess I shouldn't be surprised, since she doesn't hide her extreme desire to see me marry this horror of a man.

Begrudgingly, I follow Mom and Carlito into our house.

"I'll be right back," I tell them while I head for the stairs. "I need to go change."

"Okay," Mom replies, slipping out of her shoes, leaving them in the foyer closet, and then going to the kitchen.

"Wait." Carlito's tone crawls with a roaring whisper as he grabs my upper arm, his fingers viciously piercing into me and making my skin burn.

Glaring, I whirl around with pursed lips. "Yes?"

"What's with the fucking attitude?" he chides with the odor of his liquor bathing my lips, twining with his nasty breath.

I internally hurl in disgust.

"Got something to say?" he throws out.

*I have a lot to say, but I'm also not stupid.*

"I'm tired. It's almost three a.m."

He clenches my arm tighter, his drunken expression turning hostile and his nostrils flaring. "Who was that guy you were talking to at the wedding?"

"No one." My lips contort with a grimace from the pain he's causing. "He's a doctor. A friend of the groom's. He found out I'm doing my residency and was asking how I liked it."

"Remember whose ring you're wearing. You don't fucking talk to other men. You hear me?" he barks in a whisper as he lowers his face to mine, the tequila on his breath slithering into my mouth. "If you tarnish my name by acting like a whore, I'll make you pay for it. You understand?"

My heart beats like a hammering drum.

"I'll ruin your fucking name so badly, no one will wanna marry you," he snarls.

"Maybe that wouldn't be a bad thing," I shoot back, grinding my teeth until they rattle as I stare into his dirt-colored eyes.

His upper lip twitches before he thrusts a fist into the air.

I draw in a quick, shallow gasp, my eyes popping wide as his knuckles near my jaw and press into me.

"I can't wait," he threatens with that soulless expression beating into mine.

I know what he means. He can't wait to hurt me.

He relieves some of the pressure on my arm from his continued grip, and I take that second to pull away. I rush upstairs without looking back, my chest heaving. Shutting the door behind me, I lean against it, my eyelids drifting to a close as the tears fall, slow at first, then rushing out like a colossal storm. I sob soundlessly into my palms, my entire body breaking and trembling in the wake of my tortured pain.

Crying is all I have. I'll always suffer in silence.

Fingering the ring he once gave me, I pull it off, leaving it beside my feet. There was no real engagement. Our parents met in our dining room, with us present, and Carlito handed me a ring like a collar for a shackled animal.

After a few moments, I hear my mother and Carlito talking. Prying the door open a little, I listen in, wanting to know if they'll talk about me. At first they don't, but then I hear the conversation switch to the wedding.

"So, I was thinking we can move the date up a little. Maybe by three months?" Mom's voice climbs up, going all sugary. "I spoke to your mother and made all the arrangements, and she's fine with it. I know how much you're looking forward to marrying my daughter."

The blood drains from my face, and my eyes go round, a cold shudder running up my arms.

*No. She can't do this to me.*

"That's fine by me. The sooner, the better," Carlito agrees fiercely. "I need a good woman in my life."

"I know you do, and my daughter is a perfect match for you." I hear the smile in my mother's voice.

The cell phone in my hand vibrates and I find Chiara's name on the screen. I quickly answer, telling her everything that's happening, and that I can't live this life anymore and I'd rather die.

She thinks there's something we can do, but we both know that's a lie. It's over.

"I'm glad we're on the same page," Mom continues. "My girl isn't getting any younger, you know. She has to start having children, which I'm sure you want too."

"I definitely do. A lot of them," he chuckles.

I hurl; the whimpers coming out of me sound like they belong to my ghost.

Chiara remains quiet, and I don't blame her. What can she say that she hasn't already?

"We should give my daughter the good news," Mom adds. "Where in the world is she, for God's sake? Raquel?!" Her shouting whips across my skin. "Come down already."

*Oh, no. I can't face them. I have to get out of here. I need to find a way out of this house before she finds me.*

"I have to go," I tell Chiara before hanging up. "I think she's coming to my room."

Rising from the floor, I slip into a pair of sneakers from the closet, still in my black cocktail dress and coat, then grab the handbag I dropped beside the door.

My mom will kill me for this, and Carlito will be more than enraged that his soon-to-be wife is running around in the middle of the night in a slinky dress, but I don't care about the consequences. I just know I can't be here. I'll break down in front of both of them once they mention the wedding, and that will make Carlito mad. The last thing I want is for him to get angrier at me.

Deciding to take the back way out of the house in hopes of leaving before my mom gets up here, I tiptoe down the stairs, knowing she won't see me from where they are. All I have to do is get downstairs and dart right around to the back door, then run outside. I can call an Uber once I'm far enough away.

A chair scrapes across the floor just as I hit the last step. My heart pounds in my ears as I dash the last few steps toward the door and turn the knob.

"Raquel?" Mom calls. "Is that you?"

Her footsteps trudge over the carpet, getting closer. My anxiety clutches its furious grip around my throat, squeezing as I gently pull the door open and close it behind me.

Then I run like hell.

# Two

# RAQUEL

There's a bar I go to, miles from home. It's my secret hideaway. No one knows about it, and I'm especially grateful for that right now.

I can't believe I got away. I heard the door open as I kept running. I heard my mother screaming for me to come back, but I only ran faster. Once I was a safe distance away, I called for a car.

I don't even know why I ran. I know I'll be coming back soon with my tail between my legs. But there was no way I could've plastered a smile on my face as she told me the wonderful news of my wedding.

Carlito knows quite well how much I despise him, and it only makes him want to marry me more. He enjoys torturing me. I know he would have enjoyed it if I'd cried when they told me about the push of the wedding date.

I sip on a Cherry Coke, foregoing the alcohol since I already had some at the wedding. My cell has been ringing nonstop with my mother's name flashing on the screen.

"Ugh!" I snap, smacking the phone facedown on top of the bar.

But she doesn't stop calling. She never will. With a loud, exaggerated grumble, I decide to answer.

"What do you want?" I practically bark.

"Where the hell are you! What do you think you're doing, young lady?!" she shrieks.

I can picture her blonde highlights swaying haphazardly as she walks around the house like she always does when she's upset.

"Carlito is out searching for you! Do you know that? This is humiliating! Do you even *know* how your behavior is reflecting on this family? Don't you get how this makes me look? How could you humiliate me like this?!"

"Humiliating?" I whisper-shout, bitterness crawling from my tone. "*You're* humiliated? What about me?! I can't even choose the man I want to marry! You and Dad chose that horrible piece of shit for me. Someone who treats me like crap, manhandles me like I'm his possession, and cheats on me around town. That's all you think I'm worth?"

"Carlito is a perfect match." Her agitation comes clearly through the line. "He comes from a great family with—"

"With money?" My pulse spikes in my neck. "That's all it'll ever be with you." Angry tears streak down my face. "I don't even matter, do I?"

"Why do you think we're doing this? For *you*!" Venom drips from every syllable. "He can provide you a good life and a proper family. You foolish, ungrateful child! What else could you want, huh?!"

"What about love?" I scream a little too loud, causing a few older men around the bar to glance at me.

"Love?" She laughs. "Oh, God. You really are a fool. Love is for losers, darling. People who think they can fall in love and have it all are only lying to themselves. Life isn't a fairy tale, Raquel. Time to grow up." She exhales sharply. "I have given you *everything* you could ever want, and all I ask in return is your obedience. I will *not* tolerate this behavior. Your father *will* be hearing about this, and he'll be just as disappointed."

Something clatters in the background, like she's knocked into something.

"You *will* stop your immature nonsense and come home right now!"

"I'll come back when I damn well please!"

"Raquel, I swea—"

I end the call, my breath lashing out of me and my heart squeezing in my rib cage. My hands tremble as the phone falls out of my grasp and rattles beside my glass.

I've never spoken to my mother that way. Not once. But the rage inside me is too great to contain. I can't take it anymore. I can't stand them thinking they can control my every move.

Covering my face with my palms, I take deep breaths. I hate this. I'll never find a way out of this soon-to-be marriage. Not unless I forge my own road. One that ends with my demise.

"Sounds like you need a *real* drink," says a deep, seductive voice.

I let my hands gradually drift from my face, simultaneously wiping the tears away.

A handsome, tattooed stranger greets me, the corner of his mouth tipping up into a flirty smile.

*Where the hell did he come from? And how did I not notice him before? He's not the type of man a woman can ignore.*

Thick brows frame large, round eyes, the color of rich mahogany—strong, yet comforting. His hair is combed back, but a whisp of it falls slightly past his forehead, the rest of it full and tempting at the top and buzzed at the sides.

My eyes fall to his right arm, which is filled with tattoos. There are elaborate black vines and black roses filling the top of his hand and knuckle. A skull hides beneath the flowers on his forearm, and the sharp vines continue up his arm like tiny teeth.

He screams masculinity and hard edges, but the softness in his smile and those eyes is what draws me in.

He's as intricate as his tattoos—a complication I shouldn't find attractive, yet I do. One thing I've come to enjoy while working as a resident in a hospital is reading people, and his story already smells like trouble.

"I probably could use a strong one," I snicker in response, no joy left in my voice. "But it's also crazy late and I need to eventually get home in one piece, even though I wish I didn't have to."

He doesn't say anything. He just assesses me with his sultry gaze, his fist resting under the dark brown stubble that rides up his angular jaw.

He's dangerously beautiful. That's the only way to describe a man like that. The kind of man who looks both sinful and sensual. The kind who holds both danger and temptation in the spark of his gaze.

The hint of his floral tattoo covers the skin of his neck, the rest hiding beneath his gray t-shirt that I'd very much like to remove just to see what's beneath.

That's a reckless thought.

What does it matter how attractive he is? I'll either be dead or married soon. On any other day, I'd enjoy the attention from a man like that, but not today.

Not anymore.

Not ever.

My life is over.

And soon it will be for good.

A realization hits me: I have no intention of going home. I'll find a way to die today. It's the only way I'll ever truly live.

He lifts his glass of honey-colored liquid and brings it to his mouth, his eyes still on mine. "Don't worry, sweetheart. I can drink for the both of us."

He takes the liquor and downs it in one sip, drinking me in with his eyes at the same time. I can't stop myself from watching the bob of his Adam's apple as he swallows.

Placing the glass back down, he lifts a finger to call for the bartender, but his darkened gaze is still on me, assessing me so ferociously, it's as though he knows me.

But that's nonsense. We've never met before.

I have the sudden urge to hide, like he can see me. All of me.

And I don't mean my skin. I mean my heart. My soul. All the pain I hide there.

I'm immersed in it. Suffocating.

The power of his intense gaze is practically ripping away the fabricated layers of my life, leaving nothing but bare bones that rot with my every breath.

"You must have a good story to be here dressed like that," he adds, his stare cascading over my body, lingering on the thin shoulder straps of my tight black dress.

His jaw tenses. My body flushes from the perusing way his eyes ride down my curves, like he's already picturing me without my clothes on.

"Long story." I clear my throat as my eyes dart from the hollows of his cheeks to the rippling, brawny muscles of his chest and arms that are practically exploding from under his tanned skin.

The smirk on his face bends over his full lips once I find his eyes, and I realize he's caught me gawking. Color rushes to my cheeks, and I instantly turn to the bar, my entire body all warm and flushed.

His chair drags across the floor, pulling closer until the side of his knee touches mine. His breath cruises over my neck.

Hot.

Heavy.

Tempting.

All of him is.

It's clutching my body in an erotic undercurrent. One I've never felt this strongly before. I'm afraid to turn, to glance at him.

*Why am I so turned on by a stranger? This is crazy.*

I know it's been a while since I've been with someone, and this man is beautiful, but this alluring, electric energy pulling me in needs to stop.

"I'm not against you objectifying me." His voice caresses over my skin, his words gliding lower, filling the emptiness with rousing need. "Please continue. I'm rather enjoying it. It's been a while since I enjoyed something this much."

My heart rate kicks up a notch—okay, a bunch of notches—mingling with the ball of knots meeting my insides.

I should be afraid, sitting here with this man who clearly wants me and could probably hurt me. But does it matter if he does? What do I have to lose? I have nothing to live for anymore.

"I—I wasn't looking," I lie as I risk a glance, an exhale dropping harshly from my lips.

The smile dancing on his mouth and the glint in his eyes tell me he knows I'm lying. His gaze flickers past my face and down my body, making me squirm. He looks at me as though he wants to taste me, like the liquor still on his breath. The eroticism slinking in those copper hues should drive me away, but it only pulls me deeper, like quicksand.

I want to be desired. Hungered for.

I crave it. I've never felt this level of lust before.

Maybe this is my chance to be someone different. I'm not the Raquel I was yesterday. Today, I can be someone else.

The old Raquel had a chance to live.

The new one doesn't.

I can finally be carefree with a man and not give a crap. What do I have to lose? He might be just what I need to help me forget the awfulness of my existence, even if just for a few hours.

He focuses on me, and my body instantly comes alive, begging me to surrender to the temptation. He's an angel in a devil's body, and deep down, I want to know how it'd feel to be corrupted by the likes of him.

Chiara has hooked up with strangers before, but I've always been the relationship type. I need the emotional connection before I dive into someone's bed. But why should I let that stop me now? I might not be alive tomorrow.

I wasn't lying when I told Chiara I wanted to die. That's the only choice I have. The only choice my family left me with.

"So, what was that all about on the phone?" he asks, angling back a bit, yet still uncomfortably close.

"Aren't you nosy?" I pop a brow as some of the stress leaves my shoulders.

"You were practically giving the whole bar your life story, baby girl."

He gives me a crooked grin, roughing his fingers through his voluminous strands, and I instantly shudder at the sentiment, at the way those large hands move.

"If you wanted to keep things a secret…" He leans into my ear, his lips a drop away. "You probably should've used your inside voice."

My body breaks with heat and goose bumps from the soft seduction flickering in his tone. I'm not sure if there was sexual innuendo hidden in those words, but it sure felt that way.

I grow even more conscious of his proximity, and each time he talks, it sounds like he's reading a dirty poem.

"Yeah, well, rough day," I mutter, trying to hide behind this intense attraction as he pulls back.

"I'm sorry." His flirting is now gone, replaced with a wave of concern.

"Me too," I sigh, remembering the events of tonight all over again while my lungs squeeze with every breath I try to inhale. "You know, maybe I will have that drink, after all."

I call for the bartender, raising a finger to get his attention, but as I do, the stranger's hand falls to my forearm, and my skin instantly tingles. His touch is rugged and rough, everything a man's touch should be.

I turn to find his steely gaze locked on mine, and it's like I'm being held in place. I'm captivated by those eyes, smooth and comforting, like a mug of warm cocoa on a winter day. What I wouldn't do to wrap my hands around him.

"I'd love to get you that drink." His voice drifts low as his eyes dart to my lips before capturing mine again.

"Yeah. Uh, okay." My fingertips flutter over my neck. "Margarita, please. No salt."

He nods, reluctantly drawing back, his hand now raised as he orders for me. Not even a minute later, I'm sipping on my drink, my mind completely forgetting that this bar is going to close in under an hour and I'll have to face the music of my untimely death.

I don't even know how I'll do it. Maybe I can drink myself to oblivion and then hop in front of oncoming traffic.

No. Too messy.

I could probably hire a hit man to take me out. I do have my credit cards on hand. Much easier than doing it myself. But who could I find that quickly? Probably no one.

"Do you come here a lot?" His question pulls me from my dreadful plans.

"Sometimes. You?"

"Same. But there aren't always beautiful women here who can't help but stare at me every chance they get." He tightens his lips, trying to contain that amused grin.

"I really wasn't staring." I roll my eyes, doing a crappy job at playing it off. "I was simply admiring your, um…shirt? What is that, cotton?"

He chuckles all deep and gravelly, that roguish smirk deepening. *Holy hotness.*

"Wanna feel it?" He yanks the fabric on his chest, that inviting smile of his pulling me to do the same.

"Uh, no." I shake my head with too much force as my heart thuds louder and louder. "Maybe next time."

"Think now is your only chance, sweetheart. By the sound of it, you're about to get married."

I rake a hand through my hair, my eyes landing on the bar. "If I had any say, I wouldn't be."

"Hey."

His palm is once again on my arm, and I quite like it there. I turn to him, finding a frown gripping his features.

"You don't have to do something you don't want to do."

"I wish it was that easy." My brows knit tightly.

Lifting up my drink, I finish it in one sip, then call for the bartender to order another.

"Are you sure you want to do that?" the man asks, moving his hand away.

I realize I still don't know his damn name.

"Great," I grumble flatly. "Now a complete stranger is telling me what the hell to do."

"I didn't mean it that way." Leaning sideways, he rests his right elbow on the bar and the other hand on his bouncing thigh. "I want you to be safe getting home."

"I'll be fine, uh…" My face twists with a scowl. "What's your name?"

"Dante."

"I'll be fine, *Dante*. Thanks for your concern."

"Aren't you going to give me your name?" He picks up his drink, looking questioningly at me.

"Raquel."

"Well, Raquel, I didn't mean to offend you."

"It's fine. Story of my life." I shrug nonchalantly, palming my hands together and then relaxing them on the bar as I stare ahead.

I don't even know why I'm talking to him. I know I won't sleep with him, no matter how much I wanted to convince myself I would earlier. It was nice pretending. And it's not as though we can be friends. I'll be dead.

Or if I'm not, Carlito will kill me.

Dante orders another drink for me before his hand slides to my shoulder, his index finger casually slipping under the strap of my dress.

Tingles break over my skin, coating me in electrifying heat and making my nipples pebble beneath the thick material of my dress.

I hope like hell he can't see them.

"Clearly, it's not fine," he rasps, causing me to turn my attention to him.

My breaths fall hastily from my lips as my eyes jump to his mouth. It might be the alcohol, but wow, his lips are so delicious. What would it be like to kiss a man that attractive? To feel truly desired by someone I want in return? I wouldn't know.

I haven't been properly kissed or fucked in years. Not since my parents announced my marriage to Carlito two years ago, when I graduated from medical school. Carlito hasn't dared touch me that way, and he won't until we're married. Then he'll do whatever he wants.

My heart clamps and tears ache behind my eyes, threatening to show their face. I tuck them away, not wanting to ruin my day even more by crying in front of a bar full of people for the second time. This man probably thinks I'm nuts already. I don't want to give him any more reasons to think that way.

Dante rubs the back of his neck, and my chest climbs with every fired breath as I watch his triceps flex. His gaze zeros in on my breasts, probably noticing my nipples poking through the dress.

"Last call," the bartender announces.

Dante sharply turns back to the bar, finishing the rest of his drink in one quick swallow and slamming the glass back down. I swiftly finish mine, not knowing how I'm actually going to take my life once I get out of here.

What if Carlito finds me first? Though he's never actually hit me, I can tell he's itching to put me in my place. The rage trickles within his eyes every time I'm around him. Once it's filled to capacity, the wrath will rain, and I'll be its victim for life.

"So, what's this fiancé of yours like?" Dante asks, his warm gaze trapping me in an invisible cage I'd be more than willing to climb into.

I've never seen a man with such beautiful brown eyes before. They're soulful, while the rest of him is all male. The rippled muscles of his biceps stretch sinfully as he crosses his arms, causing me to gape for longer than appropriate.

Again.

But this time he doesn't say anything. His eyes are still perched to mine when I glance up.

"He's not exactly my fiancé," I mutter, peering down at my lap. "And he's awful. My parents arranged it, and I have no choice in the matter."

His hand snaps to mine, gripping it tightly in his, a thumb softly dusting over the top as he looks at me. My attention slithers back to him as my body stirs with a jolt, quiet awareness pouring through me every time his skin touches mine.

"I'm sorry you're hurting." His tone is as soft as his touch; he's now rubbing slow circles over my hand. "But everyone has a choice. Some are just harder to make."

I'm breathless. Lost to him. Unable to pull away.

He's right. We all have choices we're sometimes too afraid to make. I need to stop holding myself back.

Maybe I shouldn't feel this way, but I can't help this haze of attraction between us. I need to know where it can go before everything ends for me.

"This is probably crazy," I whisper, looking back up at him. "But—"

"But what?" The smooth cadence of his words bathes me in tranquility.

And in the next three seconds, I change the course of my fate completely.

"Want to get out of here?" The question jumps out before I have a chance to take it back.

My heartbeats slam in my rib cage, afraid he'll say no—or maybe afraid that he'll actually say yes.

His eyes widen for the briefest of seconds, and then he's on his feet, towering over me and tugging on my hand. His lips curve with a wicked smirk.

"I thought you'd never ask."

I breathe a sigh of relief, wrapping my fingers around his and letting him take me as far from here as possible for as long as he'll have me.

# Three

# DANTE

She's so beautiful with her long, wavy black hair and brown eyes so dark they're almost the color of midnight. She's a lot shorter in person, especially with no heels on. She's five-three while I'm six-three. My brothers and I are all tall, taking after our father.

Thanks to my constant surveillance, I knew she'd be at this bar. After I watched her run from her house, I beat her here.

Raquel Bianchi is predictable that way. She likes to hide out in this crummy hole-in-the-wall bar whenever she's upset. I would've been really pissed if she'd chosen to go elsewhere.

I've been keeping tabs on her for a year now, intercepting all her calls and having my men follow her when I couldn't do it myself.

When my brothers and I set the plan in motion to hurt the

Bianchi brothers, Raquel was always the chess piece I was born to play. We knew how much she meant to her father, and we knew how much they hated us.

At first, when I saw her photo while we planned our revenge, I only wanted to trick her into marriage to punish her father for hurting our family. Marrying his daughter would do the trick. But then we decided we could use her as a bargaining chip to get her father out of hiding.

Not that I'll ever give her up, but I could easily convince her father I would trade her life for his. Unlike Faro, he'd probably choose to save his daughter.

Little does Sal know that Raquel will be mine, and she'll stay that way, even though she doesn't know it yet. The Bianchi men have always thought they're better than us. The thought of the Cavaleri boys marrying a Bianchi woman would be hell to them.

I can't wait to let her father know the happy news…right before I put a bullet in his skull. It's too bad he won't be attending the wedding, unless it's in a coffin.

I have no plans of falling for my enemy's daughter. Raquel may be innocent, but she still shares their blood. We may be married soon, and I'll even fuck her, but I'll never fall in love with her. A loveless marriage is all we'll have.

She can blame her father for that. He stained her with the blood of his mistakes, and for that, she'll always pay. I might not be as cruel as Carlito, but marrying me will be its own prison. This little bird will never truly be free.

I can provide her with something Carlito can't, though: a life not ruled by fear. She'll never have to be afraid of a man hurting her again.

Tonight, after I left Viper, one of the dance clubs my brothers and I own, I went to the wedding she was attending and made sure

Carlito wasn't doing what she didn't want him to do. I blended with the crowd, completely unnoticed amongst the hundreds of people in attendance. When they were heading out, I followed them back to her parents' house.

I've gotten to know her soon-to-be ex-fiancé quite well. He likes to frequent Tips & Tricks, a strip club owned by the Bianchis, of which Chiara is the manager.

Whenever he's there, I find a way to be there too, securing a table right next to his or joining him when he texts my burner. My men keep me up to date about his comings and goings too, so I know where he'll be before he even does.

After the first conversation I struck up with him, he thought we were friends for life or some shit. The man can drink a whole bottle of liquor and sing like a canary, with a stripper or two on his lap while he spills details about what he'll do to Raquel once they're married.

I feel sorry for her. I'm even sorry for what I plan to do to her. The lies I'll tell to get what I want. But it's necessary. My brothers and I have waited fifteen years to avenge the deaths of my father and eight-year-old brother, Matteo, who are both dead thanks to her uncle Faro and his brothers, one of whom is her father.

Because of her family, I had to run away with my oldest brother, Dom, and my younger brother, Enzo, when I was only twelve. We lived on the streets for a year before finding shelters to survive in.

We had to do a lot of ugly shit to make it out alive, like robbing people and stealing candy bars from convenience stores so we could eat. Our past is filled with more awfulness than any kid should ever endure. But we did, because of them.

Faro wanted us dead. Before he killed my father, he swore to him that he'd kill us too. So we had no choice but to get as far away from his whole family as we could.

We got lucky eventually, when Dom met Tomás Smith while working at a coffee shop when he was sixteen. Tomás offered us a job, a safe place to live, and more importantly, someone who could look out for all of us. Dom was just a kid, only a year older than me, when we ran, but he did whatever he could to keep us safe. With Tomás, we finally were.

We didn't think the day would ever come when we'd be on top—when the Bianchi brothers would fear us—but now they do.

They hid like roaches after we burned the first business they owned: a laundromat they used to run guns and manage their illegal operations. We've been solidifying our plan for vengeance for a year now, making sure all the cards are laid out perfectly. The time has finally arrived for every one of them to pay the ultimate price.

We not only took out the laundromat and their men, but we torched a warehouse they used for business dealings, killing every member of the Palermo crime family inside.

We've been looking for Faro and his brothers ever since the laundromat went up in smoke, needing our pound of flesh. We'll find them even if we have to burn everything to the ground to do it.

Faro recently tried to end the war he started long ago by making a deal with Dom in exchange for his daughter, but that blew up in his face. None of us will ever accept anything the Bianchis have to offer. Nothing will end the bloodshed.

Nothing but their deaths.

We've waited too long for the day when we can make them pay. It's the only goal we've had in the last fifteen years, and I will see it through until my dying breath. Nothing and no one can come between me and my vengeance.

Not even someone as beautiful as Raquel Bianchi.

"So, where are we going?" she asks, oblivious to the trap I'll be setting soon.

"My place." I peer over at her, veering my car into the right lane. "Is that okay?"

She shrugs, her eyes drowning in sadness as she glances at me from the passenger side of my powder-blue McLaren Speedtail.

"I have nowhere else to be," she throws in casually, her lips bending with a scowl.

I kind of hate seeing her upset. It's probably because I've been following her for so long; it feels like I know her.

She doesn't deserve any of this. Not what her family planned for her, and not what I'm planning. But sometimes life beats down on people who don't deserve it, leaving the evil ones unscathed. It's unfair, but it's reality.

My brothers and I didn't deserve the shit we got either. Matteo didn't deserve to never know what it means to live, but he was killed anyway.

When I heard what Raquel said to Chiara earlier tonight, about how she wanted to kill herself, I knew I had to make our introduction today. Give her the opportunity to accept the offer that'll change her life forever.

If she doesn't accept, I'll have no choice but to take her against her will. It's much easier if she's not kicking and screaming. Not that it'd matter. None of the men securing my place would give a shit.

When she finds out the real truth about me, it'll be far too late. She'll be Mrs. Cavaleri for the rest of her life, whether she wants to be or not.

This is, until death.

I never expected her to want to leave with me tonight. I had this plan of flirting my way into her panties and then letting her know I need a wife, but she's made things a lot easier…so far.

"Hey." I reach out my hand for hers, tucking her fingers in my palm. "It's gonna be okay."

"No, it won't." Bitterness grows in her eyes. "It'll never be okay."

"You don't know that. You never know where your life will take you." I glance at her in between focusing on the road. "I mean, did you ever expect to meet a handsome man at four in the morning?"

She half laughs, half cries while swiping under her eye. "No, I actually didn't."

"So you *do* think I'm handsome." I lift a brow, my lips turning with a grin as I catch the light in her eyes from the smile now on her face.

"You're okay, I guess," she giggles pitifully, sniffling and taking her hand back. "A lot better than the man I'm being forced to marry, that's for sure."

"It's funny." I pause, setting my plan in motion. "You want to get out of a marriage, and I want to get into one."

"What do you mean?" Her head tilts to the side, eyes laser-focused on me.

"Well…" I make a left turn, cruising down a bare street. "There's this property I badly want to secure. But the problem is, the owner won't sell to me."

"Why?" Her brows furrow.

"I have to prove I'm a happily married man first."

Her eyes widen. "That's crazy."

"Yep." I shrug. "The owner is old and has his rules. Something about a married man being better suited to take care of the house. If I want his place, I have less than a week to find a fake wife who can live with me for three months and pretend to be mine." I turn right, nearing my house. "I kind of told him I was already engaged and the wedding is in two weeks."

Her mouth falls open.

"Now you see the problem?" I grin.

She nods with a nervous laugh. "A little."

"He wants to see the marriage certificate once it's finalized," I explain further. "And after he's happy that I'm married for three months, he'll sign the contract for the property."

I fucking hope she buys this shit, or I'm going to have to do what Dom will be doing to Chiara tonight: lock her away in a room until she accepts her new world.

"Do you have anyone in mind?" Her eyes narrow.

*Yes. You.*

"Not yet. It's a hard ask, even with all the money I'd offer her in return."

*And the pot has been sweetened.*

"Money?" Her tone rises with excitement. "How much money?"

"I think a million tax-free would be fair. What do you think?"

Her brows shoot up. "I'll do it!"

"What?"

I turn my head to her as I park the car in my driveway.

"Are you serious? You should really think about it," I push, but internally I'm grinning like a bastard, knowing I have her where I want her.

"I don't need to think about it."

She reaches for my arm, clinging to my bicep with all the desperation slinking in her eyes. I feel it and hate that I do.

*I'd let you fly away if I could, little bird, but I can't. You're mine now.*

Will she be this desperate to escape me when she learns of her new fate?

It shouldn't matter to me. None of it matters. Not her pain, and not what I have to do. It's all irrelevant. The only thing that I care about is avenging the deaths of my family.

"Look…" She drops her arm away from me. "I don't have anywhere to go. If I go home, I'm afraid my mother will send me to the altar the next hour. And my fiancé? He's a real asshole. I'm scared of what he'll do once he gets his hands on me. So even if you're some crazy psycho killer…" She laughs. "That's okay. I was considering offing myself tonight, so you'd be saving me the trouble."

Those words slam right into the center of my chest.

*Fuck. This woman.*

"Raquel…."

I lift up my hand, my fingers inching toward the sharp contours of her face. My palm finds her cheek, and I love how well it fits.

"Don't say that," I whisper, my thumb feathering softly over her skin.

She blinks the tears away, but they can't hide from me. I see them. I feel them rotting through the marrow of my bones. I hate that I feel sorry for her, but I can't block it out. The sensation overcomes me. She's such a good person; it kills me to see that amount of pain in her eyes.

"I'm sorry for my sob story." Her voice cracks, dripping with emotion. "Maybe I was meant to meet you. Maybe you're my one chance to have a fresh start, somewhere they can't find me."

*I wish that was true.*

"I'll help you. I promise." My lips betray her even while my eyes pretend that I'm a good man.

She melts into my touch, her eyelids drifting closed as her breathing evens.

"If you're serious about this, then I'll get you whatever you need to start a new life once your three-month commitment is up,"

I add. "I'll hand you a new identity, a passport, and you can pick wherever the hell you want to go. No one will stop you."

*I'm such a bastard.*

"You'd do that?" Her face lights up, those eyes glistening.

"I'd do that. No questions."

There's so much hope on her face, and it won't be pretty when she realizes none of this is real.

"Thank you!" she cries, throwing herself at me and wrapping her arms around my neck, her small sobs denting the armor I've built around my heart to keep her out of it.

*Stop caring about her. She's nothing.*

But I can't seem to.

My arms go around her, tugging her even closer, wanting to protect her and not understanding why.

She's the daughter of my enemy. Why do I care what happens to her? Why do her tears make me want to rip out Carlito's heart and feed it to her father?

Getting into his car was a risk I was willing to take. What else did I have to lose? My life was already a living hell. Before today, I'd never have dreamed of getting into a car with a man I'd only just met.

But things have changed drastically.

When I thought the wedding was six months away, it still seemed like enough time to do something, but three months is nothing. It'll be here before I know it.

Whoever Dante is, I know one thing: he has money, and a lot of it. From the moment I saw his car, I knew he had to be rich. McLarens aren't cheap, and his costs a good two million. I know a thing or two about cars. It's my side passion. I love luxury cars, especially sports cars.

Once we got to the house, I knew my suspicions were correct. His house is not merely a house, but a sprawling white mansion covering acres of land.

We sit on his cream suede sofa, my toes curling over the soft, shaggy white rug. An electric fireplace is in front of me, and a raindrop-style crystal chandelier hangs overhead. My palms surround a warm mug of coffee while he sips on his.

Considering the daybreak has come, I welcome the caffeine permeating through my pores. But honestly, I'm no longer tired. Not like I was when I got home from the wedding. It must be the anxiety spinning me out of control.

"What exactly do you do?" I ask as he takes another sip from his mug before placing it down on a square glass table before us.

As soon as I walked in, I noticed all the bodyguards stationed around the premises. Each one is tall, built, and scary enough to give me the impression that they'd kill anyone who dared walk inside uninvited.

Why would he need them?

"I run some companies," he throws in coolly.

"They must do well," I murmur, glancing up at the cathedral ceiling and the black-and-white contemporary artwork perched on the walls.

"They do okay." He grins, telling me they do way more than that. "And what about you?"

"I'm a second-year resident at a hospital in the general surgery program." My eyes are back on his. "I have three more years to go."

"Whoa. So you're not only beauty, but brains too? Damn."

My cheeks burn from the compliment. I'm not used to the praise. My parents were never the type to hand compliments out.

His tongue takes a leisurely swipe of his lower lip as his gaze subtly glides down my body, but I notice it, and I like it.

"Look, before we do this, you need to know some things about me," I say, realizing he has to know the truth about the type of family I come from and what they'll do if and when they find out about us.

He angles his body toward me even more, one thigh raised on the sofa.

"Now I'm intrigued. Tell me everything." The smirk on his face makes my stomach flop and tighten. "But I promise nothing will scare me away."

A tiny, severed laugh breaks from my lips. He has no idea if that's true. Not until he understands what he's getting into. I'm so desperate for this to work. It's my only way out. But once he learns the truth, he might not want to marry me.

Pulling in a long breath and closing my eyes for a mere second to gather the nerves, I tell him everything, from who my father and uncles are, to the kind of life I've led, to being forced to marry Carlito. I give him every dirty detail.

He's contemplative for a moment while my heart does somersaults as I wait for him to say something, anything. I anxiously run my finger over the handle of the mug.

"That's all?" He chuckles deeply, his eyes gleaming with humor. "I thought you were going to tell me you were a part-time serial killer or something. Not that it'd be a deal breaker either."

"You really don't care that I'm the daughter of a mobster? It doesn't worry you?"

"Not at all. You don't have to doubt my ability to keep you safe, Raquel. I can do that one-handed. And, as you can see…" He waves a hand toward the men he employs. "I have plenty of help too."

I exhale a sigh of relief.

He scoots closer, his hand settling on my knee. "You don't have to worry anymore. I'll protect you."

A tentative smile appears on my face. I want to trust him, but I'm worried I can't. I know nothing about him. Not even his last name. Does he really stand a chance against my family and Carlito?

I guess we'll find out soon.

"So, how is this arrangement between us going to work?" I ask, needing to start the process so he can't change his mind.

"Well…" He moves his hand away, picking up his mug again. "My lawyers have already drafted a contract, which we'll both sign. They'll just add your name to it today. I'll also need you to sign the papers so we can get the marriage certificate. Then, once the three months are complete, you'll get your money and all the documentation, as promised."

"And what about the other stuff?" My cheeks are burning, but I need to know if he expects anything sexual from our marriage.

He smirks, knowingly. "You mean will I fuck you?"

"Mm-hmm. I know I came home with you and all, but that was before all this." I wave a hand in the air.

"Don't worry, baby. I won't touch you." His tone lowers. Deep. Masculine.

My body shivers with awareness, the prickling over my skin spreading past my arms.

"Not unless you want me to. And you *might* want me to." A devilish smirk crosses his face.

"I won't," I quickly say.

I'm no longer sure if that's true. My heart is racing to the speed of roaring flames. I was so ready to have a one-night stand, but now we can't. Not when I'll be seeing him for three months.

His hand extends, and I'm caught in his gaze, like a moth dizzy from the moonlight. My pulse picks up speed and my stomach writhes with nerves as his knuckle strokes down my cheek.

"You sure about that?" he asks.

My breathing stills, imprisoned from his unrelenting gaze. His raspy tone slides between my thighs, making me crave whatever is happening between us.

I can't let it go there. Not now. Not when I'm not here to stay. I don't want to form a connection with him only to leave it behind. I have to keep him at arm's length while I'm here. I have to fight this intense attraction to my soon-to-be husband.

*God help me.*

"I'm sure," I assert with all the confidence I can muster.

My hand wraps around his powerful wrist, drawing it away. My cheek tingles where his touch was, the feeling so foreign it almost feels surreal.

"Whatever you say, beautiful. I'm here to make you happy. You'll be my wife, after all."

"In name only." I quirk a brow, still feeling the effect he has on me.

"Right. Of course." He grins. "Oh, and before I forget, I'll need your phone. You won't be able to have it in the time you're here, or your family will be able to track you."

"Right. Okay. But I have to text my cousin Chiara. She has to know I'm okay, or she'll turn the world upside down to find me."

"That's fine, but don't tell her anything other than you're safe. Don't say a word about me or our location."

"Of course. I understand. Oh, I also need to message my boss and let her know I'll need a month off for a family emergency, or they'll come looking too."

He nods in understanding as I remove my cell from my handbag and go to my messages, typing one out to Chiara, then my job. My boss and I have a pretty good relationship, and though I know I should call her, I don't think I could lie as well over the phone.

### RAQUEL TO CHIARA

Hey. Just wanted you to know I'll be gone for a while. No, I won't off myself. Don't worry. But I did find a way out. He's rich, hot, and promises to get me out of the country soon. And if he kills me, then he kills me. Just kidding. I hope. Love you.

### RAQUEL TO JOB KERRY

Hey, Kerry. I'm sorry to do this at the last minute, but I wouldn't if I didn't have to. My family is going through an emergency right now, and I had to go out of state with my parents for a month. I understand if my position won't be there when I return, though I would very much like it to be. I don't have great reception here, so I'm sorry if I don't get back to you. -Raquel

"Here." I hand him the phone, and he takes it, turning it off before stuffing it in his pants pocket.

"All right, let me show you to your room so you can maybe take a nap." He sets his mug down and rises to his feet while I do the same.

"That sounds nice, though I can't say I'm tired."

"Weirdly, I'm not either," he remarks as we walk side by side out of the room and toward the large foyer.

I follow him up the spiral staircase, gripping the bronzed banister as I take slow steps, noticing every detail of his home, one I imagine is the type a celebrity would live in.

"I have a lot of men around the place, as you might have noticed," he says over his shoulder. "Don't let that concern you. I like to protect what's mine. Can't be too careful these days."

"I understand." I climb the final step, crossing into a wide hallway and seeing room after room until we stop at one.

"Here we are." He parts the door, his smile as welcoming as the bedroom.

"This is nice." My feet fall over the dark hardwood as I stride further inside the massive bedroom.

I silently take in everything: the misty gray upholstered bed with a dark gray abstract rug beneath, the two white armchairs perched by the floor-to-ceiling windows, and a square glass table sandwiched between them.

"Where is your room?" I ask with my back to him.

"You're in it," comes a husky answer.

His breath glides up my neck, making goose bumps scatter across my arms.

*Wait. What did he just say?*

I whip around to find amusement flanking his features.

"You mean we have to share a room?" My eyes go round.

"We do." His body moves dangerously close to mine. "Did I forget to mention that?"

A tiny, crooked smile snakes over his mouth, and I know right away that he purposely left that part out.

"We should have separate rooms." Agitation rolls into my voice. "I don't think this is a good idea."

"Why not?" He draws nearer, his body only a finger's length away from mine.

"Well...I...um..." I stammer, my eyes darting between him and the floor.

I'm acutely aware of his taut muscles being too close to my skin and his exhales drifting past my lips.

"Are you afraid of me, Raquel?" The back of his hand reaches out, tracing my jaw.

*God, he loves to touch, and I love being touched. I'm in so much trouble.*

"No." My rapid, audible breaths betray me, calling me a liar.

"Good. Because I can behave myself, even with you sleeping beside me." His tone oozes with sensual prowess as our gazes align with fierce intensity. "The question is, can you?"

I clear my throat, hoping to clear my body of all thoughts of him at the same time. "Why is this even necessary? Why can't we have separate rooms?"

"Look…" He marches away toward the door. "You don't have to do this if you don't want to. The contract hasn't been signed, so you're free to go. I can drive you home now if you want."

"No!" I practically jump a step. "It's…it's fine. I'll stay here. With you."

"You sure? I don't want to push you into something you're clearly not ready for." He moves a foot toward me, killing some of the distance he's created.

"I'm sure. We'll figure it out."

"I know this is a lot…" That softness in his gaze that attracted me to him back at the bar is back. "But if we don't appear truly married and the seller somehow finds out, then my deal with him will go to shit, along with the money and documents I promised you."

*I can't let that happen!*

"I understand, Dante."

"How about this?" he counters. "How about we get the marriage certificate done today, but we wait on the contract while you try this arrangement out for a week? Like a trial period. Then, if you're fine with it, we'll sign the paperwork. But if you want out, I'll have the marriage annulled and find someone else to make my wife."

The way he says that word, wife…I kind of don't want him to find anyone else.

I jerk my head back. "You can get a marriage certificate that fast?"

"I know some people." He winks.

He must be someone big in the business world.

"Yeah, the trial period seems fair."

I'll agree to anything at this point. Whatever he needs me to do, I'll do it just to avoid marrying Carlito.

"What's your full name, by the way?" I think it's time I know the last name of the man I'm about to marry.

"Cavaleri."

*Raquel Cavaleri.*

I toss the name around in my head, liking the sound of it, even if it'll only be mine for a short while.

"How about we get some breakfast?" he asks, jarring me from my thoughts. "I don't know about you, but I'm starving."

It's close to six a.m. now, and my stomach growls right on cue, as though hearing his words.

"Come on, hungry fiancée," he teases on a laugh. "Let's get you fed."

"Fiancée?" I taunt as we head back down the stairs, me beside him. "You haven't even given me a ring yet."

"Would you like me to get down on one knee too while we're at it?" He slams me with another show-stopping smile, glancing at me sideways. "I can definitely make that happen if you want, wifey."

"Shut up," I giggle, playfully swatting him on his chest with the back of my hand as we reach his enormous white kitchen.

He captures my wrist in his palm, his gaze darkening and his touch tightening, causing my core to throb just enough to know how turned on I suddenly am. His gaze drops down to my lips.

Hooded. Wanton.

I pant, unable to contain my emotions. And that's when his touch softens as he lets me go, striding toward the fridge. I lower myself onto one of the black stools beside the kitchen island.

*What the hell was that? And why do I want it to happen again?*

"What are you in the mood for?" He opens the fridge, his hand disappearing inside like nothing just happened between us.

"You cook?" My words fall incredulously, my body still feeling the effects of his dominating touch.

"That's right, baby girl. I hope you're ready to be spoiled." He peers at me over his shoulder, haunting me with those captivating eyes. "My brothers and I all know how to cook. We're pretty good too."

"Impressive," I remark, still drowning in that spell he has me under whenever he looks at me or touches me. "Pancakes sound good."

"Any special kind?"

"I do like them with blueberries."

"Lucky for you…" I hear his smile as he delves inside the fridge. "I have some fresh ones."

He gets to work laying out the ingredients, then takes out a pan and bowl from a cabinet. He tosses the milk and flour into the mixing bowl, and the sight of his forearms flexing and those muscles straining as he mixes, the veins beneath his tanned skin bulging angrily, has my toes curling. The impulse to run my fingers over all that virile power overwhelms me. But I sit here, ignoring the urges rolling up my body.

After he finishes the batter, he removes some plates and forks, handing me one of each, then retrieves a ladle, pouring a spoonful of batter onto the sizzling pan.

When the first one is done, he puts it on my plate. He's very comfortable in the kitchen, and wow, that only makes him more attractive. A man who knows how to cook well is one of my downfalls.

"You're staring again," he teases with a handsome smirk, clearly enjoying the attention.

"I…um…."

I poke the pancake with my fork, destroying the poor thing, as my heart pounds.

"Okay, fine," I throw in, my eyes slamming to his and my pulse quickening. "You got me. I was totally staring, okay? You're hot. Unobjectively, insanely gorgeous." I shroud my face with a hand. "There. I said it."

*Oh my hell. Why did I just do that?*

"Damn. Hot and gorgeous in one sentence?" He chuckles. "Give it to me straight, though. On a scale of one to ten, with ten being Henry Cavill…" He throws another pancake on my plate. "How hot are we talking here?"

"Ugh!" I groan, my fork clattering against the plate as I drop it and cover my face with my hands. "You're not going to let me live this down, are you?"

"Not a chance in hell, baby." Deep laughter fills the room, and then his hand lands on mine, his fingertips fledging over my knuckles. "It's okay to be attracted to your husband. It's normally required."

There's hilarity in his voice as I peek up at him and find amusement glinting in the auburn hues of his eyes.

"We're not even married yet, and you're already my husband?" I tilt up a brow. "You sure move fast."

"You'll be my wife later today, Raquel." He hits me with an intense gaze, his voice growing huskier. "Might as well get used to the title."

"How come this feels like I'm signing up for a bad reality show?" I cross my arms over my chest, eyes turning to thin slits. "Are you hiding cameras anywhere?"

I look both ways for effect.

He laughs, walking over to the counter to add some pancakes onto his plate before turning off the stove and finally taking a seat across from me. "Nah, sweetheart. Whenever there are cameras involved, it's always because she wants them there."

He winks, and I feel it shooting down my body, like a lightning strike in my panties, except a lot more exciting. I stuff a piece of pancake into my mouth, chewing until my breathing calms and I can formulate a response that doesn't sound ridiculous.

"Oh, you're into that?" I finally ask.

*That's what you came up with? Obviously, your future hubby is into fucking with cameras. He clearly just said that.*

He cuts into his breakfast, curiously glancing up at me. "You're not?"

The sensual nuance of that question tremors over my body as my exhales grow louder. I pop another giant piece of my food into my mouth so I don't have to answer. Maybe I could be into it? I was never that adventurous in bed, and neither were my partners.

But I have a feeling sex with him would be something I've yet to experience. Something I never will. Sleeping with my husband is not an option, even if it's all I can think about.

No sex. No feelings.

I need things as clean as possible so that in three months, I can move on with no one holding me back.

"You don't have to answer," he adds, his gaze doused with lustful hunger. "We'll have plenty of time to get to know each other. Properly."

*Properly? What the hell does that mean? And do I really want the answer?*

I've never had a problem figuring out when a woman wants me. And Raquel Bianchi definitely does. She's practically ripping off my clothes and wants me to do the same to her. If I wanted to fuck her, all I'd need to do would be push her just enough to make her beg for it. She seems a little shy, and that makes me want her even more. I bet underneath all that, she's fucking wild. I enjoyed toying with her about the cameras a little too much.

If she was on them, I'd watch those videos on repeat.

But I have to be careful with what I say. I might know her more than she realizes, but I'm only a stranger to her. A hot stranger, apparently. It was damn adorable the way she blushed when she said that.

"I have to go to work in a bit," I tell her as we continue to enjoy breakfast. "Feel free to go to the pool or roam around. Eat anything from the fridge. My house is your house." My hand combs through my hair. "Oh, and in a few hours, my cook will be stopping by."

"You have a cook?" Her mouth drops open just a little.

"Of course." I cut into my pancake. "I might know how to make a meal, but I don't have the time to do it. You'll love Janet."

"I don't mind cooking for us." She shuffles in her seat while I eat, looking at her empty plate before I catch her eyes again.

"Really?" I lower my voice, gazing at her.

Her cheeks brighten into a deeper shade of pink the more I drink her in.

"Do you cook naked? Because that's the only way I'd want you cooking for me."

I can't stop teasing her, pulling her beyond the comfort level she's used to. I want those cheeks to blush again.

"Not usually." She bursts into a nervous laugh, her lower lip trapped between her teeth…and yep, there are those pink cheeks again. "I much prefer to cook with clothes on."

I don't stop staring at her as she talks. I don't think I could if I wanted to. The way those heart-shaped lips move…goddamn, she's stunning.

"How do you know if you've never given it a shot?"

She shakes her head, the smile still on her face. "It's one of those things. When you know, you know." She pulls herself closer to the plate, looking questioningly at me. "Is that a requirement of our arrangement? Because if so, we have a lot of negotiating to do."

"Really? Like what?" I place my fork down and sit back, palms on the top of my thighs.

"For instance, I'm never kissing you." She raises a single

brow. "Ever. No matter how hot I already said you are, to my utter humiliation."

"Don't forget unobjectively, insanely gorgeous." My mouth bends with a smirk.

She half scowls, half suppresses a grin. "Oh, believe me, I haven't."

"Don't be embarrassed for having good taste." I pick up my fresh cup of coffee and take a long sip, my playful gaze stuck to the narrowing of her eyes.

Raquel can throw in whatever terms she wants at me. Whatever's written in our contract won't matter. It won't be real. Unlike our marriage.

She'll be mine. She just has no idea.

Yet.

"I'm also not fucking you." She goes all serious.

"Damn, did I just like hearing you say that word. Can you say it again, but lower this time?"

My cock grows heavy, hard, while her eyes turn to humorously glaring slits. Her arms cross over her small chest that's just enough for my palms. My hands tingle to touch her there. To touch her in every place she hides.

"Anything else?" I ask, unable to keep that smirk off my face.

"I'm not touching you either."

"That's so broad. Is there any wiggle room on that one? I was kind of hoping to snuggle."

"Absolutely *no* snuggling." She barely stifles a laugh.

"What if we watch a movie, you in my arms, and we end up falling asleep together?"

She sits up straighter. "Why would I even be in your arms to begin with?"

"Maybe you were cold? Maybe you were lonely?" My voice

deepens, my gaze boring into hers. "Maybe you just liked how my body felt next to yours?"

Her cheeks flush as she bites the corner of her lower lip, and my dick jerks, wanting to be there instead.

"That…uh, that'll never happen." But there's too much uncertainty on her features.

"Never is too strong of a word," I add. "Let's wait to see what happens."

"Nothing will happen." Her words are sharp, edging, like a sword. One I'll have too much fun melting until it's no longer a threat.

"Whatever you say, wife."

"Don't say it like that!"

"Hey!" I lift up my hands in defeat. "I'm agreeing with you."

"Uh-huh, but your voice isn't."

"I can't control what my voice thinks. It's got a mind of its own, like some of my other body parts."

She skims a shaky hand down the side of her neck, calling for my palm to wrap around it, to squeeze as I'm buried deep inside her with my mouth on those luscious lips. It's like every layer of her skin is calling out to me, baiting me.

She looks around the room, clearly wanting out of this conversation. I can only guess it's because no matter how much she denies her hunger, I know deep down she wants to light our fire and feel it burn.

Sometimes when you've met a complete stranger, there's this invisible string pulling you to them. Like gravity shifting and creating something new. You don't understand it—hell, you might not even want it—but it happens on its own. That's how it is between us.

This attraction is undeniable. She can try to pretend she doesn't feel it, but it'll continue to grow until we're both consumed.

"I can't believe how big this place is," Raquel tosses out.

"It's yours now."

"For three months," she retorts, the glint in her eyes shining bright, reminding me of my darkness.

"However long you want."

"I won't be staying past three months."

"Great." My lips turn up. "You're probably annoying, anyway."

"Only after midnight." She breathes out an easy laugh.

"Remind me to stay the hell away once the clock strikes twelve." A genuine chuckle breaks from my chest.

I don't remember the last time I laughed or smiled this much with a woman. Sure, I've done it out of politeness, but it never felt authentic. It's different with her. It's like we've been friends for a while.

Her shoulders drop with a sigh, her expression growing somber.

"Thank you. For saving me." She gazes at me with too much emotion, her lips set to a frown. "Because that's what you did."

*But I didn't*, I want to say. *I lied.*

My jaw clenches with unexplained feelings.

Is it pity? Shame? I don't know.

She's too beautiful to be caught in the middle of our war. Too good to become a mere pawn on our chessboard. But every war has its casualties, and she's about to be mine.

I might not be able to love the daughter of my enemy, but I'll treat her with every ounce of respect she deserves, which is a lot more than her father did for my family. And on those cold and lonely nights, we'll keep each other's bodies warm, even when our hearts are nothing but ice.

I can't believe Carlito thought he'd ever have her. I'd move heaven and earth to keep her away from that asshole. Neither of us loves her, but I won't be cruel. Not like he'll be. Marrying her is simply a way to advance himself in the family. He's nothing but a foot soldier now, but marrying the advisor's daughter is a hell of a step up.

Too bad I just put a kink in his plans. His fiancée is about to become my wife, and I'll do what I can to keep him as far away from her as possible. If he won't stay away, there's always a bullet with his name on it.

Once she learns of my plans and the lies I told to bring her here, she'll hate me. But it's better for her to hate me here, where I can keep her away from what would've been her life.

Ever since my brothers and I set our revenge for the Bianchis in motion and I saw her photos from our initial surveillance, I told Dom she was mine. There was something there beneath her beauty. Something broken and bruised. It spoke to me. Once I learned of the marriage her parents planned, I realized we were more alike than I thought. Both of us are fighting for a way out of the life we never asked for.

Everything changed when my father and brother died. My world disappeared, its color gone as though the earth had faded into darkness. The pain only grew over the years, holding steady and weighing me down.

I don't want it. I want a life free from the ugliness in my heart. I don't want to be known as a brutal killer, but I am what I am now. There's no future, no happiness, for me when all I've ever known is vengeance. My heart is too black, my hands too bloody, to ever give a piece of myself to someone else. Who'd want it, anyway?

Love was not meant to be mine. My heart is soaked in the blood of my enemies, and nothing and no one will make it beat again.

I'll never tell Dom that I sometimes wonder about being with someone. He, out of all of us, took the deaths the hardest. Who can blame him? Who knows what would have happened to me if I'd had to watch my father and brother die like he did?

If he hadn't gone out looking for our dad that day, if he hadn't stepped foot in that warehouse, he'd never have seen them get shot to death before his eyes. He was never the same. He grew cold, distant. That probably also had to do with knowing he lost Chiara, his best friend.

He has her now. Well, not exactly. She has no damn clue that the man who kidnapped her last night is her long-lost friend.

Somewhere in that messed-up heart of his, I know he still cares about her. Maybe he can be the one to move on from the past. Maybe they can have something together, something stronger than our need for revenge. And maybe if they can, I can have it too.

Or maybe I'm being an idiot.

Raquel plays with her pancakes, absently slicing off small pieces with the fork, barely eating now.

"I have some good news and bad news," I say, hoping to bring the radiating smile back to her face.

I hate seeing women upset. That shit wrecks me. But with her, it does something worse. I don't fucking know why, and I don't want to know.

Her focus stills on me. "Let's start with the bad news."

"You don't have any clothes here."

She laughs. "Is that the good news or bad news?"

"We'll call it a draw, baby girl."

Her not having anything to wear is definitely a plus…for me.

"So, what's the good news?"

"I have Colleen stopping by in less than an hour. She's my personal shopper, and now yours. She's going to bring a ton of clothes and crap for you to sift through. Go crazy. Buy whatever you want. She has my info."

Her head whips back. "Seriously?"

"Seriously. I mean unless you plan to walk around here naked, which I'm fully on board with, by the way. On second thought…" I reach into my pocket and take out my cell. "I'm going to cancel that appointment."

"What?!" She jumps off the seat with a giggle, grabbing my forearm over the kitchen island. "No, don't do that."

Her touch forces my lungs to grow heavy. I tighten my jaw, steadying the desire to tell her to keep that hand just where it is.

"Are you sure?" I ask. "Did I mention I sleep naked? I really don't mind if you do too."

"Um…" Her eyes widen, her palm falling away. "I hope you're joking."

"Maybe." I grin, standing up and washing my plate before putting it in the cabinet.

"Are you ever serious?" Her face lights up with a smile.

I slowly walk around to her, stepping closer until my front is to her back. My hands fall around the edge of the island, trapping her.

"Only when I'm making love."

She doesn't move as I lean my mouth to the edge of her ear, my breaths fanning down her neck. She gasps, her inhales sharp, louder than the blood pulsing through my veins.

I've been around so many women, but no one comes close. No one makes me *want* this much.

Leaning my lips down to the back of her head, I kiss her hair, inhaling the scent of jasmine and wanting those long strands laced around my fingers with our bodies skin to skin.

"Bye, beautiful," I whisper, sliding my mouth down to the curve of her ear. "I'll see you later today when I bring over the marriage paperwork. Have fun shopping."

As I stroll away, her loud and hurried exhales make me wish I didn't have to go.

# RAQUEL

"What do you think of this?" Colleen asks again, holding up another floral dress in the bedroom I now share with Dante.

I've tuned her out more than once already, still replaying what happened with Dante before he left. The way he came up behind me. The way he kissed the back of my head.

My body flushes with heat from the memory. I don't know how I'll hold out for three months. The more I'm around him, the harder it'll get. He won't make it easy, I can already tell.

Right now, I wish I had pushed for separate bedrooms. He needs me just as much as I need him. Maybe he would've let me have that one thing.

"Raquel?" Colleen calls, her hazel eyes assessing me as she

smiles.

I glance up at her with what I hope is an apologetic expression. "I'm sorry. My mind is elsewhere today. I do love the other floral I tried on. The white with the blue flowers."

"Great. I'll add that to the total." She strides over to one of the suitcases she brought, bending down to put the dress she just showed me back inside.

She rummages for a few moments, then takes out what looks like lingerie.

"Um, I don't think I'll be needing those," I tell her as she drops them on the bed beside me. "I already picked the regular bras and panties."

"Oh." Her face falls nervously as she fingers her short blonde hair that's angled perfectly around her face. "Well…uh, Mr. Cavaleri instructed me to show them to you and to make sure you picked a few different sets. Would you like for me to call him and tell him you've changed your mind?"

*He what?!*

This man is going to drive me to divorce before we're even married. Why the hell would I need lingerie? What is he planning?

But I can't have her call him and possibly jeopardize our deal. I don't have any other options besides doing whatever he wants. Even if that means wearing this damn see-through white lace panty set that's currently draped over my hand.

I examine the tag.

*Holy crap.*

Five hundred for one bra is insane, but I guess to him, that's pocket change.

"I'll take all eight sets," I tell her.

Suddenly, her face lights up. "Wonderful. I'm sure Mr. Cavaleri will be pleased."

*Yeah, he sure will be…when I make his ass put it on.*

He wants to make me uncomfortable? Let's see how he likes it.

Okay, I probably won't do that, but it's a nice thought. Though I think these panties would probably be a tad too small around those thick, well-built thighs.

And here I go, growing all hot at the thought of his bare body.

Clearing my throat, I fidget with the black dress I'm still wearing, trying hard not to think about the man who saved me from hell.

Colleen removes the lingerie from my bed and adds them to another bag on the floor with the brightest smile. I've lost count of how many bags I have. There are at least thirty scattered across the room.

She must be making good commission on these sales. Between the intimates, casual clothes, swimwear, and dressy stuff, plus all the makeup and hair supplies I got, I've easily spent two hundred grand. I have never spent this much in one sitting. But hey, if that's what he wants, why not?

After she folds away all the items I didn't buy, she gets set to go.

"It was a pleasure meeting you." She reaches out a hand for mine, and we shake. "Please do call if you need anything else."

"I will. Thank you." I open the door for her as she rolls out both of the large suitcases she brought, while I follow her out into the hallway.

One of Dante's guards walks over to us.

"Let me, ma'am," he tells her, then grabs both of the suitcases, lifting them up in the air while marching down the stairs before us.

Considering he's a good six-seven and bulky as hell, he could probably carry both of us on his head too and not even sweat.

Once she's at the door, she waves goodbye as Dante's man

brings her stuff to the car.

After they're gone, I decide to run back upstairs to finally take a shower and put on fresh clothes. I strip out of my dress and panties, leaving them on the bed. Finding the bag with the bath accessories, I retrieve all the insanely pricy items Colleen brought and take them with me.

Stepping into a luxurious bathroom, I tread over the sparkling dark gray marble floor and reach the stand-up shower all the way at the far left corner. The jacuzzi on the right is making me wish I could dip inside it, but I'd end up falling right to sleep in it if I did.

Opening the glass door, I turn on the hot water that's like calming raindrops on a warm, summer day. The steam rises up my body, the scalding temperature washing away the rot.

I fill my palm with the smell of jasmine mixed with a hint of roses and rub the shampoo into my strands, the foam building until I wash it away. Then I finish off with my body.

Once I'm done, I shut off the water. Grabbing two black towels from the rack on the wall, I dry off before coming out and wrapping another towel around my hair. When I exit the bathroom, I locate a bag with lounge clothes and grab a white tank with gray yoga pants, quickly getting dressed. I should probably put all these clothes away, but I'm finally feeling tired, so instead, I slip into bed, picking up the remote.

I flip through hundreds of channels, my eyelids growing heavy and the remote jittering in my hand as sleep calls. I let it take me away, feeling relaxed for the first time in a while.

I find myself awake an hour later, according to the large round clock on the wall. My body feels run-down and my head is still groggy with sleep, but I force myself to get up, knowing I'll never get any shut-eye tonight if I continue to nap.

Flipping my feet out of the warm comfort of Dante's bed, I make it back downstairs. I start walking aimlessly around the house, not knowing where I'm going and feeling a bit uneasy as I pass guard after guard at every entry point. There are two at the door leading to the pool, then more at the other back entrances. It feels as though I'm being watched every second.

Who needs this many people defending their house? I'm not buying that this is for protection. He has to be involved in something shady. Something I probably don't want to know about. The less I'm involved in this kind of stuff, the better.

I wanted no part in my father's dealings, and I sure as hell don't want anything to do with whatever Dante has his hands in.

All I want is to live my life in peace without being controlled. I know how dirty my father's hands are, and I've always wanted to be far away from that. And Dante, even with all his obvious secrets, can get me there.

I don't know where I'll go once our marriage is over. Maybe a small village in a country that can use my medical skills. I might never finish my residency now, but I still have a lot to offer the world. It'd be a waste not to put my knowledge to use.

My dream has always been to become a doctor and help those who need it. I never imagined my dream would fall short of reality. But as much as my heart breaks at knowing my hard work will never be realized, it's a small price to pay for escaping the clutches of a man who'll drain all the happiness left in my life.

I don't even have my medical supply bag, the one I never leave the house without. How the hell did I forget to bring it? Then again, at the time, I really did think I was coming back home.

The bag contains all my essentials, from sutures to stethoscope. I don't feel the same without it. It's like a piece of me is missing. I guess that's another thing I'll have to get used to.

After walking through what feels like the entire first floor and discovering a home theater and a game room with a full bowling alley on one side, I make it back to my room—well, our room. Removing all the clothes from the bags, I begin to hang them, leaving aside a hot-pink two-piece bikini. There are two walk-in closets in his bedroom, one completely empty, like it was meant for me. Like he knew I'd need it, which is obviously a crazy thought.

The closet itself is more like its own room. You could place a king-sized bed in here, plus a dresser, and still have plenty of room to run around.

After everything is put away, an hour has passed, and I'm ready to take a dip in the pool. With my hips draped in a black cover-up, I make it back down, heading toward the garden. The two guards there open the doors as soon as they see me coming.

"Ma'am," they say in unison with a curt nod, their expressions stern.

"Raquel is fine," I throw in.

When I see their demeanor hasn't softened, I smile awkwardly before heading out.

"Wow," I whisper as the scent of freshly cut grass on the acres of bright green land before me permeates my senses.

The long, rectangular pool to my right is beautiful, but there's something else that catches my attention. A circular fountain on my left is surrounded by white benches, perfectly placed flowers in bright colors all around it.

It's so tranquil. I take a seat, my legs raised up and slanted to the side as I breathe in the fresh air. My eyelids grow heavy, and I realize that the hour-long nap from earlier didn't help at all.

# DANTE

While I'm at work, I try hard not to constantly watch her on the cameras I have throughout my property. The app on my cell makes it easy to access them wherever I am. My brothers and I all have them in our homes. We need to be aware of every move the Bianchis try to make against us.

When I return back home so we can have lunch together, I already know she's outside napping on one of the benches. I had this place made in memory of my mother. She always loved flowers and the water.

We had a lake not far from our home, and it was one of her favorite places. And every week, Dad would bring fresh flowers for her. She'd have the biggest smile on her face. I still see it, even though her face is distant now, washed away with the memories.

I miss her. I always will. I miss all of them.

I pull in a long inhale as I make it to where Raquel lies.

I've been standing over her for minutes now, watching the peacefulness drip from her body, listening to the steady breaths falling from her lungs. She looks too breathtaking to wake up, and that bikini molded to her tanned curves makes it harder for me to look away.

I saw her with Colleen earlier and loved knowing how uncomfortable she was with that lingerie in her hand. She'll be using every single damn piece. And when I rip it off of her, I'll buy her even more.

I stifle a groan from the images in my head of her straddling me with those eyes on mine. My hand is on her arm, my fingers sliding up and down as I savor the softness of her skin, wanting to know how soft she is between those thighs.

"Wake up, sweetheart." My tone is low, my hand still touching her.

She grumbles, her body moving a little, but her eyes remain closed.

"You have to eat. Janet made lunch for us already."

"Dante?" She yawns, her eyelids rising and her hand jumping to her face and rubbing away the sleep.

"Yes, wife," I say, liking how that word rolls off my tongue. "It's me."

She smiles, eyes still heavy. Her body stretches deliciously, giving me a chance to let my gaze roam free. I take my time, memorizing the bends and dips of her frame.

"What time is it?" She sits up.

"A little past noon." I reach a hand for hers, and she takes it, getting to her feet.

"I'm sorry. I hope it's okay I slept here."

We walk hand in hand, her feet moving to the beat of mine. "Of course it is. I told you, my house is yours. You never have to ask me for permission."

"Thank you." She glances at me, her lips tight in the sweetest smile, making her eyes glisten.

She's so goddamn breathtaking, especially when she looks at me that way. Like I'm her savior. Someone who brought her out of hell. And maybe I did, in a way.

But I'm about to bring her another. This paradise will fade when she learns all the things I've been hiding. I plan to keep my secrets buried until the clock runs out, until I have no choice but to reveal the truth. I'll delay the pain for as long as possible.

We enter the kitchen, where Janet is setting two plates of

handmade sushi and tuna avocado salad out for us.

"Hi there." Janet looks to Raquel, her shoulder-length strawberry-blonde hair swaying as she moves toward us.

"Nice to meet you," Raquel says, reaching out a hand for hers as they shake.

"You as well. And what a beauty you are." Janet peers at me with a knowing smile, like she's glad I actually brought a woman home. She doesn't exactly know why.

"Isn't she though?" I wrap an arm around the small of Raquel's back, pulling her to my side, while she discreetly tries to push me away.

"Stop fidgeting," I whisper into the shell of her ear. "She thinks you're my girlfriend, so you're supposed to be pretending to be in love with me, and right now, you're doing a shit job of it, baby."

She clears her throat, her lips spreading into a smile as fake as she thinks our marriage will be.

"Thank you for the compliment, Janet," she throws in, her tone sweet as fuck. "I'm so incredibly lucky to have met an amazing man like Dante." She circles an arm around the middle of my back, squeezing my ribs, almost hurting me. "Isn't that right, babe?"

She tilts her face to me, the smile still sitting on her face. I suppress a laugh at this entertaining show she's putting on.

"That's right, my love. You *are* incredibly lucky." My lips fall to her cheek, staying there for far too long, as I groan almost silently while I inhale her scent.

Her chest jumps with tattered breaths, her fingernails biting into my flesh and causing my teeth to grit discreetly.

"Well, I will leave you two lovebirds to your meal. I'll be back later to make dinner." Janet is already out of the kitchen.

"Thanks," I mutter as I pull away.

"I thought I said no kissing." Raquel goes all whispery and

hoarse, her gaze full of desire she's awful at masking. "Keep those lips to yourself."

"Actually…" I let my knuckles slowly brush down her cheek, swiping lower and falling in between her tits. "What you said was that *you're* not kissing *me*. No one ever said anything about what I'd do."

"Dante…" she murmurs. "Don't."

Her brows tighten, her lips parted, cheeks flushed.

"Don't what?" I ask, my voice filled with the same need staring back at me. "Don't do this?"

I lower my lips down to her jaw, kissing her softly, inhaling the scent of her floral shampoo.

"Oh, shit," she moans deeply, her ass hitting the island as she moves back a step. "I can't."

"You can't what, sweetheart?"

My mouth moves down her neck; her head falls backward, letting me have all of it. My tongue circles around that spot below her ear, and she practically jumps with a louder moan, her hand finding my hair and pulling as I nip her lobe. I drag back with a growl, my lips nearing hers, so close I can taste the rapid waves of her exhales and feel her heart colliding with mine.

I should kiss her. I should show her what I know we could be together, even if that's the only thing we can ever have.

Her eyes align with mine, our gazes threading tighter and pulling me deeper. Her breaths fall faster now as my pulse wages a battle it can't win.

But instead of taking what I want, I jerk away, knowing the only way I want those lips on mine is if she puts them there first.

By the time I'm through, Raquel Bianchi will be so turned on, so enslaved to her desire, her lips will be begging me for what her eyes are asking for right now.

"Let's eat." I casually pull up a stool behind her, taking a seat.

She continues to appear flustered, finally moving to sit beside me after too many seconds.

"You like sushi?" I ask, popping a piece into my mouth.

But I already know the answer to that, which is why I asked Janet to make some.

"It's one of my favorites." Her voice strains as her fingers run up and down her neck, exactly in the spot my lips just were.

"I'm glad."

She's quiet for a moment before she speaks again. "Why did you tell Janet I'm your girlfriend?"

"I don't want people to know my business regarding our deal." I drag my chair closer to hers. "It was easier to explain your presence that way."

She nods, her eyes darting from me to the food.

I lift up another piece with the chopsticks Janet left.

"Open your mouth," I tell her.

She does without hesitation, those hooded eyes on mine as I slip a piece past her lips. And even the way she chews makes me want to throw her on the table and part her thighs for a taste of something else far better.

I continue to feed her, and she doesn't protest.

I could get used to this.

Could get used to her.

But I shouldn't.

# *Seven*

# RAQUEL

I can't believe I let him kiss me earlier. Well, not kiss me exactly. More like fuck the hell out of my neck.

My lord, he's good with those lips and that tongue. I can just imagine what they could do to other parts of my anatomy.

My skin warms at the memory from half hour ago. I'm losing control with this man. I'm someone else with him, like I've shed a layer of myself. The part that's been caged is finally free.

I don't have anyone to answer to. No family to disappoint. No future husband to anger. Well, except this one, but I don't think he's anything like Carlito. At least I hope not.

"Are you ready to do this?" Dante asks from beside me, clutching a pen in his hand as he waits for me to sign the paperwork that'll give us the marriage certificate.

Am I?

No. But it's as ready as I'll ever be. In three months, I'll be starting a whole new life. A fresh start is something I never thought I'd have.

Taking a shaky breath, I turn my head to my right and find him staring back at me.

"I'm ready." I pick up a pen, adding my name on the line.

That's it. It's done. Just like that.

The blue ink glares back at me, condemning me or praising me. I can't be sure.

*Holy shit. I just married a stranger.*

Dante grabs the pen from me, folding the papers up. "All right. I'm going to take this to my contact, and we'll have the certificate in a few hours."

"That's really it?"

"Yeah, sweetheart. What did you expect? A wedding?" He smirks. "I mean, I can arrange that too. I kind of want to see you wearing a white dress."

"Not on your life," I laugh as I swat him playfully on his arm, knowing he's only teasing.

"Never say never." He winks. "Oh, and I have a little wedding gift for you."

"Dante." My brows pinch with a heavy sigh. "I'm not really your wife, so you don't have to spend money on me. You already went above and beyond with the clothes. And that lingerie. Seriously?"

He chuckles. "Think of the lingerie as your 'just in case' stash."

"Just in case what?"

His gaze turns hot and heavy-lidded as his hand hungrily jumps to the back of my neck, roughly drawing me closer and making my mouth flirt with a hint of his. His lips just barely graze mine, and my breathing stills, a tremor running down my spine.

"Just in case you decide to find out what it feels like to fuck a man actually worth your time."

I gasp, and my lower lip drops, accidentally sliding over his. My eyes widen, my breaths hitching, louder than any thunder shooting across the stormy skies.

His palm wraps tighter around me, our lips still stroking softly over one another's, his roughened exhales bathing my mouth.

I want more than anything for him to kiss me.

My core clenches and throbs.

*Just do it.*

But he doesn't. He turns away instead.

"Fuck," he groans, his hand clutching the back of his head.

A few seconds later, his eyes are on mine, playfulness fitting over his face like a mask.

"About that surprise," he tosses out. "Wait here while I get it."

He marches out, practically two steps at a time, while I release an audible sigh, gripping the edge of the table.

I've only been here half a day and I already want to fuck him.

*Awesome.*

*Not.*

He comes back in carrying a black leather satchel.

It's a nice handbag. Very much my style, but I'm not sure how much I'll be using it, considering I won't be going anywhere. But maybe I can once I'm out of here.

"Thank you," I say reaching for it as he comes to stand before me.

His lips slant up into a lopsided grin that has my stomach knotted up. "Open it."

"Okay?" I curiously unzip it once I place it on the table.

Then I gasp, tears springing into my eyes.

*No way.*

"Wha— How?" I stammer, running my finger past the stethoscope.

There's practically everything I had in my own bag, plus more.

"So you like it?" he questions knowingly.

"Are you kidding me?" I wipe a tear or two from my eye, not believing he did this. "I love it. I had one, but I left it at home. You don't know how badly I needed this. But it's too much. How did you even know?"

"I figured every doc needs her stash." He slips his hands into his black trousers, his shirt pulling against the muscular width of his chest as the buttons practically beg me to undo them. "You've helped me more than you realize. I wanted to do something in appreciation."

"This is amazing. Thank you," I whisper, zipping up the bag as my gaze finds his, unable and unwilling to let it go. "You've been so good to me."

His eyes search mine, his jaw twitching, the breaths slipping from his lungs fighting for space with mine.

"I have to go," he says gruffly, ripping apart that spark of connection that was there seconds ago. "I'll be at work all night. Damn overseas clients."

"Okay." I don't know what else to say from the change in his demeanor.

He starts to walk away, but suddenly freezes in place.

"Don't wait," he throws over his shoulder. "Go to sleep without me. You're safe here."

I feel so alone already. This house is too big for just me.

"How will I reach you if I need you?"

*How will I survive without a phone? I'm so cut off from everyone.*

"If you need me, ask one of my men to call me. I'll always be available for you."

"Thanks." I wish he'd stay a little longer, but his back is already turned.

"I'll see you later, sweetheart."

# DANTE

"Sir, we're positioned," Roger alerts Dom through his walkie-talkie as our van comes to a stop. "We see some movement inside. Two men so far. Both armed."

Roger is one of those dudes who, by day, seems like the nicest person alive—and I guess he has to be, considering he runs a martial arts school—but no one would know he's one hell of a killer, and an ex-army sniper.

"We're going through the back," Dom tells me, Enzo, and the other men in the van with us. "Keep your masks and gloves on at all times. Kill any man inside."

I slip on my black face mask and slide into my black gloves. The semi-automatic pistol in my hand will come in handy tonight as we shoot the enemy at Tips & Tricks.

One more Bianchi business will light up the night like colorful fireworks. Destroying everything they own has been part of our plan from the get-go. Little by little, we will take everything: their sources of income, their power, their daughters, and—finally—their lives.

My brothers and the men hop out one by one, with more guys exiting from the van behind us. Taking cautious steps, we walk the quarter block to the back entrance of the club. It's quiet here, with the crickets singing our anthem as we reach our destination.

It helps that one of our tech guys killed all the cameras in a three-mile radius. Every motherfucking cam has been sleeping for hours, keeping us hidden.

Once we reach the club, Dom stealthily peers inside, then lifts up two fingers, indicating he sees two targets. Grabbing the keys he took from Chiara when he kidnapped her, he unlocks the door, nodding once before he pushes it open.

Then all hell breaks loose.

Bullets fly from all directions. Two men come at me, their pistols pointing as they shoot. I duck down, kicking one man in the ankles before I fire back, then raise up the gun to take out the second guy before he has a chance to kill me.

Two others come running from the back of the bar, firing at me. Something pierces me near my shoulder, burning, but I ignore it. The adrenaline is what's keeping me conscious.

*Pop.*

I duck as a bullet comes flying past my face.

*Pop.*

This time I'm the one firing, shooting one guy in his thigh before getting another round into some other motherfucker. The man with the leg wound groans in agony before I let the bullet rip into his chest.

Silence thickens the room, and as I focus, I realize our enemies are all dead.

"Fuck!" I grumble, clinging to my left arm and hissing in pain that's now sharper than before.

"What happened?" Dom runs over.

"I'm hit."

He yanks up the sleeve of my hoodie, and I find blood oozing out from the top of my arm, right under the shoulder.

"Fuck. We have to get you to Raquel. She's the closest." Dom sounds alarmed as he removes his hoodie and tightens it around the wound, applying pressure.

We normally use Ricky for this kind of shit. He's a vet Tomás knew, but he's a lot further away from here, and since Raquel is closer, it does make more sense to get her to fix me up. I don't know how I'm going to explain a bullet wound, but I'd better make something up quick.

Just as we're about to leave, Dom and Enzo keeping me upright, we hear the sound of a woman's whimper.

*What the hell? No one's supposed to be here. Did we kill someone innocent? I'll never forgive myself if we messed up this badly.*

"Did you hear that?" Enzo hisses.

Dom nods, gesturing toward the bar with a tilt of his head.

*Go,* he mouths.

Enzo lets another man take his position beside me so he can investigate.

The pain in my shoulder is stronger now. I shut my eyes, taking long inhales, while listening to Enzo talk to the woman and ask her to get out from behind the bar. But she refuses, and it sounds like she has a weapon pointing at him.

Did he say Joelle?

But I'm no longer listening. I just want to get the fuck out of here.

"Come on, man!" Dom shouts. "Dante needs help!"

I open my eyes and find Joelle, a stripper from the club, in Enzo's clutches. She's the one Carlito and the rest of the Palermo men love to play with. I guess my brother wants to take their girl away. Not surprising, knowing how much he likes her, even when he pretends she means nothing.

From athletes to celebrities, Joelle brings in the most expensive clients. The Bianchis are not only going to lose their club, but their favorite girl too.

Once we're in the van, they lay me down across the bench seat in the back. A minute later, we're rolling down the street, and I still have no idea what I'm going to tell Raquel.

# Eight

## RAQUEL

"**M**a'am, wake up," someone calls to me from somewhere far away.

It's like a dream I can't seem to grab hold of.

"We need your help. Wake up," the same voice says again.

My eyes pop open, and that's when I find two of Dante's men standing over me. At least that's who I hope they are, or I'm in some serious trouble.

"Wha…" I sit up, my eyes darting from one to the other. "What's going on?"

"The boss needs you, ma'am. He got hurt tonight. A robbery."

"What are you talking about? Where is he?"

I rush to my feet, thanking myself for not wearing short shorts to bed and deciding on some loose black pajama pants and a black tank top instead.

"He's in the kitchen. He was working late," the tall man informs me. "He was coming out to his car when he was shot."

"Shot? What?!" I jog down the steps, wondering why the hell he isn't in a damn hospital.

"Yeah," the man goes on, keeping up with me easily. "They took whatever cash was in his wallet, then put a bullet in his arm when he tried to chase after them."

"Fucking idiot!" I grate in frustration as we descend down the final step. "Everyone knows not to chase after the criminal."

"I'm sorry, beautiful wife," Dante says from a distance. "I'll remember that for next time."

That's when I see him, the light in his eyes set to a dim as he slumps in a chair beside a table, a white shirt covered with a small red stain enveloping his arm.

"Seriously, Dante?" I throw my hands in the air once I approach. "The first night we're married, and you've already managed to almost die?"

"I did say I was sorry." He smirks, but it's weak, like he's in a lot of pain.

Shit. I'm such a jerk, talking to him about this while he's hurting.

The doctor bag he bought me is already on the table, waiting for me.

"Dante, I hope you realize I can't do much here. Why didn't you just go to a hospital?"

"Would you believe me if I said I don't have insurance?" He grins, his teeth gritting now as though every word is a struggle.

"I don't know what the hell you're hiding, and I don't think I want to know, but I can't help you. What if the bullet is really deep in there? I can't remove it here without risking more damage."

If he doesn't want to go to the hospital, there has to be a reason. It's not like a robbery was his fault, unless he's lying about what happened.

*Who is he really? What did I get involved in?*

"It's a flesh wound, baby. You're all I've got, so you either let me die or clean me up. But leave a nice scar so I'll have a good story for the ladies."

"What ladies?" I arch a brow as I draw near, deciding I'll do my best to help him, since it's obvious he won't be going anywhere.

"Oh, you know." He winces as I unwrap the shirt from his arm and find the hole has stopped bleeding. "The ones I'll spend my nights with when you're long gone, sipping cocktails in Maui while I die from missing you."

"Uh-huh. Yeah, okay." I hand the shirt to one of his men. "You? Lonely? I find that hard to believe."

"You're a hard woman to replace, Raquel Bianchi." He looks deeply into my eyes. "I can already tell."

I'm so used to him teasing me, but I'm shocked to find no humor in those words, nor his gaze. He means it.

"Well, you'll have to learn to go on without me, Dante Cavaleri."

"Ouch. You're an awful, awful woman."

"The worst," I tease. "Now, come on. Get up. Let's go to the sink."

He stands, moving with me, his bare skin and hard muscles a sight I can't enjoy under the circumstances.

"I don't think I'll have a hard time replacing you, though," I tell him with a quirk of my lips as I remove a bottle of saline solution from my bag.

"Wow. You're really trying to kick a man when he's already down." He rests his forearm right at the edge of the sink.

"It's what I do best." I crack a smile, spilling half the bottle of saline over his shoulder and making sure it's clean before I examine him for any bullet fragments.

He sits back down on the chair as I grab some forceps.

"This is gonna hurt," I warn.

"Baby, nothing could hurt quite as bad as that mouth of yours giving me shit while I've got a hole the size of Texas."

"It's not that big," I scoff playfully. "Don't be so dramatic."

"Oh, you're gonna get it."

His grin deepens, and I have an insane urge to kiss him.

"Are you ready?" I swallow down my growing attraction, moving the forceps toward his arm and placing my other palm on his wrist.

He nods once, then I begin.

"Shit," he hisses as the metal meets his flesh.

"Remember this pain the next time you play Rambo."

He groans, flexing his jaw, and I can feel his eyes on me. His gaze is so dark and warm, I have to steady my pulse to concentrate.

I continue working, making sure there's nothing inside. And there isn't. I stitch him up and apply some gauze before wrapping the wound.

"You'll need antibiotics. Where do you plan on getting those?" I glare at him.

"I know a guy who knows a guy." His mouth curves into a smile as he takes a seat back on the chair.

"This isn't funny, Dante. You'd better get them, or you could develop a serious infection."

He looks at one of his men behind me and jerks his head to the side. They march out on command, and once they're gone, his gaze seductively slinks from my face down to the curve of my hips before riding back up.

"Come here, baby." He pats his lap, his eyes eagerly drinking me in.

"Uh…" My brows slam upward. "There's absolutely no way I'm sitting on you."

"Wanna bet?"

Before I can make my escape, his uninjured arm snakes around my ass, gripping me tight and setting me right on his thighs.

"Dante…" I stress, my feet dangling over his other side. "We're supposed to keep business and pleasure separate, not mix the two."

He gazes up at me with hooded eyes, his lips nearing the middle of my chest.

"Who made up that rule? Because it's pretty stupid," he rasps sultrily, making my insides curl deliciously in the wake of his alluring voice.

"Thank you for taking care of me, wife."

All I can do is groan as his hot mouth lands over the top of my breasts, still covered with clothing. His lips pepper me with soft kisses, and my nipples strain from the sensation.

My hand settles on his head with a loud gasp, my fingers sinking into the silken weight of his hair as the thick strands awaken my senses. I clutch for dear life, pulling a little too roughly when his teeth scrape along the curve of my breast. He breaks with a savage growl, his hand twisting up to my hair and yanking hard as he clenches his teeth.

"If you make those sounds again…" he warns, his gaze capturing me as his breaths fall rapidly over my mouth. "You're gonna find yourself fully stretched with my cock inside you."

My pulse leaps out of my throat, my inhales fighting with my exhales. My body wants him, but I can't give in.

No emotional attachments.

"I…I should go," I warble as I quickly stand up.

He lets me go with a sigh.

My feet barely move. My back is to him as I take a step away, then another. But I stop, my shoulders swaying with heavy panting.

I stand here, fighting my feelings for someone I don't know. I've never craved a man like I do him. I never knew what it felt like to be desired this badly.

But I know now. I want to know how it feels to be touched by him. I want him to show me, even if it's for a short time.

The chair drags across the floor, the sound rocking my already tumultuous heart. His footsteps thud, and I suck in a sharp breath, my stomach in tight knots.

He comes closer, his body heat warming me up from the inside out. I whimper, unable to contain the flutters when he's this close.

"I want you." His erotic, husky tone whips over my skin as his hand roughly clutches the back of my neck, spinning me around, landing me harshly against him.

My chest flails with heavy waves of emotion as my lips part. His gaze is piercing, and I can't help but be pulled into those gorgeous eyes and that face bent with want.

"You make me insane, Raquel."

He looks at me so deeply, so intoxicatingly.

"I'm sorry," he rasps as I swallow the lump lodged in my throat.

And before I can ask what for, his lips slam to mine.

He kisses me like a man hungry for more. Like his life ends and begins with me. The moans and groans mingle with our breaths as he pushes me up against the wall with the weight of his body. I knock roughly into the hard surface. His injured arm hangs by his side, his hand palming the curve of my hip.

I cling to the back of his head, my fingers sprawling and drawing him even closer as his erotic growls vibrate against my mouth.

He angles his face to kiss me deeper, his tongue rolling with mine, his teeth biting into my lower lip before we move in sync again, finding a rhythm too difficult to separate from.

I could kiss this man for hours. It's filled with passion and beauty. The first kiss to rival all first kisses I've had in the past. Nothing will ever come close.

After what feels like forever, yet not long enough, he pulls back. Both of us pant as his forehead falls to mine.

"I've wanted to kiss you for a long time." His gravelly whisper seeps with sensuality, wrapping me with so much hunger that I ache for him.

"We've only just met at the bar," I sigh, attempting to calm my stuttered breathing. "Can't be that long."

"It feels longer than that."

"I guess it does," I breathe.

"That kiss…Raquel." He takes a long inhale.

"You weren't so bad yourself." I grin, my eyes closed as I enjoy the intimacy of the moment.

"You're a hard one to impress." There's a smile twined in his words. "I promise to do better next time, wife."

"There'll be no next time," I pretend to argue, no longer sure who I'm trying to convince.

"We'll see about that." The edge of certainty in his voice is obvious.

And he's probably right. After that kiss, I don't think I could stop him.

I drag in a slow breath. "You should go to bed and sleep. You need to heal."

"Only if you come with me." His lips sink to mine in a soft caress, and my insides flip around as though disconnected from my body.

"Okay," I murmur as he draws back, the corners of his lips climbing with a heartfelt smile.

And I feel it somewhere inside me, like it's found a permanent space within my very soul. Our eyes stay locked on one another as my body courses with the awareness prickling my skin. When he looks at me like that, I'm grateful to be alive. Grateful I found him. Or that he found me.

His hand grabs hold of mine, and he leads me out of the kitchen and up the stairs to our bedroom. When the door shuts behind us, I hide away the nerves, watching him as he comes toward me, our gazes once again fused into one molten wave.

"Let's go to bed," he says softly, the back of his hand coasting down the side of my face, making my cheek tingle from his touch.

I nod, letting him twine his pinky around mine as he brings me to the bed and flips the comforter over to make room.

I climb in first, with him close behind. My body alights with renewed hunger, the passion from before lingering and stamping over any thoughts that tell me this is wrong or that being in bed with him, this near his body, is not right.

But he feels right, and in this moment, that's all that matters. Life is too short to live in the shadow of regret.

He slides his right arm under my body, shifting me to him, while his left arm rests over my middle.

"Sleep well," I say.

He sighs contently. "With you, I will. Goodnight, sweetheart."

My eyelids flow shut, my heart full of happiness. I'm bathed by the serenity of this moment, not wanting to ever be without it.

And yet, I wonder how I can feel this way, knowing I've just stitched up a man I barely know.

"**H**ow's the arm?" Enzo asks the following day as he sits across from me in my office at work. "She make your boo-boo feel better?"

He chuckles, leaning back further into the black leather armchair.

"She sure as fuck did." I push my feet out, crossing my arms.

No woman has ever taken care of me. Not until her. The way she tended to my wound so gently, it made me feel all kinds of shit I don't want to admit out loud.

"She's damn good at taking care of me. Jealous? Joelle still hate you?"

He throws up a middle finger. "It hasn't even been a day. She'll come around." He grins smugly. "It takes time to love me."

"So I guess you'll be waiting a while, then?" My head tips to the side with a mocking laugh.

"Yeah, yeah. You got jokes? You know I don't need her. I've got plenty of women on speed dial. But damn, that body would look so good tangled in my sheets."

"I'm sure she's dying to get right in your bed with all the women you fuck in it."

Joelle was never part of our plan, but I guess some opportunities just find themselves. And my brother's always had a thing for her, from the first moment he laid eyes on her. He'd usually come with me when I'd go to meet with Carlito, but once he saw her, he started inviting himself each time I went.

"Okay, a little clarification." He lifts up an index finger, shaking his head, pretending he's got his feelings hurt. "I don't fuck anyone on my bed. I've got other beds around the house for that."

"Wow. I'm damn sorry for the confusion," I snicker. "But she still won't want your ass once she sees the women there. What are you going to do with her, anyway?"

"I'm gonna keep her until I get bored." He shrugs. "Then move her to a different country so the Bianchis never get her back. She's worth a whole lot of shit to them."

"I know that. But what is she worth to you? And before you start…" I lift a palm, cutting off any of his bullshit before it begins. "I know you like her. So instead, how about maybe take care of her for a while? I'm sure she's not used to that, being around those fucks."

I wait for a wise-ass comment, but it never comes. He stares over my head, as though considering what I'm saying.

"Nah." He shakes his head. "She and I are like oil and water, hot and cold. She doesn't give a shit about me. She and I at the club was just her working, nothing more."

His jaw tenses with the edge in his voice. And I know immediately by the look in his eye that she hurt him.

"Even a cat with the sharpest claws can be tamed," I say.

"You a fucking poet now?" He picks up a pen and tosses it at me with a chuckle.

I catch it easily, staring at him with a grin.

Enzo likes to hide behind his big heart, as though showing it off makes him weak. He might be the youngest one of us at only twenty-five, but he grew up quickly like we all had to.

Each of us deserves to find something meaningful, something true, whether it's a woman or something else that makes us happy. But I worry we're doomed to walk behind the life we could have, instead of alongside it.

While spending some more time with Enzo, we hear something slam in Dom's office right next to mine, so we rush there.

It was his burner cell connecting to the wall after he received a text from Faro, threatening to kill us like he did Matteo.

The fucking Bianchis still don't respect us. They don't quite comprehend the kind of men we are now. We care about nothing more than killing them all.

We've risen from the ashes, completely reborn. We're the devils marking their graves. They may have been the ones to fear then, but we're the ones to fear now.

And the angel sleeping beside me has no idea that the man who swore to protect her will be the one taking out her father.

I haven't been able to stop thinking about waking up with Raquel curled around me. I want more of that—more of *her*—even when it's the last thing I should want. I didn't realize the sparks we'd have when we were finally face-to-face, even while knowing how badly I wanted to fuck her when I followed her around all that time.

I know I can stop myself from falling in love with her, but I can't stop myself from wanting her. And I don't think she can either.

As a thank-you for helping me with the arm, I had Janet make a steak and lobster dinner for tonight, knowing those are some of her other favorites. The garden by the fountain has been arranged with a table for two, and candles with rose petals have been scattered across it.

Probably a little too much, but I think she deserves it after everything she's been through with Carlito and her family.

Once I park my McLaren, I enter the house, finding her cuddled on the sofa in the den with the TV on. She sits up as soon as she sees me.

"How's your arm?" There's concern scribbled all over her face.

"As good as new," I lie.

The muscle is still throbbing, especially when I move it.

"Uh-huh." She narrows her eyes. "You suck at lying. You know that?"

*I guess not as much as you think, baby.*

"Man, I have so many things to improve on." I walk up a step, then some more. "And now that I remember...how about you come over here so I can practice kissing you again? Maybe this time, I'll get it right."

She rolls her eyes, lips teasing me with a hint of a barely there smile. "Not on your life, Dante Cavaleri. I'm not that kind of girl."

"Really?"

I'm in front of her now, roughly cupping her jaw, my gaze pinning her in place.

"It didn't seem that way this morning, when you were rubbing this ass all over my cock," I say gruffly, grabbing a handful of her ass cheek.

Her exhales instantly grow ragged, her face flushing crimson. "I must've been asleep."

"Who's the liar now, wife? You know you can't resist me just as much as I can't resist you."

I lower my lips to hers, softly kissing her once. Twice. Even though her lips don't kiss me in return, that rapid breathing greets me.

"How about you stop denying you want me?" My words roll over her mouth. "How about we see where this goes?"

Her chest rises faster now as my lips feather over hers, softly caressing.

"Whether it ends today or months from now, the world is ours, and we don't need to know what happens next to enjoy the days we have."

"I want to," she confesses. "But I can't."

"Why?" My voice is low and deep as my mouth still brushes over hers, while my hand is tightly circled around her lower back.

"You scare me, Dante. I've never felt this much intensity for someone, this much attraction." She sighs, like it's a bad thing. "I like you, and I don't want to like you because I'll be gone in three months." Her eyes fall to the ground. "And maybe you're used to fooling around, but I'm not."

"Hey." With a finger, I tip up her face to mine. "Don't put a label on this. Not before we've even had a chance to figure out what we are. What we could be."

*What the hell am I saying?*

She's right. We can't be more. I can't love her. I'd be betraying my brothers. My family. Everyone. At least that's how I see it.

But she is my wife, and she will be forever, so I'm not okay with her calling us a fling.

"I can't stay here." Her eyes beg for understanding, shrouded by so much pain. "Even if I were to fall for you at the end of this, I couldn't stay. They'll always find me, and they'll kill us both."

I cup her cheek, wanting to touch her every chance I get. "You don't have to worry about them hurting you, or me. I'll slit every one of their throats to keep you safe. You hear me?"

Her gaze alights with tears. "You don't mean my father, right?"

When I don't answer, her stare widens.

"I don't want anyone to die, Dante. I just want to be left alone."

"Sometimes the only way to find peace is to take someone else's away."

She inhales sharply, looking at me with a twinge of fear.

"Who are you?" The question comes as a whisper, one full of bewilderment, like she already knows the answer.

But she doesn't.

She doesn't know I'm both the prince from her fairy tales and the monster from her nightmares.

# RAQUEL

I was right about him, or at least I think I was. There's a danger behind those heavenly eyes. One I'm only starting to see, even while it's not directed at me.

But those that have met that side of him must fear it when they smell it coming, like the thickening of the air right before the storm comes crashing down.

For some reason, I don't fear him at all. I don't think he'll hurt me, and I hope he doesn't hurt my family. Though he probably could.

Once I leave, I won't have to worry about anyone fighting. There'll be nothing to fight about. I'll be gone.

He holds me in his protective arms as we sway together to a soft ballad playing from the speakers he arranged in his garden.

I couldn't believe he planned such an intimate dinner. The food was amazing. It's as though he knows all the things I like.

After the plates were cleared, we shared a huge piece of tiramisu, another one of my downfalls. And just when I thought the night was over, he surprised me with music. And damn, does the man know how to move.

"I love dancing with you," he says softly.

His eyes are on mine, stealing my breaths away, and I'm not sure how many I have left to give. His arms hold me around the small of my back as we dance the hours away, lost to the melody. To each other. The sun dips away, the fiery sky cast in a spark of orange and red.

"I love dancing with you too," I sigh contently, smiling with a heart so full, I can't contain it. "You didn't have to do any of this for me, but I love it so much."

"You deserve it, Raquel."

One hand glides up to my face, and every time he touches me so tenderly, it wakes up my insane desire for him, curling with the warmth of a fire he's set in the pit of my stomach.

"A woman like you deserves to be treated this way every day. Don't ever forget it." His knuckles drop to my lips. "Know your worth, baby, because I do."

My heart flips erratically, joining my stomach.

*Can I keep you?*

Why couldn't my parents have forced me to marry him? I'd definitely have been on board with that. I don't know if this is how he treats every woman lucky enough to be with him, but I'm glad I'm on the receiving end. It's nice to be with a man who isn't trying to hurt me for a change. He smiles, like he's heard my thoughts.

And as he leads me into another dance, I giggle shamelessly when he spins me once before I'm back against him—body to body, heart to heart, soul to soul. It's like we're creating our own music. Our own lyrical bond. But when the music finally ends, when the words stop swirling around us, I don't know where either of us will be.

Another song picks up, and it's as though we're consumed by each other. The touching, the feeling of our hands and bodies, all of it…it's overwhelming. Being with him tonight has somehow brought us closer together.

My head rests on his shoulder as the song ends, and he kisses my hair.

"Did I mention how beautiful you look in this white dress?"

I lift up my head with a grin. "Uh, I think you may have mentioned that before and after you kissed me."

"We kissed?" He tilts his head sideways, his lips quirking up. "When?"

I roll my eyes on a laugh. "You're an idiot."

"Only when you're around." He bites his bottom lip, his hypnotizing gaze crawling over my face, getting me all hot and thoroughly bothered.

"How about you remind me, baby?" he asks, his tone smoldering. "Was it a good kiss?"

My nipples harden under the tight confines of the silk material.

"It was perfect," I say hoarsely, remembering him whisking me off the last step as soon as I came down wearing this dress he bought me.

"Describe it." He gazes down at my lips, eyes hooded. "Don't skip a detail."

This time, I'm the one with my hand reaching up toward him, the stubble on his jaw grazing my palm. I stare deeply into his eyes, my thumb running across his lips, wanting badly to feel them.

"How about I show you?"

And then I do. I capture his lips with mine, and the most erotic growl erupts from this man as his hand slams to the back of my head, the music long forgotten. Our lips part in a frenzy, his tongue stroking mine in hurried circles, hands clawing at our clothes.

My long fingernails land on the back of his shirt, yanking the navy button-down out from beneath his black pants as his mouth sucks on my tongue while I moan. My nails rake up his back; the feel of his smooth skin on my fingertips has my heart pounding and body screaming for more. He groans as I let my nails sink in deeper, loving this side of myself I never knew existed.

His hands are under my ass, and I'm lifted into the air, my thighs coming around his waist. Our lips are unbreakable as the kiss grows more intense, and I'm unsure where he ends and I begin. He lowers me onto the cool grass, his thick cock rubbing circles over my achy clit through the thin shroud of my panties.

"Touch me," I beg, my voice so needy I barely recognize it. "I want to feel your hands on me."

It's stupid. I know that. I'll grow attached.

But right now, my rational side is gone. I want Dante like my every breath is his and his every breath is mine.

"Are you sure?" he asks, his brows bowed with wanton hunger.

"You don't seem like the type of man to ask for permission."

"I'm not." He brushes his lips over mine. "But I'm asking, baby."

"Touch me, please. I've never wanted to be touched by anyone as badly as I want to be touched by you."

"Fuck," he growls through gritted teeth.

Suddenly, his hand slowly glides from my knee up to my inner thigh. A finger hooks into my thong, roughly yanking it to the side, exposing me to the whisk of cool air.

"I've been thinking of this pussy ever since I met you."

"Yes," I whimper as he rubs two fingers on each side of my wet slit, careful to avoid my clit.

"I've wondered how you like to be fucked," he continues. "Rough? Gentle? Both?"

The tip of his finger invades me, easing an inch inside.

My breathing intensifies as my walls clench around him.

"I've wanted to know how you taste." He lowers his mouth to my neck, teasing my earlobe with his teeth as he enters me fully, sliding in and out slowly.

"Dante, please," I groan with desperation.

"Mmm, I like how my name sounds on those pretty lips." He circles his finger inside me. "Say it again, and this time tell me how you want it."

His lips leave kisses down my neck as he stretches me with another finger.

"Yes, just like that! Fuck me how you fuck the other women," I beg, knowing I'm soaking his fingers.

"There are no women but you, wife." He thrusts in and out, harder this time, hitting my G-spot so deeply that stars flicker before my eyes. "Now tell me, how should I make you come?"

My heart races, the intense way I'm turned on giving me strength to tell him what I really want.

"With your mouth," I confess. "With your fingers. Hard. I want…I've never…"

But before I can tell him that the three guys I've slept with in the past have not been rough at all, that I want someone to be, my thighs are in the air and over his shoulders and his face is a centimeter away from my pussy.

"If rough is what you want, baby, I can give you that." Without looking away from me, he reaches his long tongue out, taking a slow swipe from my entrance right up to my sensitive clit.

I rattle under him, my moans a mix of whimpers. It's been years since a man's gone down on me. My God, I've missed this.

I grasp on to his hair, pushing him back down onto me. His laugh vibrates over my needy flesh as his tongue runs up and down, hitting both sides of my clit, while two fingers enter me, ramming with a tortured tempo. My toes curl as his tongue and fingers continue to wreck me with sweet agony, the combination bringing the orgasm to the cusp of its breaking point.

"Yes, don't stop," I groan, rotating my hips over his mouth. "I'm gonna come."

He slams inside me over and over, the tip of his tongue flicking faster at the same time. My hips arch like I'm trying to escape the orgasm that's about to blow my body to shreds. And with another thrust, I come violently, screaming his name, not caring who hears it.

He climbs up my body, kissing me hungrily. His hand reaches under my dress and cups my breast, pinching my nipple in between two fingers.

"Turn around," he demands as his lips leave mine, his gaze still clouded with desperation.

I flip over, desperate for him too.

"Fuck me," I demand, turning my head toward him and sticking out my ass. "With your cock this time."

"Shit, baby."

His hand finds the edge of my dress, lifting it over me, and his palm lands hard on my bare ass, making my skin burn from the harsh touch. I whimper as two fingers slip inside me, fucking me all over again. His hand wraps around the front of my throat, gripping roughly and pulling my face backward with renewed possession as another wave of an orgasm grows.

I'm a prisoner to his gaze as I moan out his name, needing to come, the pleasure even more powerful than before.

"I *am* gonna fuck you," he promises through gritted teeth, his voice sealed with an oath. "It won't be today, but we both know it'll be soon. And we both know how much you're gonna beg for it to happen again and again, wife."

Those words shoot straight to my core, like an explosion. I shouldn't love that title, but I do…when he's the one calling me that.

He curls his fingers inside me, pounding into my G-spot like a demonic possession, his breath hot and hungry at the shell of my ear.

"Oh, God, Dante, I'm…I'm coming!" I cry, my body sparking to life.

"Mmm. Such a good little cunt. Takes my fingers so well." He pumps me faster. "I know it's gonna take my cock just as good."

The dirty talk pushes all the right buttons, wringing out every ounce of pleasure from me. Once my tremors still, he slides his fingers out, cupping my pussy as he bites and kisses my neck. And instead of removing his hand completely, he glides two fingers up to my ass.

"Dante, what are you—"

"Shhh."

His palm tightens around my neck, pulling me toward him, and then his lips are on mine, our tongues falling to a slow rhythm as the tip of his finger enters my other hole.

My muscles lock, stiffening around him. No one has ever done this to me. No one even asked to. But he doesn't have to ask. I'd let him do just about anything.

He draws back a few inches, his lips falling away from mine. "I'm going to own that tight little hole too. Isn't that right?"

"Yes," I groan, feeling another orgasm rising like a tidal wave.

"You need to come again, don't you, sweetheart?"

"Yes," I admit, unashamed.

And he lets me. With my neck and my pussy at his mercy, his talented fingers bring me to the brink, the rush unlike anything I've ever felt before.

I don't know how I'll ever be able to live without it now.

# Ten

# DANTE

**W**hat happened between us last night was bound to happen eventually, and we both know it'll keep happening.

She's like a drug.

Her beauty, those deep brown eyes…they fuel me like no one before her. The attraction between us lights me on fire, and I can't deny it's there, burning through my walls.

She has no idea I have cameras all around, including in the bedroom we share. She doesn't know how much I enjoy watching her whenever I'm at work, like I'm doing right now in my office.

Raquel walks out of the shower completely naked, the ends of her dried hair dipping to her ass. I grow harder, my cock surging to move inside her the way my fingers did last night.

She felt damn good and tasted like heaven, and every time she said my name, it made me want to make her come all over again. I haven't been able to stop thinking about it.

My door opens unexpectedly, and I fumble with my phone like I was caught doing something bad. And I guess I was.

"What you got there?" Enzo wags his brows as he strides inside. "Watching porn on the job again?" He tsks, sitting down on the seat across from my desk. "Don't make me report you to the boss."

"Is he even here?" I ask about Dom, who's the CEO of the hotel chain Tomás used to run before his death.

Enzo and I are on the board of the company, and all three of us also co-own the nightclubs we started together.

"Nah. He's probably torturing Chiara again," he chuckles. "I really can't believe she doesn't know who he is. I bet she'd remember me though."

He says it like he was some hot shit back then.

"You were barely in puberty. You didn't even have hair on your balls then, baby bro. She wouldn't know who the fuck you were."

We're lucky we never came face-to-face with her at the strip club she runs. But that place is so dark and creeping with so many people, it was highly unlikely.

"Screw you, man." Enzo's shoulders rattle with a snicker. "You sound bitter as hell. I'm sorry if you're not getting any pussy, but don't take it out on me."

"I get all the pussy I need."

"Really?" He rubs his palms together. "Finally, this conversation just got interesting."

I crush a paper in my palm, one intended for the trash, and toss it at his head. "I'm not telling you shit. Get out of here and go work or something."

"I'm done, actually. I was heading out in a bit." He gets to his feet. "Marissa texted for a quickie."

"Which one is she?"

"The one with the pink highlights, or whatever that shit is called."

"All you had to say is the one who gave you head in the VIP room."

He bursts out laughing, and I do too, remembering that night filled with too much booze and too many women. It was weeks ago, but it might as well be a lifetime.

"All right, I gotta get out of here too," I tell him, putting away the files I was working on and following him out of the office.

"Have fun with Marissa," I throw over my shoulder as he heads toward his car.

"Have fun with Raquel." He smirks knowingly.

*I plan to.*

# RAQUEL

I decide to take a pre-dinner dip in the pool. The days are still in the low seventies, which is my perfect weather. I hate the New York summer heat and humidity, and so does my hair.

Dante's men pay me no mind as I strut out the door to the pool, but I know they're aware of everything as they stand there like statues. It's weird. I'm not used to it at all, but at least I feel safe knowing they can protect me if the need comes.

I don't know what my father will do if he finds me before I can get away. It's probably nothing compared to what Carlito will do. I don't think my father would physically hurt me, but I can only guess how mad he is. I'm sure he has men out searching for me, with Carlito leading the pack. My dad is very protective of his family name—all my uncles are—and I bet once he found out his precious, dutiful daughter ran away so she could avoid marriage to a man he deemed her match, his head was rolling.

I wonder if this caused him to come out of hiding from whoever it is that's after my family. Maybe it's a good thing I'm here. Not only am I safe from Carlito, but I'm safe from the men after my father too.

Dad was always kind to me growing up, but I knew I was nothing more than another soldier in his army. Someone whose job it was to obey. He treated me like I was his little angel, but also like his commodity, an object to shine and make pretty. I was supposed to remain a virgin until marriage, but little do my parents know, I haven't been a virgin for a very long time.

To their knowledge, I never had a boyfriend, but I did have a few short-term ones behind their backs. It got difficult to sneak around, though. I was constantly lying and telling them I was going out with friends from work when I was really out with a guy.

The women in my circle are nothing more than toys for the men in their life, whether it's their fathers or their husbands. Our opinions don't matter, and our happiness sure as hell doesn't. All that matters is that we do what we're told when we're told. I can't stand it. And I can't wait to be away from it forever.

I reach the pool, grabbing a chair floaty from beside it, then climb down into the perfectly heated warm water. Lying over the float, I close my eyes. The sun blazes down on top of me, and I love the heat on my skin.

The music plays from the speakers set around the garden, music I put on before I came out here. Dermot Kennedy's voice fills my ears; the song "Better Days" hits me right in the heart. A song about finding the light in the darkness. I hope I find my light soon, because the dark has been overpowering me for too long.

Just as I'm about to hop back in the water, I feel a hand grip my inner thigh. My pulse throbs in my ears as my eyes fly open. I find Dante smiling and his tanned, tattooed skin glistening with beaded droplets of water.

"Oh my God, you scared me!" I pant, a hand landing on my chest while my eyes refuse to unpeel from his body.

His legs are hidden in the water as he backs away into the shallow side of the pool while I drift over the deep end.

This is the second time I'm seeing him without his shirt on, but unlike when he got shot, I can actually enjoy the view this time. He shouldn't wear clothing. Period. His stomach is shredded with an eight-pack, and my fingers are itching to trace his abs. To feel them.

And getting a better view of his tattoos is like looking at a piece of artwork. The ink starts on the right side of his neck, drifting down his shoulder and forearm before finally wrapping around his knuckles. But it doesn't stop there. The black vines and matching roses also spread over the right side of his torso, with a large skull on his chest, surrounded by black flowers.

It's as though his body is cast in both light and darkness. A man split between two worlds, caught in the middle with no way out.

"My sincerest apologies, wife. You looked so good lying there, I needed to join you. How was the shower earlier?" He comes toward me, placing a hand on my thigh.

I jerk with a wild stare.

"How did you know I took a shower?" I slap his hand off me. *Has he been watching me? Is he some creep?*

I wait for an answer while he combs a hand through his hair, looking a little unsure of himself.

"Dante?" My voice is thick with ire. "You'd better tell me right now. Do you have cameras on me?"

"How mad would you be if I said I did?" He grins.

I snarl, splashing him with water and huffing out a breath.

"I can't believe this!" My tone is clipped now, inhales rattling inside my lungs. "How could you not tell me you've been watching me doing God knows what!"

"I'm sorry, baby. Let me explain."

"No. Fuck you!"

I try desperately to climb out of the chair, but his palm lands heavy on my knee.

"Let go! I'm leaving! You, this house, everything. I don't need this. I've had enough of being controlled by my family. I don't need it from a damn stranger." I fight to get his hand off, but he calmly keeps it there. "You must be some sick perv to be watching me!"

"That's not it, sweetheart. Let's talk."

But I don't want to hear it. Instead, I try harder to get out of this stupid chair, even as he clutches to me with pleading eyes. But instead, I flip right into the water.

It envelops every inch of me as I tumble into six feet of water.

Down. Down.

Drifting.

Floating.

Not doing a thing to climb out.

Is this what drowning is like? To fight for air? To fight for life? The way I've always been fighting. The way I'll probably never stop.

Strong hands grip my waist, bringing my head up to the surface.

"What the hell are you doing, Raquel?" There's fury laced in the cadence of his voice, worry carved over his face. "You trying to die? Because I'm not gonna fucking let you."

"Oh!" I throw my hands in the air. "So you're going to tell me what the hell I'm allowed to do now too?! You…" I poke him in the center of his chest. "Don't get to do that. You hear me!"

His jaw twitches, his eyes narrowing as his Adam's apple bobs, while his hands drop to his sides, forming clenched fists.

My heart races from my own anger, but also from the way he looks at me, like he's not sure if he wants to give me a thorough spanking or throw me up against the wall and fuck me. Maybe all of the above.

How the hell am I still attracted to him, knowing he's probably some kind of sicko?

*Oh my God! I walked out of the shower naked today!*

I know he's seen me almost bare already, but that's different. I had no idea I was being spied on!

I sneer, turning away from him in an attempt to get out of here, but before I can, his hand whips out, clutching the back of my neck, yanking me flush against him.

"Did I say you could go?" His lips hover over mine. "We weren't done talking."

My eyes turn to thin slits. His dark, heavy gaze breathes me in like a serpent assessing its prey as I push at him.

"*I* was done," I hiss. "Let me go, you asshole. I have nothing else to say to you. Oh, and you can take your sorry ass to the couch tonight because there's no way in hell I'm sleeping next to you."

"I thought you were leaving." His lips coil into a devilish smirk, his fingers delving deeper.

"I am. Tomorrow."

He chuckles low. "Well, if you think I'm going anywhere except my bed, you have me mistaken for someone else, sweetheart."

His inhales are sharp as his lips sweep past mine. My heart squeezes, taking my lungs with it. I fight the climbing whimper.

My body is drunk on the feel of him. My toes curl within the water, and my nipples bead, craving his touch. My breaths grow shallow as his chest rubs over mine.

"I'm sorry," he says, his gravelly tone lacing through my veins like poison.

My anger begins dissipating, like a candle flickering until it gives out.

"I think we need to start over, because I can't stand you being mad at me."

He rotates my body, dragging me to the edge of the pool by the back of my neck. His muscles press up behind me in the water, forcing me to curl over the hard surface with my cheek pressed onto the cold, damp stones.

"If you want me to stop watching you, I will," he grunts against my neck, his lips flirting with my skin.

His other hand begins climbing up the outskirts of my thigh until his palm reaches my hip, a finger hooking under the thin strap of my black bikini bottom.

"I have cameras all over my property," he explains. "It's only a means of protection, baby. I never expected you to be here, in my bed, under my fingertips."

His hand wanders down to my core, cupping me there, massaging, coaxing the orgasm he's already set ablaze. I melt into him, forgetting why I was even mad in the first place.

"Why couldn't you tell me?" I ask with a barely threaded whisper, arousal coating it. "I would've at least made sure you only saw my good side."

A sexy, masculine chuckle falls from his mouth just as two fingers slip my bikini to the side, exposing me. "Every inch of you is your good side, sweetheart."

I gasp as his fingers slice in between my lips below, rubbing my clit in small, torturous circles.

His men are everywhere, but luckily, none are facing us. Thank God for the music masking whatever is left of my dignity.

My hands fight to hang on to the edge of the pool. The need to cry out, to let him know how good this feels, overwhelms me.

"You liked me watching you, didn't you, Raquel? You liked knowing I was hard today seeing your naked body after the shower."

"Yes," I confess with a whimper, unable to deny it.

I like being dirty with him. I like knowing I can turn him on so easily. It's empowering.

He rubs my clit faster now, causing me to grasp his thigh with a hand. My nails practically pierce his skin as I fight the astounding need to scream out his name.

"Dante!" I whisper hoarsely. "We can't do this here. Your people are everywhere."

"I thought you liked being watched?"

I moan low, my body in a state of craze at the thought of coming with all the men around to hear and see me.

"We can't." But I don't sound sure at all.

"We can. And you will. And you'd better use your inside voice, baby girl, because I won't be gentle."

I remember when he said those words to me that first time we met at the bar, and it sets me further on fire.

Two fingers slam hard inside me from the front.

"On second thought…" he groans. "I want you to scream. I want to hear what a little slut you are."

I bite into my lower lip, barely suppressing the moans from the way he moves inside me, so deep, so hard. And that dirty talk has my pussy convulsing around him. I almost don't care who hears. I'm so high on emotion, I'd let them all watch me get fucked.

His thumb circles my clit as he thrusts in a hurried pace, his panting hot and heavy on the side of my neck as his mouth taunts me with passionate kisses. His thick length digs into the small of my back, and knowing he's hard for me, that I turn this gorgeous man on, is making me want to drop to my knees and watch as every inch of him enters my mouth.

"They know what's happening," he warns. "My men know I have my hand on this sweet pussy. I bet they want a taste."

He fucks me without mercy. Without fear.

"It's too bad I don't share." He curls his fingers deeper, rubbing my G-spot just right, while his dirty words lure the fire from my core.

My body is his to command, to own.

"I should fuck you right on the ground so they can all see how much you love my cock."

"Dante, please. Faster," I beg. I can't take this torture anymore.

He spins me around, lifting me up onto the surface so my back is against the ground and my ass is in the air while my calves wrap around his lower back.

"What are you—oh my God!" I gasp as his fingers slide into me again, the new position even better than the last.

I no longer care who sees me. My mind is somewhere far away, where only he and I exist. He pushes even deeper while my walls tighten around him for survival.

He moves quicker, his eyes clinging on to me. I climb higher, my center throbbing, and with one more slam of his fingers, I come.

"Dante, yes!" I cry, my wild breaths threading in my voice and overshadowing the beat of the melody climbing from the speakers.

His movements slow as I descend from the high, and his fingers reluctantly pull out. His body falls over me, his other hand fisting my hair and yanking me back as his lips capture mine in a brutal kiss.

Biting.

Sucking.

Both of us groaning with pleasure.

Captivated.

He pulls apart only a fraction, growling as he slips the fingers that were just inside me into his mouth and sucks them dry before kissing me again with renewed passion.

Both hands are laced in my hair, tugging, as he angles me and kisses me deeper.

"I think we broke all the terms of your contract," he rasps around my lips.

"There's still one left to break," I sigh, wanting him inside me so badly.

"Then maybe we should go upstairs and see what else we can break."

I pant, nerves falling into the pit of my stomach as my eyes widen a little.

"We don't have to if you're not ready." He kisses the edge of my lips, and the sensation tingles down my arms. "I have you for three months. There's plenty of time for that."

"You sound like you're more in control than I am," I huff out.

I want him, but I'm also nervous about it.

He rights himself, allowing me to face him. His hand falls to mine, and our fingers thread together.

"Believe me, I'm not. I'm doing my best to respect you, but I'm not sure how long I have left in me, baby." He kisses the other side of my lips. "I've never wanted anyone this badly before."

My chest grows heavy; my heart weighs a million pounds. "Neither have I."

He cups my cheek, his gaze dripping with emotion as we remain silent, just staring at one another. And my eyes sting with this overwhelming feeling of being connected with someone so strongly.

"Let's go upstairs and get dry, then have dinner," he says. "I have a business meeting tonight, and I want to spend a little time with you before I go."

"Will you be gone all night?"

*Please say no.*

I want his arms around me while I drift off to sleep. They make me feel safe for once.

"I might be."

"Oh." I glance down, unable to hide the disappointment.

"Hey…" He tilts my face up with a finger. "But I promise not to get shot tonight." He winks.

"That'd be nice. And I hope you've been taking your antibiotics. Don't make me count them."

"I promise." He salutes me. "I've been a good little boy, listening to my sexy doctor."

"Shut up." I swat him playfully with a jerk of my lips.

He clenches his jaw and pulls in a deep breath. "You do that again, and I'll fuck you right here, right now."

I gasp, swallowing the sudden lump in my throat.

*I want you to*, I'd like to say.

But I keep the words to myself, knowing that once I sleep with him, I'll only want him more.

But I know it'll happen soon. I just have to figure out a way not to fall in love with him when these three months are up. I need to keep my heart locked away somewhere he can't find it.

My body is all I'll let him have.

# Eleven

## DANTE

I'm trapped.

Raquel has captured something inside me. Something I never meant to give her. I'm starting to like her a little too much. The need to fuck her has become all I can think about, but that's not all. I'm starting to care about her, and I can't do that.

It all dawned on me earlier today while I was at work, when I couldn't fucking wait to see her. Then at the pool, when she fell into the water, this crazy feeling of intense worry latched on to me with a fury. And when we kissed, I never wanted it to stop.

Why is it this easy with her when she's the last woman on earth I should want?

Taking her was never just about revenge. During the time when I followed her, I witnessed how miserable she was when no one was looking. I felt it inside my bones, the hurt she was carrying all alone. I wanted more than anything to help her. But I didn't know I'd grow to care for her this way. It scares me more than anything ever has.

I can't let myself fall in love with her. I can't give her that part of me. If I do, it'll be a betrayal to my family. A betrayal to everything we've vowed for the last fifteen years.

But how do I expect to stop my growing feelings while living with her, especially when I don't even stay away? How the hell am I supposed to keep myself from feeling something I never thought I wanted, especially with a Bianchi, the family who hated us growing up?

When Dom and Chiara were friends back when we were kids, he'd hear the shit her father would say about our family. Dom told us everything, and we never forgot.

It never made sense, though. We were like anyone else in the neighborhood. A simple middle-class family living to get by. There has to be a reason why they hated us. And if there is, I'll find it.

I take great pleasure in killing our enemy, in destroying everything they value. It stills the raging of my heart and the rotting of my soul. It calms the demons that soak my veins. If Raquel knew this side of me, she'd never see me the same way again.

Maybe I should let her meet the monster. Maybe then she'll stay away.

I can't continue treating her the way I've been. I have to push her away, so far that the sweet taste of her lips can't touch me in my dreams. She belongs across the line, in enemy territory. For as long as we're married, the battle lines will be drawn, where there'll be no confusion for either of us.

Touching her, kissing her…it was all a mistake. A damn foolish one. One I won't make again. I thought I could have her body and not let her fall into my heart, but I was dead wrong.

The only way I can have her is with a purely sexual relationship. No kissing, just fucking. That gorgeous woman is my wife, after all. I can try to cage my heart, but I sure as fuck can't cage my cock.

I'm certain I can get her to comply to my terms, at least for these few months where she believes we're only married for both of our convenience. After that, she'll hate me so damn much, she probably won't want to fuck me anyway.

My hands bend into tight fists at the thought of not being with her the way we have been. At the thought of making her think she means nothing.

"Hey, Dante," Ellie calls as she walks into the VIP room of Vixen, one of the three clubs my brothers and I own.

*Shit. Why is she here?*

"Ellie, hey. How you been?" I shift uncomfortably on the red suede couch.

The music blasts from the DJ booth below as she takes a seat beside me, too damn close. Vixen is a two-story nightclub, with all the VIP rooms on the second floor and enough space to dance.

"I've missed you," she purrs in my ear, her long fingers massaging the top of my thigh.

She pulls back her gray eyes, leisurely scanning my face and body. Her hand goes to her short brown hair that's longer in the front, framing her face.

"Have you missed me?" Her bright pink lips tilt up.

"I've been busy," is my cool reply.

What else am I supposed to say?

*No. Sorry, babe. I don't even think about you. I'm only capable of thinking about one woman, apparently, and it ain't you.*

"Is that a polite way of saying no?" She giggles, and it annoys the fuck out of me for some reason. It never did before.

She's pretty and we've hooked up more than once, but I have no interest in that anymore, not since…

*Raquel.*

God damn it. I can't stop thinking about her no matter how fucking hard I try, and I *am* trying. Kind of.

Ellie was my regular hookup for the past few months. I enjoyed her company for the purpose it served, but things are different now, and I'm not willing to be with her or anyone else. Even if my wife is the daughter of my sworn enemy, marriage is still a promise of loyalty, so I'm not fucking Ellie, even if I wanted to. Which I don't.

"I invited her here for you," Enzo whisper-shouts from my left, grinning as though he's done me some kind of favor.

"Who the fuck asked you to?" I bark out with a little too much irritation.

"Shit. What'd she do? Bite your dick off or something?" He chuckles, only amusing himself.

But I'm not laughing. I glare, which gets him grinning.

"Do you remember that time we messed around in the bathroom?" Ellie keeps fucking talking at my right. "You're still the best I've ever had."

She bites the edge of her lower lip, wrapping a loose strand of her hair around her finger.

Goddamn, she doesn't get the hint. I need to be firmer or she'll never drop this.

"Look, Ellie, you're great and everything, you really are, but I've started seeing someone, and I kinda like her."

*That's only half the truth. I'm not seeing her at all. We're actually married. Surprise.*

"Oh." Her eyes widen a bit, her lips parting in obvious shock. "I'm sorry, Dante. I didn't know."

*Me either.*

This is the first time I've admitted to liking Raquel out loud.

Ellie straightens her back, angling her face sideways, her eyes on me.

"Well, you deserve to be happy." She runs her long, black nails through the front of her hair, her features bowing with disappointment. "I was kind of hoping it'd be with me, but I guess you never saw me that way."

"I'm sorry," I offer, because it's the only thing I have.

"Whoa!" Enzo says a little too loudly. "Did you mean you like Raquel?"

"Shut the fuck up!" I yell into his ear. "I don't need Dom hearing that."

Dom is currently pushing a girl off his lap, clearly pissed, judging by the expression on his face. The only reason he came tonight was to meet with a big-time investor we need to expand our empire. We plan to open a few more clubs, but we need capital.

Johnny, the man we're trying to impress, looks like he's having a grand old time, dancing with two women who are about thirty-five years younger than he is. He's sixty, and looks decent for his age. And damn, can he drink…and his taste is as expensive as the yachts he owns.

"Shit." Enzo interrupts my thoughts. "You're serious about liking Raquel?"

"No, I'm not."

But Enzo knows me well. Both of my brothers do.

"You're a fucking liar." He bumps a fist into my shoulder.

"It doesn't matter. I'll never be with her. Leave it at that."

"Bro, you're already married. You're with her in every way,

whether you like it or not. That's what you wanted. What's wrong with also liking her?" His brows pull in confusion. "It's not a crime."

"Her fucking name! That's what!" I practically shout in his ear. "Or did you forget that?"

"That's what has your balls twisted?" He lets out an exaggerated laugh. "So what? She didn't do shit to us, man. She may be one of them by blood, but she's not her father. She didn't hurt our family."

"Being with her is a betrayal to our family name. To everything we stand for."

"Says who? That's you talking. Not any one of us." He clasps my shoulder. "Listen, bro. I know you and Dom never listen to me—I'm the kid brother and shit—but I'll tell you one thing. Life is too damn short to get hung up on names. If you like her and if she likes you, then it's worth it."

I shake my head. "It doesn't matter anyway. Once she finds out who we are—who I am—it'll be over."

"Or, maybe it won't." He smirks. "Maybe there's a chance that she'll eventually forgive your corny ass."

"Wait a damn minute." I pull back, giving him a hard stare. "Are *you* giving me advice on relationships? The brother who swears he'll never give a girl a ring?"

"So?" He shrugs a shoulder. "That doesn't mean I don't believe in it. I just don't believe in it for me. You're different. You always were."

"Okay, Dr. Oz," I half tease, not wanting to admit he could be right or let his words sit in my head too long.

Raquel and I can't be anything but two people sworn into a life we didn't create. It was handed to us by her father and her uncles, and that's all we will be.

"Don't you mean Dr. Phil?" Enzo asks.

"I don't fuckin' know," I chuckle as I grab him in a chokehold, my knuckles roughly rubbing the top of his head. "Look at you, being all grown up."

"What the hell, man?!" He fights me off with a laugh, the heaviness of the conversation long behind us. "Don't mess up my hair. I'm taking Tatiana back to my place."

And he's back.

# RAQUEL

I wake to an empty bed, the space beside me cool to the touch. My stomach drops more than it should.

Did he ever come home from his business meeting?

I glance at the digital clock on the nightstand, noticing it's seven in the morning.

Why should I care if he stayed out all night with his tongue down some woman's throat? But my gut boils over with an insane amount of jealousy at the images of him doing what he's done to me to someone else.

I pull in a long, frayed inhale.

We're nothing. He doesn't owe me an explanation.

Three months. That's all this is. A fake marriage. No attachments.

That's what I told myself from the start.

So why am I having such a problem now?

No big deal. He's just a guy I hooked up with. That's all.

*You like him. He does crazy things to your pulse and even crazier things to your body. Don't deny it.*

I huff out a defeated sigh, scolding my own thoughts as I flip my legs out of bed. Prodding across the floor to run into the bathroom,

I quickly brush my teeth before jumping in the shower. Once I'm dressed, I head for the door, intending to get some breakfast.

But as soon as I open it, he's there. Well, more like his bare chest is.

"Dante? Where have you been?" I try to avoid staring at his chiseled muscles and those thick slopes of his arms.

His jaw tics as his eyes land on my tight, green tank top. My breaths intensify every time he looks at me so hungrily, so depravedly.

My reaction is almost instantaneous. I can't stop my eyes from slowly sliding down his bare torso. He shouldn't be allowed to walk around without a shirt on. It's unfair.

And those gray sweats…my God. They ride too low on his hips, exposing a hint of the V leading to that thick shaft I felt not long ago.

I grow achy and warm between my thighs, the need for him to touch me only getting stronger.

"I was out," he finally answers, but there's something cold in his tone.

"Are you okay?"

"I'm fine." The words whip across me like an arctic chill. "I was coming to get you for breakfast."

"Oh. Thanks." My lips flicker with a barely there smile, muddled with the confusion stemming from his mood.

"No big deal." He starts walking away. "So, you coming or what?"

"Uh, yeah. Did you just get home?" I shut my door, joining him down the stairs.

"Nah. I got in pretty late." He avoids my eyes as we make it down.

"Where did you sleep, then?"

"In another room."

*Thud.*

*Thud.*

My pulse slams in my neck, my heart rate kicking up to an uncontrollable pace.

"Oh. I thought you'd, um…" Nerves clog my throat.

"Thought what?" he asks with an edge.

"Thought you'd join me when you got home."

*Why do I sound so needy? What the hell is wrong with me?*

We make it to the kitchen, where Janet greets us.

"Good morning, you lovebirds. I hope you slept well."

I glance at Dante, who looks pissed. The irritation might as well be branded on his face.

Janet gives him a curious look, and her stare narrows as he grabs a plate of pancakes and sausage from her, keeping his eyes glued to the food.

"Well, let me leave you two," she adds, grabbing her black handbag from the counter. "Enjoy your meal. I'll be back for lunch."

"Thank you," I tell her. "This looks great."

"You're very welcome. Have a good day."

"You too."

As soon as she walks out of the room, I spin toward Dante with a hand on my hip.

"What the hell is wrong with you this morning?" I shout through a whisper, hoping she isn't still close enough to hear us.

The front door closes before he answers.

"Excuse me?" He drops his fork against the plate; the sound resonates through the space.

"You heard me! You haven't been yourself since the moment I saw you today. What's going on? Did I do something to piss you off?"

He inhales deeply, rubbing the back of his neck, but still managing not to avoid me. "I had a lot of time to think last night. About us. And—"

"And what?" The words drip with a thick trail of annoyance. "Say whatever you clearly need to get off your chest."

He sighs. "We need to keep our arrangement to strictly business. No more messing around. No more sharing a bedroom."

My shoulders tense up, my muscles going rigid. Confusion and nerves settle in the pit of my stomach.

"What happened to your precious deal? What happened to your seller finding out if we don't share a room?"

"He won't. I'll make sure of it."

"How convenient!" My exhale practically slices out of me.

Why is he doing this? And why do I care? Isn't this what I wanted from the beginning? For us to have different rooms? To not grow attached? Well, problem solved.

Maybe he met someone else. Someone more interesting than I am. Why else would he do such a one-eighty?

He probably regrets marrying me now that he met her and wishes he could be with this new woman instead. Now he's stuck with me because he feels obligated to help.

"Fine," I say, standing up and taking my plate to the garbage. "Whatever."

"What the fuck are you doing?"

"What the *fuck* does it look like?" I grin, my narrowed eyes level to his as I toss the food in the trash.

That could've fed a homeless person, and here I am throwing it away like it's nothing. But if he plans on treating me like shit while I'm living here, then I don't have to eat his food. Well, at least not right this moment. I may have to re-think lunch.

"You're clearly mad, so your answer is starvation?"

We lock eyes as he cracks an amused smirk, arms crossing over his chest.

"I'm not mad." I bend my lips into a snarl. "At all."

"Right," he mutters. "'Cause you look real happy."

"Put on a damn shirt!" I yell, my hands raised in frustration. "Who eats naked?"

"I did tell you I enjoy being naked." He stands, fingers at his waistband. "The pants are just for you. I can always take them off. I know how much you want it."

"I hate you!" I drop my plate on the counter with a clank. "Stay the hell away from me."

And I mean that. I'm done with Dante Cavaleri, fake husband or not. We can cohabitate for the next few months, but he can get the hell out of my way while we're doing it.

"Won't be a problem," he calls out after I'm already steps away.

"Great!" I shout back. "Asshole."

And I know he heard that.

How did I go from worrying I'd fall in love with him to not knowing how I'll survive without his kindness?

# Twelve

# DANTE

I'm an absolute dick. I hurt her, and I hate myself for doing it. I'm stuck between two worlds. One where all I want is to repeat what we did by the pool and give in to the attraction, while the other stops me before I'm in too deep.

I stayed away from her after breakfast yesterday, spending most of the day in the office. And today, it was pretty much the same. Now, I'm heading to Viper with Enzo to help him with some business, and I'm already late. But the real reason I'm going is to avoid her. Anything not to see that glimpse of anger combined with a bit of sadness on Raquel's face. The same look I saw yesterday.

Why the hell did my life have to be so damn complicated? But I know I'm doing the right thing by my family.

I think.

"Fuck!" I grip the back of my neck in the elevator at work, making my way down to my car in the garage.

It's killing me not to go home and throw her on the bed and apologize the right way. Man, I want her. The chemistry between us is worth exploring. If she were anyone else, not connected to the family I despise, I'd make her mine without a drop of hesitation.

Getting into my car, I drive a few miles to the club, knowing Enzo is already there, probably drunk or fucking someone in the bathroom.

But now that I think about it, I haven't seen him do that shit the last few times we've gone out. Maybe he's growing tired of it. I'm not a choir boy either, but I'm way more particular with who I stick my dick in. My baby bro is not that selective.

Parking the car, I make it past the long line of people waiting to get inside. The music booms from the open door while two bouncers check IDs in the front.

"Hey, Petey," I call out to one, nodding my head in greeting.

"Hey, boss."

I walk inside, where the smell of sweat and too much perfume invades my senses.

Why the hell am I even here? I should be home in bed with her instead.

I wonder what she's doing. It's not like I can pick up the phone and call her. I could call Lou, the main guard at the house, and ask for her, but what the fuck would I even say?

I head for the bar, ordering a whiskey neat and drowning in the burn flowing down my throat. As I stare at the dance floor, the people move to the beat, sandwiched between each other, not giving a shit about anything but the music. Unlike me, standing here thinking about a woman I shouldn't want.

Turning back to the bar, I stop myself from ordering another, knowing I have to drive home. A hand clamps over my shoulder, and I'm about to bark at whoever it is, in no mood for some drunk-ass motherfucker, but I find Enzo there instead.

"Finally got here, huh? I already took care of everything, by the way!" he shouts over the music. "You're welcome!"

"Great. Then I'm leaving."

"What? Why? Have a few drinks."

"I have a headache."

He chuckles. "You don't get headaches."

I stare hard. "I do now."

"Why are you really leaving?" There's a knowing smile on his face that I want to wipe off.

"I don't know."

He shakes his head, amusement fitting his features. "Just go to her already."

"How I feel about her is irrelevant."

"Wow. So you didn't even listen to a fucking word I said to you last time, did you?"

"I heard." I grin.

"Man, you're an idiot. If Joelle had a real thing for me, I'd go for it."

"Are you saying you like her?" I jerk my head back. "You don't like anyone."

He flips me off, his mouth set tight. "You make me sound like a heartless asshole. Shit. I like people. I like *you*. Not right now, though."

"Fuck you," I chuckle. "You know what I mean. You told me you're not getting serious until you're at least forty." I lean closer as the song changes to a louder one and the bass begins to pound under my feet. "What happened to that?"

"Joelle and I are never gonna happen, so that won't be a

problem." He stares past me contemplatively. "She's the only one who's gotten to me, even back when she'd dance for me at the club." He looks over at me again. "There was something about her. Something I wanted. And after everything between us, I knew I had to have her as soon as I saw her the night we burned down the strip club."

I knew he liked her, but I didn't realize how much.

"I enjoy getting under her skin," he adds. "It's so goddamn easy to provoke her."

"You haven't fucked her yet, have you? And you were giving me a hard time with Raquel?"

"Please." He shrugs. "If I wanted her, I'd have her. But it's complicated."

He actually looks serious.

*Shit. He's got it bad.*

I can't picture him in love. I'm so used to seeing women hanging all over him, I've never imagined it ever being just one.

"All right. Well, I'm out," I tell him. "Try not to catch any STDs tonight."

"Yeah, go tend to your *headache*. Maybe she can stroke your pain away." He smiles, looking proud of himself.

This time, I flip him off before walking back out of the club, pushing my way through people as I make it to the exit.

I say goodbye to the bouncers and head to my car, wondering if Raquel is in bed and if I'd be able to sneak inside and watch her sleeping, even for a moment.

I park the McLaren in the garage and climb out. The house appears quiet. It's a little past midnight, so I'm sure she isn't up. I slip my keys out of my pocket and open the door, hearing music coming from somewhere inside.

I turn, looking inquisitively at Elliot, one of my men. "Who the hell is here?"

"No one, sir."

He shakes his head, looking slightly nervous, like he's afraid I'll fire him or something. He's new, only a few months in, so I get why he'd be worried if he fucked up.

"Then what's with the music? You guys throwing a party or something?" I laugh, but it never reaches my face.

"Nothing like that, sir." He takes a step forward. "Miss Raquel wanted it on, and—"

"She's up?" I interrupt, already marching toward the den.

Why would she be up so late? The need to see her, to…I don't know what, because I'm supposed to be staying the hell away from her.

I'm a damn confused motherfucker.

Rounding the corner, I step into the room, expecting to see her on the sofa or something, but she's nowhere near there.

Instead, I find her on top of my glass coffee table, a martini glass in her hand, bloodred liquid swaying in perfect rhythm to her hips.

Her eyes are closed as she dances barefoot, completely ignorant of me standing there. My jaw flexes.

"What the hell are you doing?" I snap. "Are you trying to get hurt up there?"

Her eyelids drift up as she registers my presence, and her gaze grows large before a huge smile crosses her face.

"Dante!" she slurs, grinning as though unable to rip the thrill from her face.

Her eyes are streaked red, matching that drink. It shouldn't make me this damn happy to know how excited she is to see me, but it does.

"Are you drunk?" My voice slithers with irritation.

"No?" she giggles, taking the glass to her lips and downing the contents before looking back at me. "Maybe a little?"

What is she thinking? Why the hell would she get drunk all alone without me? These might be my men, but they're still strangers and she's a gorgeous woman—a drunk-as-fuck gorgeous woman. A woman I practically fucked in front of some of them.

The thought steels my cock. I want to repeat that again, except right here this time. If she were sober, I wouldn't be able to keep my hands off of her.

She's damn sexy dancing up there. I should've been watching the cameras tonight. I can't expect the men to call me just because she decided to fucking drink and dance in tiny jean shorts and a tight-ass shirt.

"How many drinks did you have?" I grate out, my palm itching to teach her a lesson.

"More…a lot. A few." She giggles again like this is somehow funny, her feet unsteady as she shuffles around.

"Get your ass down here, Raquel. You're about to fall right through the goddamn table."

"I'mmm having bun." Her eyes widen with a curl of her lips. "I meant fun." She laughs hysterically.

"I'm putting you to bed. You're drunk. Get down, or I'll make you. You don't want that."

She frowns. "Mmm. Why so serious, husband? Maybe you want a dance?"

"No." I tame my wild heart, wanting more than anything to flip her over my shoulder and bring her upstairs.

But instead, I wait to see where she plans to take this.

"That's too bad, 'cause I feel like dancing again," she says, drenched in sensuality.

The song changes, and her eyes lands on mine with a sultry expression. She doesn't move at first. Her chest swells with harsh breaths while her eyes slide to my lips, and then lower until they land on my dick.

*Fuck.*

My cock jerks, needing more than just her eyes. Needing all of her. Those lips wrapped around it. That body, mine for the taking.

I can't tear my attention away from her. I'm compelled to look into those large, hypnotizing eyes.

And then her body moves.

She sways her hips side to side, her gaze still locked on mine as she dips lower, her hand slinking down in between her tits.

Where the hell did she learn to move that way?

The empty martini glass rests in her hand as she gyrates. The lyrics of the song are pure sin; the thoughts of what I want to do to her are probably illegal.

She rights herself, her body unable to let go of the beat, drowning in the music as she gives me her back. Her long, black hair is up high in a ponytail I'd very much like to wrap around my wrist while ramming inside her from behind.

My hard-on throbs while I watch her, not wanting to disturb the sight before me. It's like my own private show.

Her hands fall to her hips, slowly lifting the thin fabric of her black tank top up a little bit at a time, until my eyes fill with her bare skin. She pulls it up higher, her bra strap visible now, right before she lets the shirt drift down to the floor. I suck in a breath, my heart pounding in the wake of my hunger, the music sounding louder…or maybe it's my own damn pulse.

I can practically see the edge of her round ass peeking through those shorts. The desire to sink my hand under them, to thrust my fingers inside her like I did at the pool, is all I can think about.

She pivots toward me with the corner of her lower lip trapped within her teeth and her nipples hardened in the confines of the see-through bra she's wearing, the one I bought her. She's no longer dancing; the song has now switched to another.

"Did you like my dance?"

Her chest rocks with the tremble of her breaths. And my eyes try to stay glued to hers, but they wander to those perfect breasts instead. The ones I want to feel in my hands and taste on my tongue.

There's no one here but us. I might have let my men hear her, but they would never be allowed to see her. That's all for me.

I take a step toward her, wanting nothing more than to strip off every shred of her clothes and show her what I truly want. But she's drunk, and I swore to myself I'd stay away even if she weren't.

She's a Bianchi and I'm a Cavaleri. We're sworn to hate each other.

But how can I hate someone so beautiful?

The beats of my heart can't be tamed, not when she's so close. The very essence of her soothes away the demons that haunt me, that tell me to make my enemies pay and make them all suffer. But it seems that now I'm the only one left suffering.

The woman I want is someone I'm not allowed to have, but that doesn't seem to stop my heart from wanting her even more.

I want to tell her how sorry I am for pushing her away, to beg her to forgive me, but I can't do that now. Not when she's too drunk to remember.

"You're so beautiful, Raquel. I can't believe you're mine."

*Forever.*

"Yours?"

She half laughs, half moans, her eyes falling to a slow close and her knees wobbling. She's so pitifully drunk that it's kind of adorable.

A smile finally appears on my face. I can feel it in my veins. That warmth you get when you feel good. She makes me feel that way.

"Let's go, baby," I tell her. "Let me get you to bed."

"Will you be joining me, or did you find someone better?" she asks, her eyes on mine again.

"Give me your hand." I stretch out my palm for hers, confused by her question.

Why would she think that? Because of breakfast yesterday? She thinks I've replaced her?

*Shit.*

Her fingers curl over mine, and as she takes a step down, she loses her footing, almost falling. But before she could land on her ass, I scoop her up, one arm under her knees, the other cradling her back. I stare down at her, and she looks up at me. I'm caught in the moment, my pulse throbbing louder.

"You're cute," she whispers, and I taste the alcohol on her breath like it's my own.

"I thought we already established that I was hot?" I tease as my lips lower.

Her breathing is ragged and uneven. "Whennn did we estabish that?"

"You mean establish?" I grin.

"Yeah, that." She purses her lips to stifle a giggle.

"Oh, baby. I don't think you'd remember even if I told you."

"Mmmnot that drrrunk," she purrs, eyelids fluttering with every slurred word.

"Come on, my drunk mess of a wife. I think it's bedtime."

I carry her out of the room, climbing up the stairs, and she loops her arms around my neck.

"You're so strong," she sighs.

I flex my biceps on instinct, enjoying the attention and that lustful look in her eyes.

"Why the fuck did you have to be drunk?" I practically growl, my cock chafing up the inside of my jeans.

"Whatta you mean?"

"Nothing, baby. How about I tell you tomorrow?"

"Mmmkay." She lays her cheek over my chest, her hands stroking up and down the back of my neck.

Once we reach her bedroom, I kick it open and bring her to the bed. Leaving her there for a minute, I run off to the dresser and pull out one of her t-shirts.

"Let's put this on," I say.

"Okay."

She lifts her arms haphazardly while I somehow manage to dress her. Her hands go to the button of her shorts, but she struggles with it.

"Cannn you take it off?" she asks, innocently looking to me for help.

"Sure, sweetheart."

My fingers slowly undo the button, then the zipper, my inhales rolling through me as I slide the shorts down her long legs, her thong peeking out. It takes everything in me to fight this insane need for my own wife.

I quickly lift her up and place her under the comforter, needing not to continue looking at her half-naked body. She lies down, snuggling and making the cutest sounds as she hugs the pillow, looking up at me with a smile.

"Don't goooo," she begs. "Sssstay with me."

I pull in a harsh inhale. "Okay, I'll stay."

Not as though I'd be able to leave now. Not when she asked that way.

I turn off the lamp, sitting on the edge of the bed while she moves a little to make room for me. When I'm beside her, she slides closer, her face nuzzling into my chest as my arms come around her, pulling her into me even more.

I shut my eyes, enjoying the calmness she gives, dragging me into a place where happiness resides. The real kind. The kind I'd never thought I would ever taste.

But it's there, teasing me. Blinding me with its power, like a mirage, and hiding all the monsters lurking under the shadows.

Her fist claims my shirt, her nails biting into my abs. The exhales falling from her lips are warm and heavy. And before I can ask what she's doing, her hand glides lower, until it lands over my cock.

"You're hard." Her voice is shaky, but the stillness in the room is louder than any sound she makes.

"I am."

I groan as she strokes me once, then again. An animalistic growl cuts out of me, my hips arching into her hand without realizing.

"Does that mean you like me again?"

I hiss as she tightens her hand. "I like you very much." My head falls back with a curse the harder she strokes. "I never stopped."

The sound of my zipper dragging splits across the room. I grip her wrist softly, not really fighting what she's about to do.

"Let me touch you."

Her tone is laced with desire, swaying me into dangerous territory, and I jump in headfirst. She somehow undoes the button of my pants, and then her hand is there, closing around the crown of my cock.

"Fuck, Raquel," I grit.

This is wrong. I shouldn't let her do this.

"You don't like me anymore. Do you?" She strokes me harder, causing my balls to ache.

"Raquel, baby, you've gotta stop doing that."

"Answer me," she demands.

My eyes fall to hers, and even in the partial darkness, I see the fire burning in her eyes.

"Tell me why you were such an asshole?" she slurs in the cutest way. "Did you find someone else?"

She tightens her fist around the head, making me wince with a curse.

"Is my husband having an affair?" Her breaths grow heavy, her drunk voice raspy and sexy as hell.

Those eyes wait for an answer, and I want to lie, but when she stares at me this way, that look tethering into my very being, I can't. My hand drops to her cheek, cupping her gently, wanting so badly to kiss away her worries.

"I'd never cheat on you, Raquel. Not if this were fake or if it were real. You have me, even when things make no sense, even when they get too hard. I'll be here for you, baby. Always." I'm sure she'll have no recollection of what I said, but I had to say it, maybe for me.

Tears fill her gaze as she lets go of my cock, her other palm landing over her mouth. "That was so beauti—"

Her eyes bulge as she suddenly hops off the bed like she's caught fire, running into the bathroom.

And then she hurls.

"Shit," I mutter as I rise to my feet, stuffing my rock-hard cock back inside, unable to zipper my jeans while I follow her.

"I've got you, sweetheart," I reassure her as I gather her

ponytail in my hand, rubbing her back while she lets it all out into the toilet bowl.

Lucky it wasn't the bed. I'd have a fun mess to clean.

"Shh, it's okay," I say as she dry heaves.

When she finally stops, I grab a towel from the rack and wipe her mouth.

"I'm sorry," she cries, tears cruising down her rosy cheeks.

"It's okay, angel." I kiss the top of her head. "It happens. You'll feel better tomorrow, I promise. Want some water?"

She shakes her head with her brows huddled close, her frown too cute. "I don't want to throw up again."

"Okay. Sleep will make you feel good. You'll see." I snatch the garbage pail from the floor just in case, walking back out with her.

Putting the pail on her side, I drop a hand under her thighs and lift her into my arms, kissing her forehead before putting her back to bed.

"I won't go anywhere. I'll be right beside you the whole time."

"Mm-hmm."

Then it's quiet.

I hold her close, not wanting to ever leave and hoping she can forgive me for pushing her away. I can't do it anymore. I don't want to hurt her, even though I know I will once she finds out why she's really here to begin with.

# Thirteen

## RAQUEL

"Shh," someone whispers behind me.

An arm is curled around my stomach, clutching me tight.

I whimper, unable to open my eyes. My stomach is churning like a windmill, my head drumming like a rock concert is playing inside it. Pain radiates in both temples, beating so heavily, I drown in the pain.

"It's okay," says a man's voice. "Go back to sleep. I'll be here."

"Dante?" I groan, and even that one word causes the nausea to rise up my throat.

"Yes, sweetheart, it's me."

I want to ask how he's here, why, but I can't manage talking anymore. I close my eyes and drift away, hoping for clarity when

I wake up.

Light flickers through my eyelids, floating over me. I try to fight it, my stomach queasy. How much did I drink? Why would I do this to myself?

I turn onto my back, rubbing at my temple, the headache from earlier fading, but still lingering. I remember hearing Dante's voice, as though in a dream. Was he really with me, or was I hallucinating? I recall everything before I got drunk, like finding his bar and stealing a bottle of vodka and cranberry juice.

What was I thinking?

But after the first two drinks, the third came easily. Then I can't be sure how many more I had. I rarely drink, so my tolerance isn't that great to begin with. And between the issues with my parents and Carlito, and now Dante treating me like shit on top of it, all I wanted was to release some of that stress.

The night whirls through my mind like a tsunami with images flashing before my eyes, the room spinning a little as I stare at the ceiling above. Bits and pieces from last night slam into my head, like hopping on the table and dancing. I can see a man watching me, but I don't see his face. He's like a black shadow lurking off to the side.

Was it Dante?

"Ahh! Why can't I remember!"

I shut my eyes, pulling at the memories, trying to find what else I could've done.

*Oh my God!* My heart pounds. *Did he and I do anything? Did we sleep together?*

"Shit." I finger my hair, tugging it in frustration.

Oh, no! What if it's even worse? What if I did something with one of his men?!

No, I couldn't have. I wouldn't have. I'm not even attracted to any of them. The only man I want is Dante, and even after everything, I still do. So no matter how drunk I was, I'd never do that.

*Right?*

I'll never drink again. Not remembering what I did or didn't do is not a feeling I want to relive. I'm not that kind of woman.

I have to find out what happened. I won't be able to live with myself if I don't. And if I want to fill in the blanks, I should probably get out of this bed eventually.

Slowly turning my head toward the nightstand, I peek at the clock, finding it to be one thirty in the afternoon. I don't think I've ever woken up this late in my life.

Forcing myself to get up, I swing my feet gently, sitting at the edge of the bed and taking stabilizing breaths, and then finally rising to my feet.

But before I can move to the door, my eyes land on a white piece of paper with something scribbled on it, and two white pills and a bottle of water beside it. I pick up the note and read over the words.

I hope you're feeling a little better. Take the meds I left. It's for the headache you definitely have.

P.S. I'm hoping you'll strip for me again, but sober this time.

-Your objectively insanely gorgeous husband.

Oh my God! I stripped for him?

No way. He must be lying.

My cheeks warm as my eyes scan the paper over and over, as though the words will somehow change and become less humiliating.

What did I take off? Everything? Just my shirt? I mean, he's seen a lot of me already, but still! How will I ever look him in the face again?

Sitting back on the bed, I let my face fall into my palms, hating that I managed to make such a fool of myself in front of I don't even know who. He better not have let me embarrass myself in front of anyone else.

"Ugh!" I groan, shaking my head.

After a few minutes of feeling sorry for myself, I decide to face the music. We live together. I'll have to see him eventually. Might as well rip off the Band-Aid and get it over with.

Standing up, I quickly grab a pair of sweats, then brush my teeth before heading for the door. Once I open it, the nerves decide to have a dance party in my stomach, dipping and rolling like a roller coaster. The damn headache still lingers in my temples, even with the meds, and I hope some caffeine can make it a little better. Heading down the stairs, I tiptoe toward the kitchen, where I hear Janet and Dante.

"No, don't put it away. She might get hungry," he tells her. "I'll bring it up for her."

"That's a good idea. She needs something in that belly."

"After the night she had…" He laughs. "She definitely does."

There's a few seconds of quiet.

"What?" he asks her. "Why are you staring at me like I've got something on my face?"

"I think it's nice how much you like her. I can see the change in you since you met her."

Silence fills the space, except the beating of my heart. He doesn't admit to having feelings for me, but he doesn't deny it either.

"It's okay. You don't have to say anything," Janet continues. "But it's a good thing. Everyone needs someone."

She lifts up her head to find me eavesdropping.

"There she is," she says, her eyes lighting up with a smile. "How are you feeling, Raquel?"

The ball of nerves slithers up my throat at being caught standing there. Dante turns in the stool, looking at me from over his shoulder.

I was kind of hoping to hear the rest of that conversation.

But it doesn't matter, does it? He had no right to speak to me the way he did the other day. I'm sick and tired of being treated like crap by everyone. So even if he was the last man on this planet, I don't care. Dante and I are done.

"Good afternoon," he says, a lopsided grin greeting me and making me all warm. "I hope you slept well. But I find that highly unlikely."

"Leave the poor girl alone," Janet tsks. "Come sit down, honey." She pulls out a chair for me on her side. "I have a small bowl of rice for you. It'll help your stomach."

I nod as I walk over, ignoring Dante as I sit down. My stomach is still woozy, so I'm terrified to put anything in it, but I also am hungry.

"Well, I have to go," Janet tells us. "I hope you feel better, Raquel. Make sure you get as much rest as you need."

"Thank you." A flush creeps to my cheeks.

Dante says goodbye, and then we're alone. The silence thickens, and then the room erupts with the sound of my spoon clattering against the bowl.

He takes a sip of his green-looking drink, probably a concoction of something healthy to keep all those muscles in their prime.

"Are we not going to talk about what happened?" he asks.

I carefully swallow down a spoonful of rice, praying I don't hurl. It goes down easier than I imagined, so I take another. Anything to avoid asking him about my apparent strip show.

I keep staring at the rice, but I feel his eyes drilling a hole into me, compelling me to look up. And when I do, I find that sexy, crooked grin staring back at me.

"Ahh, there she is." He runs his large hand through his hair, his bulging muscles tightening from the movement.

I battle the warmth suddenly coursing up my body like hungry waves of the ocean.

Dropping the spoon into the bowl, I straighten my spine and narrow my eyes, glaring at him.

"Fine. Let's have the conversation you're dying to have," I spit out with slinking irritation. "Yes, I know I got drunk. No, I don't do this often, but I guess you could say you drove me to it. Happy? May I eat now?"

I inhale sharply while amusement plays on his mouth, deepening with my fury.

"Stop looking at me like that!" I bellow.

"Like what?" He quirks up a brow.

"I…I don't know, like you're having fun at my expense."

"Well, I am. Especially when I remember how skillfully you took off your clothes and how little you probably remember." He scratches his jaw, his eyes blazing with heated memories.

"You're lying. There's no way I did that."

"Oh, you did." He grins. "Who do you think put that shirt on you?"

I peer down at myself, and when I look back at him, it's with eyes practically falling out of my sockets.

*I was wearing a tank top last night! Oh my God! Where is it?*

I discreetly lift up my shirt, not finding anything under it besides my bare skin, a bra, and a thong.

"At first, when I found you on my coffee table with a drink in your hand, barely keeping yourself upright, I was pissed," he explains. "I wanted to strip off those shorts you had on and spank the shit out of you for getting drunk with my men around while I'm not there."

I shuffle uncomfortably in the chair at the thought of his palm making my ass burn. My pussy aches, wanting him to do it. Wanting to be at his mercy.

*Wait. Did he say I was wearing shorts?*

*Oh my God!*

"You're lucky you didn't." I glare through the haze of attraction and want, needing to fight both.

He snickers for a moment before his features turn dark. Something dangerous lurks within his eyes as he rises, his gaze boring into mine as he slowly treads up to me. I can't manage to tear myself away, and my pulse jumps in my throat with feverish anticipation.

He comes to stand at my back, leaning in, grabbing on to the chair, and spinning it around. His eyes drift to my lips, his hand reaching out and cupping my jaw roughly as he settles between my thighs.

"If I did, Raquel…if I wanted to put you over my knee and give you exactly what you deserved for that performance, you'd let me."

A low whimper slips from my lips. My heart is stampeding like crazy while my core pulsates. I want to fight him, to tell him I wouldn't let him do that, but the denial becomes unbearable to say.

His other hand finds the back of my head and his eyes line up with mine as his fingers lace through my hair, yanking hard enough for the arousal to cling to every inch of my body. The need to feel him stretching me—to feel him *everywhere*—becomes the only thing I can think about.

"I thought you trusted your men," I hiss. "If you didn't, maybe you shouldn't have left me here alone."

He groans, his lips lowering until they skim over mine. "I don't fucking trust you around anyone. You hear me? *No one.* You don't realize how gorgeous you are. How much you undo me. God, Raquel..."

I part my lips as his mouth kisses the corner of mine.

"Tell me," I practically beg. "Tell me if we—"

I need to know if something happened between us last night. But I'd remember it...wouldn't I?

He pushes himself away, letting me go completely. I feel bare, like something is missing. His gaze is wanton as he towers over me, the outline of his hard and heavy length taunting me.

"If we what? If I felt that sweet pussy around my cock?"

I nod, desperately hoping we didn't. That the first time we were together wasn't when I was drunk off my ass.

"No, Raquel, we didn't." His voice hovers with aggravation. "All you did was take off your shirt. I was glad to see you putting your see-through bras to good use, though." His gaze dips down to my chest before climbing up to meet my eyes. "You have beautiful tits, and lucky for you, I'm the only one who saw them."

I bite the corner of my lower lip, my nipples hardening. "That's all I did?"

I rub the insides of my thighs discreetly behind the kitchen island, needing to bathe in the coldest waters to quench the fire he's lit within my body.

"What happened after?"

"Nothing. I took you to bed," he sighs.

"Are you sure? Did we sleep in the same bed?"

I know we did, because I heard him. It wasn't a dream. No way. If he doesn't admit it, then I'll know he's lying about something.

"We did. But you fell asleep right away." He goes back to his seat, picking up his drink and finishing it. "I'd never touch you unless you were sober enough to remember how good I made you feel."

"O-okay," I stammer, still not sure whether he's telling me everything.

But I have nothing else to go on. No other reason to believe he's being anything but honest.

# Fourteen

## DANTE

My brothers don't know, but I've been talking to our parents over the years, for as long as they've been gone. I don't know if they can hear me, but if there's a chance they can, I want them to know I miss them. That we're doing okay.

I've spent the past three days figuring out my feelings for Raquel. I've stayed away as much as I can, sleeping in a separate room and giving us both space.

I won't be free of my guilt over having feelings for her until I talk it out with my father. I can't help wanting his guidance, wherever he is. If anyone can give me the peace I need to accept how much I care about her, my father can.

I was only twelve when he was murdered, but I remember how

kind he was. He treated every person with decency and respect. He'd be ashamed of me for what I've done to her, using her as a pawn in our game for the Bianchis.

There's one thing I do know, though. Utilizing her as a way to get her father to come out of hiding is no longer an option. We'll have to figure out another way. I'll fight like hell to keep her away from all danger, and I won't be the source of it.

"Hey, Dad," I say in my office at work, looking up at the ceiling as though he's an invisible force floating or something. "I don't know if you've seen what's going on, but things with Raquel are a mess. I thought I could keep her at arm's length, even while being married to her, but I've realized I can't stop how I feel."

My fingers dig into my eyes, my shoulders now slumped over the desk as I continue.

"I know you never hated the Bianchi name like we do now, but I thought having feelings for her was betraying what they did to you and Matteo. She's nothing like them, Dad," I explain, sighing as my eyes go back to the ceiling. "I didn't want to like her. It just happened, and I'm not willing to let her go. I want what you and Mom had. That strong kind of love. That connection you shared that I remember now, through the eyes of the man I am today."

I run a hand down my face, gripping the back of my neck.

"She could be that for me. If she'll forgive me for all the lies and bullshit, that is." I laugh, as though hearing him tell me to stop being a fool and tell her the truth before it's too late. "I'll tell her, Dad. I just need more time. Once we take care of the Bianchis and Carlito, I'll tell her everything."

And that's when it hits me: I can't keep her. Not unless she chooses me. Once she's truly safe, I'll get the marriage annulled. It's the right thing to do. The thing my father would want me to do. In the end, I want to be the best parts of him, even though I might never be.

"I'm sorry for being who I am, Dad. I know you'd never want this. I've killed too many in the name of revenge, but I'm not done yet. I won't be done until every son of a bitch pays for your and Matteo's deaths. You hear me, Dad? They're gonna fucking wish they'd slit their own damn throats when I'm done."

There's a loud knock on the door—or more like a pounding. I instantly know it's Enzo.

"Yeah?" I say before the door swings open.

"I have to talk to you. Call up Dom. Now. It's important."

Narrowing my eyes, I get out my cell. "What's going on?"

"It's about Joelle and the Bianchis."

The phone rings twice before Dom answers.

"What's up?" he asks, harshness marking his voice.

"How's Chiara?" I ask him.

He's probably still worried about her after Cain, our gun supplier, assaulted her during a charity event Dom was holding at his place three days ago.

"She's fine. She's strong. Everything's been taken care of."

I immediately know he means the cleaners have disposed of Cain's dead body. He'll never be found.

"I'm glad she's good, man," Enzo throws in.

"Thanks. Why are you calling? Something happen?"

None of us are big on talking on the phone. If any of us calls, it means some shit is going down.

Enzo pulls in a long inhale. "The Bianchis are worse than we thought."

I lean deeper into my seat, finding that hard to believe.

"What do you know?" Dom asks impatiently.

Enzo's jaw tenses. "They're trafficking women and kids, bro. Young fucking kids."

"What?" I stand, my palms landing roughly on the desk. "How do you know?"

He curls a fist on his thigh, and the anger in his face would scare any motherfucker. "Because they did it to her. And to the others she saw working at some private sex club the Bianchis started. *Kids*, man. They had *kids* working there."

"Are you fucking serious?" Dom's words loom with something menacing.

"There's more. They have her son. He's only eight. A baby, like Matteo was. They took him from her the second he was born."

"Fuck!" I slam my fist on the desk, rattling the pen holder.

Just the thought of what those children and women have had to live through has me spiraling.

"Who's the kid's father?" Dom shoots off.

"She says she doesn't know, but I don't buy it. I think she does, but she's scared to tell me."

"Does she know where they're keeping her son?" I'm the one asking the question now. "We've gotta find him."

There's one thing I don't tolerate, and that's anyone who hurts children. Every single person responsible will wish they'd never been born.

"She has no idea. But every month, they allow her to see him for ten minutes. They've been doing it since the kid was born."

"Motherfuckers!" Dom's enraged voice rips through the line.

"We need to go and find them all," I say. "And I don't mean days from now. I mean tomorrow."

"You're right," Dom agrees.

"Let us take care of it," I tell him. "Chiara needs you. Stay with her."

If Raquel was the one going through what Chiara did, there's no way I could live with myself if I had to leave her alone. I know my brother well enough to know he's torn from both ends: duty to those kids and duty to the woman he cares about. I want to take that burden off his shoulders.

"Yeah, man. Dante and I have this," Enzo adds. "We'll keep you in the loop, but you stay where you belong."

A long, silent moment passes before he speaks. "I should be there with you two. What if something—"

"We'll be fine," I reassure him. "You've gotta stop trying to protect us, Dom. It's not your job anymore."

But he can't stop. Protecting us became embedded in his genetic makeup from the moment we ran. He carries this fear of losing another brother. It's unspoken between us, but we all know it's there, tormenting him.

Not to say losing another brother is something I don't think about, because I do, but it's different with Dom. He never dealt with the aftermath of watching Matteo die, and I don't think he ever will.

"You both better be fine, or I'll fucking haunt your asses," he throws in.

"It's settled, then," I tell them. "Let's call the team and get some intel. If we find one of their men who might know something, then there's a good chance we could find where they're stashing the victims."

"I know exactly where we can start," Enzo offers. "Joelle told me they have a lawyer, Joey Russo. The guy knows everything, including where her kid is. She's sure of it."

"Then we'll start there," I decide.

A wild grin spreads over my mouth as fury rises from every ounce of my blood, like an invisible layer of smoke, filling me with the need to spill theirs.

# Fifteen

## DANTE

We didn't waste any time going to work. After a meeting with our crew a few hours later, we stopped by the lawyer's office, but he was on an "extended vacation" according to his secretary, which basically means Faro ordered him to disappear. That was all we needed to know. The bastard knows something.

But we weren't about to give up. We took Jared, the Palermos' accountant, and Victor, one of their associates. They're currently on their knees in our van. A woven sack traps each of their blindfolded and gagged faces. Their hands are tightly bound behind their backs with our weapons pointing in their direction.

"One slight move, and I'll take a leg," I warn both of them.

We can't kill them just yet, not until we get what we need.

We decide to bring them to my place instead of Enzo's. He didn't want Joelle to see them. Many of these men were not only her clients at the strip joint, but also her clients outside of it. She told Enzo how they violated her, beat her, raped her at that private sex club. If she refused the work, the Bianchis threatened to hurt her son.

So my place, it is. I have a nice basement just for these special occasions. Practically empty, no carpets or rugs, easy to clean, and—most importantly—soundproof.

Not that it matters. All the houses in my area are acres apart. The closest homes are Dom's across from me and Enzo to the left. I don't know what the hell I'm gonna tell Raquel, though.

The van stops harshly, lurching the two men forward and making them fall on their faces.

"Stand up," I demand, shoving the barrel of my gun into the back of the accountant's head while Enzo does the same to Victor.

They grumble, but make no attempt to obey. When they're not fast enough, we help them, grabbing them by the back of their shirts and dragging them out.

The darkness is everywhere at first, the daylight long gone. The only brightness is coming from inside my house. A few of our men hop out of the van, following us. The assholes fight against the gags, screaming as their legs twist over the rocky driveway.

"You should thank us that it ain't your face on that ground," Enzo says on a laugh. "This is us in a good mood. Can't tell you what'll happen if one of you doesn't start talking, though."

The door clicks open after I shove my keys into it. Dread punches me in the gut at the knowledge that Raquel will have more questions than I'm ready to give her answers for.

I considered ordering one of my men to keep her locked away in her room, but decided against it. She'll find out who I am and what I am eventually. Better start somewhere.

She should see all the parts of me: the ugly, and the parts uglier than that. Only then will she really know if I'm someone she wants to be with. If there'll even be an us after everything's said and done. Lying to her the way I did to get her to marry me is probably unforgivable.

I wouldn't blame her, though. She was always too good for me, even with the Bianchi blood spilling through her veins.

As I push the door open with my foot, Enzo and I lift the men up onto their feet and move them inside.

That's when I see her walking up the stairs with her back to me, probably heading to her room. But once she hears us, she sharply turns around. And as soon as she does—as soon as her eyes dart from the men with hoods over their heads over to me—her gaze widens, mouth parted. A million thoughts are probably swimming in her head.

"Raquel, go upstairs," I bite out.

"What is this?" Her stare shifts to me and stays there.

"Hey!" My brother gives a wave with a smile, as though this is some damn party. "I'm Enzo, Dante's much-better-looking brother. I've heard a lot about you." He glances at me with a knowing expression I want to wipe off his face. "I would stay and chat, but we have some business to take care of. I promise we'll get a chance to meet properly, though, and then maybe you can tell me what you see in him."

He winks while she gapes at him, her eyes still unrecovered from the shock. Then she turns her fearful eyes to me.

"Leave us," I tell him and my men, not looking away from her. "Take these two down. I'll be there in a minute."

Enzo shoves our prisoners forward while I continue staring at her, wanting more than anything to calm the impending storm overcasting her features.

When the basement door creaks and the sound of it closing fills the room, I slowly approach her, climbing up the first step of the stairs she's still on.

But instead of waiting for me, she backs up with every deep and hasty breath.

"Don't be scared of me," I whisper, hoping the calmness in my tone will make her stop moving away.

She shakes her head violently, her unflinching gaze telling me that fear is her only friend. "Who are those men? What are you going to do to them?"

"Nothing they don't deserve."

"Are…are you going to kill them?" Her voice jolts.

"What do you want me to say, Raquel?"

"The fucking truth!" she cries. "Who are you really? Because you sure as hell aren't some regular old businessman."

I want to spill my heart and tell her what she's begging for, but I know I can't. Not yet. Not until her father and uncles are dead, along with that fiancé of hers.

If I say anything now, she won't want to stay. And if she goes, who knows if I'd ever see her alive again? Keeping the truth from her is the only way to keep her safe.

"The truth is…" I hesitate for a moment. "Those two men are not good people. They hurt some kids really fucking badly, and my brother and I are going to do everything we can to find out where those children are."

I tread another step closer, and this time she doesn't back away.

"Can you understand that? Can you live with that?"

My heart pounds as she continues to silently stare, uncertainty muddling her eyes, her brows tensing. Seconds might as well be minutes as I wait for her to tell me she understands why I'm doing this.

"Those men really hurt kids? You're not bullshitting me?"

"I'm not, Raquel. I swear, baby. They're stealing them and hurting them in the worst way. Or at least they know who is."

"Oh, God!" A hand clamps over her mouth.

I take another step up, needing to be close to her, to kiss those lips again. I'm finally in front of her, my hands tentatively reaching toward her face, my thumbs softly swiping over the tops of her cheeks.

"Don't be scared of me, okay? I'd never hurt you. I hope you know that." I cup her face in my palms, lowering my lips to her forehead. "I'll be up to see you when I'm done, but only if you want me to."

"I...I don't know what I want." The words stumble out.

I suck in a quick breath, dropping my hands away. She doesn't want me, not anymore, and she hasn't even seen me at my worst. She hasn't seen what I'm capable of.

"I understand." Disappointment etches itself in my heart, stamping next to self-hatred.

Of course she doesn't want me.

"Go to bed, Raquel." I make my way down the stairs. "We can talk more tomorrow if you want."

I grit my teeth with my back to her, hating that the woman I'm falling for no longer looks at me the way she used to. I'm no longer her savior. I'm the darkness finding her dreams and turning them into nightmares.

"Wait," she calls, her feet prodding down the steps.

I spin toward her, hopeful she can accept me for who I've become.

She stands before me, her lips forming a thin line. "From the moment I stepped into your home, I knew there was something more to you. Something dangerous." She peers down at her feet before her eyes are back on me. "But I also saw the good in your eyes. The kindness." She slowly, hesitantly pulls out a hand to mine, forging them together. "I still see it."

I curl my fingers around hers, waiting for every single word she has left to say.

"I know you wouldn't hurt me, but I also know you're not being honest with me about who you are. I deserve to know who I'm involved with, Dante, no matter the length of time we're together. No matter how real we may or may not be."

"You're right." I pick up her hand and bring her knuckles to my lips, fastening our gazes so tightly, I never want them undone.

She grips the very essence of my soul. Whatever's left of it is hers. At least that's what it feels like when she looks at me that way and when I gaze at her the same.

It's the way my father would stare at my mom: as though his day ended and began with her smile. As though she meant everything to him. And that's because she did. I want that with Raquel someday.

"I'm sorry for pushing you away," I confess, placing her hand against my beating heart. "I was fucking scared, baby. Because the way I feel about you…I never wanted to, never deserved it. I still don't. But I want you for more than three months. I want you for as long as you'll let me have you."

My other hand wraps around the small of her back, pulling her hard against my body as I lean my forehead over hers, my eyes closing.

"You're an idiot," she teases, a tearful smile piercing through her words.

"So you tell me." I inhale her scent, wanting to commit it to my subconscious.

"Just when I thought I wouldn't forgive you for being an ass…" Her tone slices with raw emotion, yanking at my heart. "You go and say something stupid like that."

"I'm always doing something to disappoint you," I whisper, leaning my mouth against hers, brushing past the softness of her lips.

"Mmm." She nuzzles into me. "Still nowhere near as bad as my getting drunk."

"Yeah, you're probably right." I smile over her mouth.

"Hey!" She yanks back, narrowing her eyes. "You're not supposed to agree with me."

"I'm sorry, wife. There's still so much I have to learn about being a good husband."

"Dante…"

"I know." I nod, an ache forming in my throat. "You're not my wife, and you're still leaving in less than three months."

She sighs heavily. "I have to. You know that. My feelings for you, they're real too. I like you. I do. But there's no future for us."

Her hand rises to my cheek, the smooth touch of her skin on mine twisting my heart, reminding me she'll be gone soon.

"I'm sorry, Dante," she continues. "It's not because of your secrets. It's because of my life. I need to be free of them, and you need to be free of me. My family will never leave us alone, and I don't want to constantly look over my shoulder."

"You won't have to. Give me time to figure it all out." I pull her close, my lips barely a touch away. "I want you. I want this. Let us have it. Just tell me you'll give me time. Give *us* time."

"Dante, please," she whispers, the painful emotion imprinted in her voice. "Time won't help us. Just forget about me. Once I'm gone, you won't remember me. You'll see."

"Is that really what you think?" My breath skims over her lips.

"That this is just physical? That I don't care about you? Because you couldn't be more wrong."

There's so much more I could say to convince her, but this isn't the right time. I have to go and tend to business.

"Do you know how badly I want to kiss you right now?" My thumb slides under her chin.

She slants her face sideways, her features contorted with the same emotions rocking my insides.

"But I know if I do—if I taste you—I'm not gonna be able to stop, Raquel."

Her lips part, breaths falling faster, her intoxicating gaze melding and becoming a part of me. She refuses to speak; her eyes doing all the talking. I can tell how badly she's fighting our connection while wanting it.

"I don't want to leave you, baby," I tell her. "But I have to. And if you want me after what I'm about to do, keep your door open for me."

Before I go, I kiss the corner of her mouth, knowing that's all I can manage to do in this moment.

"Dante…"

My whispered name on her breath practically sends me over the edge, but with one final glance, I turn around and leave her there, standing alone, while I head to the basement to do what must be done.

Pulling the door open, I start descending down and hear the screams of one man. Guess my brother couldn't wait to start the fun without me.

"This is just a taste of what will happen to you both," Enzo says. "So, choose: your allegiance to the family or to yourself."

"I don't know shit!" one of them bellows as I take the last few steps. "If I did, I would tell you, I swear."

"No you wouldn't," I interrupt, now seeing it was Jared, the accountant talking. "That blood on your mouth, that swollen fucking eye, was just a welcome gift."

I look at Enzo.

"I think they need a little more to convince them. Don't you, brother?"

"I was saving that for you." The grin spreads over his face like a snake's bite.

I move toward the two men, each sitting on a chair, no longer blindfolded, but hands still tied behind them. They're both way older than us, probably in their forties, or maybe early fifties. There's a bit of gray at the sides of Jared's hair, while Victor has none, his brown hair thinning out at the top of his head.

One of them has to know something.

Our people can't find the lawyer yet. It's as though he's vanished. We keep hitting dead ends. It's enraging. Those kids are out there, needing help, and we can't give it to them if we don't know where the hell to look.

Approaching the corner of the basement, I open the closet, finding a small black zippered bag where I keep my toys. Not the good kind, but the kind that'll provoke anyone to talk. If they still choose to keep silent, then there's only one way out of here, and that's through painful death.

"So…" I say with my back to them as I open the bag, the sound of the zipper resonating through the large space. "Should we do this the very bloody way or the humane way?"

I take out a paring knife, plus two eight-inch chef's knives, the bright blue resin handles custom made for me. The designer had no idea what I'd be using them for, though. I remove the honing steel next, which is used to sharpen my blades.

When I rise to my feet and lay the items on the coffee table beside them, I see the fear sitting quietly across their faces, their gasping growing heavy.

"See…" I lift one knife and slowly swipe it over the steel. "My brother Dom prefers to use torches, but me, I'm old school. Knives are a lot more fun, don't you think?"

"Fuck you," Victor bites out, his lips set in a sneer. "I know who you people are. I'm not afraid of you pussies. No matter what you do, I ain't talkin'."

"They always think they won't talk, right?" I chuckle at Enzo to my right.

"Every damn time," he agrees. "You think I have time to get some popcorn before you start the show?"

I lift up one glistening blade in the air, appreciating its beauty as I stare at the sharp, pointy edges.

"You might miss the intro."

"Guess I'll stick around, then. The beginning is always the most fun."

"With the way I start…" A grin slides to my mouth. "I think so."

I approach Victor, the mentally stronger one. If I start with him and show the accountant what he'll be experiencing, I think he'll be the one to talk.

"Did you know it only takes about five minutes to die after your femoral artery is severed?"

Their eyes settle on the tip of the knife, which is pointing at the ceiling.

"But you can bleed out even faster, especially with the way I cut."

I take my time reaching Victor, and once I'm in front of him, I slowly drag the edge of the blade down his inner thigh, making sure it punctures through his jeans.

He hisses and grits his teeth as drops of blood seep through the fabric.

"I really don't enjoy this part of the process." I raise the weapon, landing it across his neck, while Jared whimpers beside him.

"He's lying," Enzo throws in with a chuckle. "He enjoys it. A little too much."

I curl my lips into a vicious smile. "Yeah, he's right. I kinda do."

And instead of bringing the knife back toward me, I slam it into Victor's outer thigh. His agonizing scream turns piercing as his flesh gives way and the blade fully enters him.

"Yes, I know it hurts. Hang in there." I pat him on the shoulder, leaving the weapon where it is.

Marching back a step, I retrieve the other chef's knife from the coffee table.

"But the good news is…" I shout over his noisy cries. "Your artery is still safe. It's important to see the positives. That's what my father used to tell us. You know, the one your boss killed."

"Oh…oh my God!" Jared's eyes widen with shock. "You really cut him."

His chest drops faster and faster with every breath. He can't seem to tear his attention away from his friend's thigh. Well, I don't actually know whether they're friends, but it doesn't really matter, does it?

"Of course I cut him. What did you think we were going to do here, buddy?" I ask, shuffling over to him with the knife still in my palm. "Braid each other's hair? Because I don't know how."

His exhales fall quicker now, his breathing shallower as the tip of one of the knives slithers closer to his eye. He can't look away; his wild stare rips through his eye sockets.

Victor still cries, his whimpers getting less pathetic by the second.

"P-ple-please don't do this." Jared's inhales rattle frantically, his eyes glazing over.

"Okay, sure, pal." I clamp a palm over his shoulder and squeeze tighter, hoping to break something. "How about you tell us where they've stashed the kids first, hmm? You can't possibly be okay with children being sold? *Raped*?"

"I don't know anything. I swear!" He shakes his head, moaning with fear. "I don't."

"Hmm." I back away. "So you've never heard of any trafficked kids and women stashed somewhere? You're saying you have nothing to give me? The guy who helps them handle their money has no idea they buy and sell innocent children?"

"Yes! I swear! I don't know shit about no kids."

"You believe him?" I ask Enzo, glancing at him to my left.

He lifts up his shoulders, shaking his head. "Nah. He probably likes little kids, that sick fuck."

"Is my brother right? Do you touch little kids? Are you protecting yourself?"

"No, no, no." His face pales, chin trembling. "I don't do that. I never touched anyone when—"

His eyes grow like their own planets as he realizes he's let something slip that he shouldn't have.

"When what?" My footsteps reverberate through the room as I walk back over to the other guy, my eyes on Jared as the knife lands sharply on Victor's cheek and slices across.

"Ahhh!" Victor screams as red droplets sail down the side of his face.

"This will be you soon, except a lot worse," I warn Jared while his face contracts in terror.

"Please! I don't know anything!" he tries to convince me.

But it's too late now.

"You still don't want to talk?" I lift the knife in my hand and slam it into Victor's other thigh, but this time, I slice the artery nice and clean, then pull out the blade.

"See, he's about to die. Slowly," I tell Jared, who's crying now. "Is that what you want to happen to you?"

"You don't understand!" he wails. "I've got a family. I've got two young daughters. I can't say shit. They'll kill them all or sell them. Please, just kill me." He peers up at me with tears lining his eyes. "Just do it."

I smell the desperation in his voice. I have no doubt they'd hurt his children after what they did to Matteo and all the other kids.

Glancing back at Victor, I give him the same opportunity.

"I can still save you," I tell him. "If you tell me what I need to know, I'll stop the bleeding."

He grits his teeth, the light from his eyes slowly fading. The chuckle from his throat brings a fresh coat of rage into my veins.

"I'm glad they offed your parents. And your kid brother too."

The blood drains from my body, like his words have sucked it out.

"What did you just say?"

The vein in my neck pounds as I repeat his words over and over in my head. Because he didn't say father. He said they killed my *parents*.

*No. It can't be.*

My eyes land on Enzo, and I can tell that the same exact question is spinning in his head too.

"You didn't know?" Victor's laughter fills the air, even brassier than before, his head falling back with amusement.

My hand snaps, grabbing the back of his neck, the knife still clenched in my other palm, ready to end this once and for all.

"What do you know about my mother, you fucking piece of shit?!"

Enzo is beside me now, a nine-mil pointing at the guy's balls. "What did they do to our mother? Talk and we'll make this quick."

His reserved wrath is coming undone. I can feel it, smell it, linking with mine.

The man finally looks at us—really looks, his eyes menacing as they drift between the both of us. "I'll tell you, no matter how you decide to kill me. I want to see agony on your cunt faces before I go."

Enzo pistol-whips him right against his mouth.

"Talk," he fires out through clenched teeth. "Now."

Victor grins, blood lining between his teeth, dripping out the corner of his mouth. "Your mother's car accident wasn't an accident. Faro was always bragging about how he arranged to have her killed when your father wouldn't pay him the protection money everyone else in the neighborhood was paying."

*What? How the hell did we not know this? And do we believe him?*

"That's impossible," I say. "She died because of a drunk driver."

"Yeah," he snickers. "That's what the cops told your old man, but who do you think paid the cops off?" His laugh is thick with mockery as he devours the shock that must show on our faces. "I'm sure your old man figured it out or Faro told him before he popped him."

His eyelids flutter as the blood seeps out his leg, killing him by the second.

"Once the kid they paid off did what he was supposed to do, which was hit your mom's car, they injected her and the kid with some shit that killed them both instantly."

The weight of his confession falls over me like stones forcing me into the ground.

"She was alive?" My world spins, despair blurring my vision.

"Yeah, very alive." He sneers. "So alive that she saw Faro's face as he killed her. He wanted to be the one to do it, even when Sal told him to get one of us to do it instead." He coughs up blood. "But that's Faro. Always wanting to be the one to call the shots."

*She was alive. We could've saved her. Someone could've helped her.*

"You'd better be telling us the truth," Enzo adds. "If you're not, we'll find out, and we'll kill every member of your fucking family."

"I have no family," he mutters, his voice giving out as the minutes trickle by, his life slipping with it. "I'm telling you the truth. Now kill me, because I won't tell you where those kids are. You can find them yourself."

*Pop.*

Enzo fires a bullet into Victor's temple before I get the chance to slash his throat. He stares hard at the dead man before us, his gaze full of torment, one we all know too well. Then he shoots another bullet into the man's heart.

But he doesn't stop. The bullets fly one by one until there are too many holes to count.

"I couldn't fucking listen to his mouth for another second," he explains, tone even, as he walks to the accountant.

The man's body trembles, stunned with heavy silence.

"You have two seconds before he slices your throat." Enzo gestures to me with a tilt of his head. "I can tell he really needs it, and I'm not one to refuse my brother."

"I'm s-s-sorry," he cries. "I ca—"

My knife cuts across his throat before he can even finish. A thick layer of crimson oozes from his neck as he stares at me unblinkingly.

I retrieve my other knife from Victor's thigh, then stroll back to the case filled with my other weapons and remove a black cloth, placing both blades on top of it.

"I'll call the cleaners," Enzo says. "And when we find the Bianchis, we're gonna find out exactly what happened to Mom."

"I think he was telling the truth." I turn toward him. "It all makes sense now. Why they hated us. How weird it was for Mom to be killed by a drunk driver during the day. Both of them dead while the cars weren't even that damaged. We saw the pictures. You know it's true."

He grips the back of his neck, the gun at his thigh.

"Yeah." He nods, his jaw flexing. "We have to tell Dom."

"I know. The Bianchis ruined our family more than we even thought."

# Sixteen

## RAQUEL

After he left and I returned to our room, I wanted more than anything to walk back down and creep into the basement. I wanted to know if he was telling the truth about those men. But I also wanted to see what he'd do to them, to know what he's capable of.

When I first saw the men being carried in like cattle and the demonic look in Dante's eyes, I was paralyzed with fear. It wasn't that I was scared of him. I was terrified of the entire situation as I realized that, once again, I'd found someone like my father.

For my entire adulthood, I've wanted nothing to do with the life of crime I was born into. But it always finds me in the shadows, as though it's a part of me, even though I've cast it away.

But I hope Dante is different. I hope he's nothing like my father.

Though we might not have forever, we have right now. And right now, I still want him.

An hour later, I'm still in the bedroom, the door ajar like he asked. Not knowing when he'll be done, I head for the shower and turn on the near-scalding water before I strip off my clothes, leaving them in a pile on the floor. I step inside, needing the heat to waft over my body and melt away the cruelty of my existence.

How did my life become such a mess?

I wonder what my parents are doing. Are they looking for me? Do they think I'm hurt?

I feel bad for putting them through this, but not bad enough to see them before I run off to another country. I'll send them a letter once I'm gone to let them know I'm safe, but never coming back. Hopefully they'll understand why I did it, but if not, I'm okay with that.

The water falls over my hair, dripping down my back. With shampoo in my palm and my eyes closed, I start to massage my scalp.

My thoughts go to Dante, wondering if he's done with…

With murder? God, even saying that is insane.

*The guy I like is probably killing someone. Right now.*

As I pick up the body wash, I hear the creaking of the door behind me, then the sound of it gently clicking shut.

*He's here.*

My body prickles with awareness as dense as the steam floating through the room, while the fog rises higher, clouding over my vision.

I can't see him. But I feel his aura, like a ghost you just can't shake or a presence feathering over your skin. But as I shift right, glancing toward the shower door, I find his dark shadow.

He pauses, his hand on the door, and my nerve endings stir to life. My body craves his touch as my pulse wakes to the intensity he brings out in me.

I don't trust myself with him. I'm someone else when we're together. Someone I don't mind being.

My body warms from the inside, wanting him here. With me.

Skin to skin.

Body to body.

Heart to heart.

This man does something to me. Something I've never experienced before, and something I never will experience again.

Chemistry, the kind we share, isn't always earned with time. Sometimes it's there from the beginning, for us to take and make it ours. And I want to make him mine, even if it's only for a moment.

The door slides open a little at a time. My body is dripping, wet, bare, ready for this man to take what's his. What I want to give him.

My heart jolts in my chest when I see his face, pieces of his hair falling over his forehead as he stares at me silently, emotions tensing over the contours of his face. My exhales fall faster as my eyes drift from his black hoodie down to his black sweats. His fingers are covered in blood.

I should be scared.

Turned off.

I should want to run. But I don't. I only want him more.

Not everything's black and white. There are a myriad of grays in the world, and he's the darkest shade of gray. My favorite color.

I back up, making room for him. The way he gazes at me full of want and need—those eyes gliding from my face past my breasts and lower to my thighs—has my body crawling with anticipation. Craving to feel him sink into me for the first time. The more he looks, the higher his chest expands, and the more wet and wanton

I become.

My palm extends for his, inviting him to join me. And without his eyes snapping away, he removes his sneakers, pushing them off with his heels before he comes closer.

Unable to hold on to another wasted moment, I move toward him, grabbing hold of his hoodie and pulling until my body smashes to him, my lips meeting his in a frenzy as my nails cling to the muscles of his back.

"Mmm," I murmur, finally giving in to what we both want so desperately.

His groan shudders on my tongue as he sucks it, while his hand lands on the back of my head, pushing me deeper into his mouth. The pads of my fingers grasp the zipper of his hoodie, sliding it hurriedly down his body until it drifts to the floor.

He separates our lips for mere seconds and anxiously steps out of his sweats without glancing away while his t-shirt follows the same path. His thick, long cock springs out, and desire tightens and throbs at my center. I'm unable to quench it, and I don't want to. I want this man inside every damn hole.

My hunger waits as my gaze feasts on him. Lustful breaths slip past my mouth; my eyes are now lined with his as he steps into the shower. He doesn't give me a second to pull in another breath before he harshly pins me to the wall with a growl.

He grips the side of my face with one hand while the other clings to the back of my neck as his lips find mine. The brutal kiss is days of desire and days of push and pull finally exploding into madness. His feral groans fuse with my depraved moans while a hand falls to the base of my jaw, fingers roughly biting into my skin as our kiss turns raw. Unbridled.

He's someone else. Someone I want with desperation. I want his hands piercing into me, marking me with a taste of him forever.

When I'm long gone, I want to remember his touch against my skin as though it never left. His hands are a constant reminder of our all-consuming attraction.

His mouth is on my neck now, kissing a fiery path down to my breasts.

"Dante," I whimper, my fingers carving through his hair.

His lips close around my hardened nipple as he looks up at me, madness lurking in the narrowed slits of his gaze.

"That's right, baby." He flicks his tongue over the hardened bud, gripping it with his teeth and pulling ruthlessly as I cry out. "Say my name just like that. Beg me to come like a little slut."

My core pulses with an ache. I love the way he talks to me when he's turned on. I grasp his soaked hair harder, the dirty words making me grow wetter. My other nipple disappears into his mouth, and he treats it just as brutally, groaning around my breast, which sends a jolt down to my pussy. I've never been spoken to this way, but I want more. I need it.

"I want you inside me. Please. I need you before—"

He shoots up my body so quickly that I gasp. His hand clasps around my throat as his mouth grazes over my lips with feral breaths.

"Before you leave me?" he growls.

Hot. Ravenous.

The look in his eyes is so possessive and domineering. All the things I never knew I wanted in a man. This is how it should be.

I wish I didn't have to go. I'd stay. I'd let him have me and make me his. But the dream isn't my reality.

"What makes you think I'd ever let you go, Raquel?" And then he captures my lips, his hand squeezing my neck and making my core quiver and clench for his cock.

His other hand rides down my body until it lands where I want him. Cupping me in his palm, he massages the sensitive flesh, making my pussy ache for release. I moan into his mouth; his teeth sink over my lower lip before he lets a finger dip inside, circling my clit slowly, then pulling away, then doing it again.

He doesn't end the torture. He keeps bringing me to the edge before yanking it away, leaving me hurting for him more than before.

"Why would you ever want to leave this, baby?" he drawls, pitching back so he can catch my gaze before thrusting two fingers inside me, ramming so deep that my eyes light up with fireworks.

My nails try to grip the wall, but it's no use.

"This pussy is mine."

"Yes!" I scream out, my mouth forming an O as he hits my G-spot mercilessly, making my legs tremble.

"Say it, Raquel. Tell me it's mine."

I can barely speak. It feels like I'm floating. Wanting Dante is like walking over a thin glass floor, set high above: admiring the beauty of the view below, but praying you don't fall down and scar yourself for life. But even still, he might be worth it.

"It's yours! No one has ever made me feel this good," I groan.

"And no one ever will."

And it's as though he's willed it so. Willed it that I'm forever his.

In one quick movement, he lifts me in the air by my waist, looking up at me. "Don't be scared, and remember to hold on tight."

"Wha—"

But I don't get to finish before he expertly flips my body around so that my thighs wrap around his neck and my mouth is level to his heavy cock. It's a sixty-nine position like I've never experienced in my life. I clutch his thighs just as he pivots my hips so that my core settles closer to his mouth, his possessive hands gripping my ass.

"Such a pretty pussy." He blows against it. "I'm gonna enjoy this."

And when his tongue snakes out for a slow, tantalizing dive, I almost collapse from the sensation. But he holds me firmer as my hands do the same around his massive legs.

I lower my lips around the crown of his cock, hollowing my cheeks as I descend slow. And when he growls around my pulsing clit, I almost come while taking him all the way deep.

I start to move, tightening my lips and taking him faster as my tongue drags up and down his length. He shudders, his groans intensifying, and my moans join him.

"Keep sucking that cock, baby girl," he grits out. "You're doing so good."

I contract around his tongue as it enters me, my body roaring with an ignited rush as the tip rolls up to my clit, sucking while his teeth rub it. I'm drenched. I can feel the warmth at my core. Feel myself slick and pulsing ravagely.

"Oh, fu-fuck!" I cry as the release creeps over me.

My hands quiver as my body rides the wave. I swallow up his thickness once again, bobbing my head faster, knowing I'm almost there and wanting him to join me.

He devours me so brazenly, everything is at his mercy. His tongue drives up from my nub to my ass, circling in that most intimate place no one has ever been.

I'd give it up to him. No questions. He'd make it feel incredible. I know he would.

The sensation there reaches my pussy, and he flattens his tongue, brushing it over my pulsating core. I shatter, gagging on his cock as he sucks me into his mouth, ripping every wave of pleasure from my body.

"You're not done, baby," he rasps, one hand somehow keeping me steady while the other clasps the back of my head, pushing me down even more as I suck him deeper. "Yeah, that's it. You take it like a good girl."

I practically choke as my eyes water, but I don't stop. His demanding ways set me off, making my body somehow need more.

His fingers thread through my waves, grasping hard as he pushes me up and down his length, over and over, until I feel him throbbing against my tongue.

"Fuck!" he roars, his hand stilling at the back of my head and keeping my mouth firmly wrapped around the base of him as he shoots spurts of his warmth down my throat.

My moans shudder over his hardened cock as I suck him dry.

"My good little whore," he growls.

Once every ounce of his release spills, he flips me back around, his hand tucking beneath my cheek.

"Don't go." His pleading reaches into my heart, making it bleed. "I can keep you safe from all of them. You'd be happy with me, baby. And I sure as hell would be happy with you."

"Dante, I—"

But he doesn't let me finish. His fiery gaze cuts through the regret in my words as his jaw pulses with ferocity, melting into desire.

"Turn around." His demand is as sharp as his tone. "I'm gonna try a little harder to convince you to stay."

And even with the orgasm I just had, I want it again. My body's heating merely from that look in his eyes. The one that says he could break me while piecing me back together all at the same time.

He grips the column of my neck, yanking my face to his as his tongue slinks out, coasting up my lips.

"Palms against the wall, sweetheart." His words curl devilishly over my mouth before he flips me around ruthlessly, not waiting for me to do it myself.

My hands slam over the wall as his fall to my back, pushing me down lower until my ass is bent over.

"Good girl. Stay just like that and don't move." He opens the shower door, letting the cold air whisk across me, causing goose bumps to prickle over my skin.

Seconds later, he's back inside, taking one of my hands and pulling it behind me before he grabs the other. I maintain my balance, my cheek planted on the tiles for stability.

"What are you doing?" I murmur, turning my head and finding those eyes fastened to mine.

Staring into them is like looking into the eyes of the devil: inviting and captivating, yet filled with murky darkness and opaque with mystery.

Who is this man I'm steadily falling for? Could he really be someone I can hold on to when all I want is to drift away and find solace somewhere safe, somewhere I'm no longer hurting?

He doesn't answer as something latches to my wrists, binding them together over the small of my back.

"Your panties look much better with you wearing them." His voice thunders over the sound of the water.

Then his palm connects over my ass with a loud snap, making my skin erupt in blistering heat.

I like being vulnerable to him. The need from within coils in the pit of my stomach, leaving me craving more of this. More of us.

Being with him is like being submerged into waves of the unknown, and right now, I want to know desperately if I'll come out unscathed.

I whimper as his fingers round my hip from behind, finding my core and ramming inside.

"I knew from the moment I saw you that I wanted you. Wanted this pussy. This body," he grates against the shell of my ear, causing my nipples to harden. "But I've realized I want more now. I want it with you, Raquel."

He grabs on to my hair, tearing my head backward.

"You make me want something I never thought I could have. And if I can't have it with you…" The sensation of his touch disappears from my core as he lines his cock up with my entrance, letting the tip push its way inside. "I don't want it with anyone else."

And then he slams his hips, sheathing himself fully into me and stretching me until it burns.

My cries slip, like drops of the water sluicing down my back, as his pounding grows harder. His tempo is savage, beastly, to the point of reprisal. My screams multiply, and I'm unable to control them. I don't want to. My body feels as though it belongs to another. Like I'm renting space inside it.

I climb higher, rising to the cusp again.

"Yes, don't stop," I plead. "You feel so good."

"Not as good as you." His hoarse voice gives way to deep, erotic grunts.

His free hand climbs over my hip and finds my clit, pinching and slapping it until I'm lost to the screaming moans that come out of me.

"Yeah, that's it. Take every inch of my cock."

With another crazed thrust of his hips, I come undone, my walls clamping around him and my screams carnal.

He tugs on fistfuls of my hair as he chases his own release

while his cock penetrates me deeper. I don't have to ask him to pull out. He does it on his own, slipping out of me and stroking his cock in his palm as I watch, getting turned on all over again.

Those eyes fasten to mine, never letting go, as his groans get closer together. Then he explodes all over my back. I feel the warmth before it drips down into my ass.

"Mmm," he sighs. "You look damn hot with your ass covered in my cum."

Heavy pants are my only response as I try to calm my erratic breathing. He pulls me up by my hair, righting me so I'm flush against him, his mouth lining with mine.

But this time, the kiss is tender, slow, yet growing with passionate heat. Building into something I'm afraid of.

I swore I'd never give him my heart, but I realize it's no longer mine to give. He's going to steal it one way or another.

# Seventeen

## DANTE

Two weeks have sped by faster than I'd like. The time with Raquel is slowly coming to an end. I've gotten to know her better and learned things I couldn't discover from mere surveillance, things that lie within her heart.

Our days together have made us closer than before, every moment solidifying a future we'll never have.

Now that I've decided not to keep her against her will, to tell her everything when the time comes, I know she'll want to be far away from me. Far from where I can convince her I'm not her enemy.

Once she finds out how badly I've been lying to her, she won't want to hear me out, and I won't hold that against her. This isn't what I wanted, but it's the monster I've created.

Two weeks ago, the day after we fucked in the shower, she signed the contract I made her believe was real. I hated deceiving her, but I had to continue the act. She can't leave yet. Not until we take care of Carlito and the Bianchis.

Yesterday, we got their location from Vincenzo, one of the Bianchis' captains, all thanks to Dom, who was pretty handy with a torch. Our men are in the process of finding out if their boy was telling us the truth.

After we killed Jared and Victor, we were hungry for information and assassinated many of the Palermo men in the process. None were willing to give up the children's whereabouts or that of the Bianchi brothers…until Vincenzo came to the rescue.

We need to locate that private club they're running with the women and kids. We've got to save them so they don't end up like Matteo.

When Dom found out that our mother was murdered, he nearly lost it. We didn't tell him immediately. He had a lot on his plate with Chiara being attacked by Cain, then taken by her father's man, Miles, who was one of our guards. The man was nothing but a mole, placed here by Faro, and we fell for it. It made trusting the rest of our crew a lot harder, but we're doing the best we can.

Dom swore the rest of the Bianchis would know death more painful than Faro ever got when Chiara shot him. I'll gladly volunteer for that.

Staring out the glass door, I watch Raquel from inside the house as she talks to Chiara on one of the loungers out by the pool. When Chiara called Raquel's phone, I couldn't deny them the conversation. I'm aware of how close they are.

Chiara already knows why I have Raquel. She wasn't happy with me, but I asked her not to say anything. I don't want Raquel to be destroyed before it's safe for her to leave me.

The very thought rips out my fucking heart. A fist tightens at my side as I try to steady the rapid beats of my pulse.

*I can't lose her.*

I told Chiara how much I care for her cousin, practically begging her to keep quiet. She swore she wouldn't say shit, but only if she confirms that Raquel is happy too, and that I've been treating her far better than Dom treated Chiara at first.

I sure as fuck hope that's what Raquel is telling her.

Though I didn't know Raquel growing up, Chiara was around whenever she could get away from Faro, her psycho father. She'd come to the bakery my parents owned since before we were born, and we'd all hang out, stuffing our faces with my father's famous chocolate cake and Oreo cupcakes. Damn, that shit was good. He used to have the recipes written in his notebook, but we lost it when we ran away and left everything behind. I often wonder if I could replicate those recipes as a way of keeping my parents close, but I'm afraid that would bring up the pain of losing them all over again.

Once I see Raquel placing the cell down beside her, I open the door and walk over to her.

"Thank you." She gives me a genuine smile, handing the phone back to me with a sigh. "It was so good to talk to her. We're like sisters. I missed her a lot."

"You'll see her soon," I tell her, hoping it's true.

"No, I won't." Her lips bend with a frown. "I can't see her before I get out of the country. It's too risky."

"She can come visit, then," I throw in, not knowing what else to say.

"I guess I can figure out how to contact her in secret, or maybe…" Her eyes light up, widening with her radiant grin. "I can call you and you can contact her for me. Like our own spy movie."

Her body stretches out, the white bikini appearing even brighter over her tanned skin, and my cock grows hard in response.

Since the first time I was inside her, we haven't been able to stop. We've fucked so many times, I think I've worn her out. There isn't an inch of space on her body I'm not familiar with.

"And what else do we do in this spy movie?" I wag my brows, coaxing another smile from her golden features.

She kicks out her foot, but before she can land it on my thigh, I grab her ankle, my gaze wrapped in a blanket of feelings too hard to admit.

"Try that again and I'll throw you over my knee and spread that pussy with my fingers for all of my men to see."

She drags in a long, sharp inhale, grinding her thighs together and swallowing harshly with her brows drawn tight.

"I thought you'd never let them see me naked." Her voice breaks.

"Maybe I've changed my mind." I grab her other ankle, yanking her hips upward and splitting her legs apart until her pussy lands on my hard-on. "Maybe they should see exactly what you do to me and why." I roll my cock over her. "You have the prettiest little pussy I've ever seen."

"Dante," she whimpers, not in protest, but with want, circling her hips like she's desperate for it, beyond caring who's watching.

My men are close enough and have their backs to us now, yards away. They won't turn around. They know better.

"Get up," I order, gently dropping her feet.

"What are you gonna do?" She flusters as she comes to a stand.

I take a seat on the lounger she was just in and pull her down over my lap so her ass is in the air and in the direction of two of my men. It's a good thing the backs of their heads have no eyes.

She looks up at the back of another man in front of her, her eyes widening as I stretch her thighs apart with a hand.

"Wider," I demand.

I watch her spread open for me even more, grabbing a handful of her ass cheek. Her swimsuit bottom rides up into the center, looking more like a thong now.

"This is such a spankable ass." My fingers explore the round, full slopes before I take a hard palm to one. "Do you think they heard that?"

She whimpers, so I do it again. Harder.

"Oh, God, Dante." She wiggles over me.

My hand is now stroking her reddening skin, so beautiful and tempting. My index finger slides the fabric to the side, exposing her damp slit.

"You're so hard," she breathes out, her sultry voice my salvation and my curse. "You like knowing how much you touching me in front of them turns me on, don't you?"

"Mmm, I do," I hum in approval, dipping my finger inside that hole. "I can feel it. Always so wet for me, aren't you, baby?"

She mumbles with a low cry as I squeeze those swollen lips together. She looks over her shoulder, and her eyes cling to mine like a raft to the ocean, drowning me in waves of regret.

I'm going to hurt this amazing woman, and I feel nothing but shame for my original plan. For even marrying her in the first place under the face of a lie. I wanted to hurt her father, but she's the only one who's going to end up hurt, and that's going to wreck me right along with her.

"Touch me," she pleads, pushing herself further into my hand.

I give her what she wants, plunging my fingers inside her wet and warm entrance with rough strokes. She tries to stifle a cry as she burrows into my calf, her moans vibrating over me. I use my other hand to spread her, working myself deeper.

"You're not doing a good job of keeping that sexy voice down." I slip out, rubbing both sides of her clit.

She peers at me with jerky, uneven breaths, and when I thrust back inside, she hides her face over me, her teeth dragging across my skin.

Her pussy soaks my fingers, practically dripping down, so I give it to her harder, wanting to break her. She tries to keep her moans soft as her nails dig into my leg while her entire body shudders, losing control.

"Scream, baby. Let them hear you. Let them hear how much you love it."

Her eyes return to mine.

"Dante…oh, God," she stammers, her brows tight. "I can't."

My palm slides into her hair, my fingers threading in the softness before I fist it, yanking her head back as far as it'll go. "I'm not giving you a choice."

Her pussy clenches around me, sucking me deeper, and I want to fuck her with a lot more than my hands.

I curl my fingers inside her, slamming into her G-spot with ferocious strength. Her untethered control melts away, replaced by gasping moans and frantic whimpers. She's not in control of her body or her mind when she's with me. It's all mine.

"That's it, baby. Look how good you can take it." I add another finger, stretching her as I continue pumping faster, deeper, not giving her body a moment to recover.

"Yes! Yes! I'm coming!" she screams, spasming around me as her nails claw my leg.

I don't stop until she stops convulsing and her breaths calm.

"Oh my God. I'm so embarrassed," she sighs, barely able to speak.

"Don't be. That was beautiful." I let my hand slip out of her, moving all three fingers into my mouth.

Her lips part, eyes watching me. My cock throbs for that pussy. We're both breathing hard, unable to keep our gazes off one another, consumed by the familiar magnetism that pulls us together, keeping the rest of the noise away.

Unable to take another moment of not feeling her wrapped around my cock, I grab her by the waist and haul her over my shoulder, fixing her swimsuit bottom so she's all covered.

"Thanks," she murmurs, her breathing hot, lining up my back.

"I'd never do anything you're uncomfortable with, baby."

And I mean that. I've gotten to know her pretty well in the three weeks we've been together, well enough to know I can finger-fuck her in front of my staff, but not carry her around while she's exposed like that.

We make it to our bedroom, where I hold her close every night. Waking up to someone I care about is still foreign. It feels like I'm someone else sometimes. Not this fucked-up monster I became. Someone unworthy of her. Someone she's bound to reject.

Raquel will always be out of my league. Her beauty will always rival my savagery. But every savage needs a gentle queen to keep him from falling deeper into the darkness.

Lowering her down my body, I cradle her in my arms, our gazes fused in unspoken promises of tomorrow. Every fiber of my intense feelings for a woman I was never allowed to have spills from my eyes.

"These days with you have been the best days I've had in a long time," I whisper. "Too long."

"Me too," she says on a sigh, her voice as muted as mine, like anything louder would destroy this moment. "I…I don't know how to leave you, Dante."

I growl in frustration, quickly lowering my mouth to hers and kissing her hungrily, ending those thoughts where we're no longer together. I need her to forget, and this is the only way I know how.

Her hands brush up the back of my head, her nails pressing and pushing her mouth into mine. We find the bed and strip away our clothes. My body tangles with hers, my gaze swinging down to find that same look in her eyes that I feel down to my soul.

There's this sacred space between liking and loving someone, a place that leads one way, whether we want to go or not. And I'm crossing over the pits of hell to get there, fighting for her heart, even while knowing mine will break in the end.

# RAQUEL

My skin may be bare, but my heart? It's completely exposed. His palm cradles my cheek so tenderly, I can't help the zap of lightning shooting through my heart. His body presses into me from above and those eyes don't leave mine as he buries his cock deep, his movements pronounced every time he thrusts.

My breaths leave in hurried pants, his just as heavy while his lips stroke mine softly as I gasp into him. He groans as his thick length stretches me, while his hand goes to my inner thigh, lifting it up a fraction, eliciting a louder moan. The new position hits me deeper, so I can barely speak.

"You're so damn beautiful, wife." His voice is hoarse with emotion.

In response, all I can do is cry out as I sink into his gaze. Every inch of me is his, right down to my soul. This feeling is so otherworldly that tears sting behind my eyes.

And this time, when his lips move across my mouth, he kisses me. It's soft. Intimate. Filled with passionate hunger. He rocks against me like we have all the time in the world, like every single second, he's capturing these moments we're creating. And I am too. Being with him right here, right now, it has me wondering how I can leave a man who makes me want this much. My hands ride up the back of his head, needing him as close as possible. I never want this to end.

How can I feel so connected to him already? This feels real, like we've been together before. Like our bodies and our hearts have always been meant to move together. And he moves me. Every single part.

He nudges back his face, our gazes aligning once more as he drops my leg. His fingers find my achy clit, stroking it unhurriedly. I fasten around him, my body shuddering and my voice growing needier the more he touches me—the more he sinks inside me—until I can't escape the strength of the release tingling through me.

"Yes, Dante. Just like that." I beg for something I know he's more than willing to give.

A deep-chested roar crawls out of him as he sinks with heavier strokes, finding a rhythm too hard for me to resist. And I fall, clutching his shoulders, my eyes tethered to his as I let him take everything I've never given another.

He spills into the condom with a groan, having remembered to wear it this time. His palm clutches the top of my head as he kisses me, his tongue thrusting with a tremble of his voice. And when his body stills, he tucks me into his side.

A deep exhale escapes from my lips as contentment overflows through my pores. The after-sex spooning has me in a state of bliss. My fingers slice in between his thick, masculine ones, and he curls his hand over mine in a tender embrace.

I've never been touched by a man. I don't mean physically.

There's this power in being touched by someone emotionally, right to the very soul of who you are. That's what it's been like with Dante in these past weeks.

And if I thought leaving him behind would be difficult then, it'll be impossible now. He makes me want to stay and fight, to get the happiness I rightfully deserve.

But is that possible? Can he really keep me safe from Carlito? Can he keep my parents away? And do I really want a life of fear, of constantly waiting for the other shoe to drop? He's going to spend his whole life protecting me from all of them. Is that fair to us?

Someone will always try to come after me. My parents will never rest until they get me away from him. I know that for a fact. They will stop at nothing to get what they want. And Carlito will kill anyone standing in his way.

Dante can do whatever he wants to Carlito, but I'll never allow him to hurt my parents. Their hearts may be in the wrong place, but they're still my family. They just think they know what's best for me, but they have no idea how wrong they are. Money isn't everything. I'd rather marry a poor man and struggle every day than fight off a man who'll spend his life hurting me.

I should call my parents. I should explain my position again and give them a chance to let me lead my own path. It's the right thing to do. They love me. I know they do.

I should ask Dante to let me call my mother just so she knows I'm okay. I really don't like worrying them, but I don't have much of an option, do I?

I decide to test the waters and ask him now after the mind-blowing sex we just had.

"So, I was wondering…" The pads of my fingers glide up and down his forearm.

"What is it, sweetheart? Tell me."

My insides turn warm and mushy every single time he calls me that. He leans over, swiping my hair away as his lips land affectionately on my neck, and my core clenches from the emotional tug of the gesture.

"I want to call my mother," I explain.

"Raquel, I—"

"Just let me finish," I cut him off, pushing myself around to face him. "She must be worried sick. I don't want her to get ill or something because of my running off."

"Baby, I can have a letter sent if that's what worries you." He cups my cheek. "But I can't let you call her. It's not safe. If they find you here and I'm not around…" His eyes drift to a close as his lips softly fall to my forehead for a quick kiss. "I'm sorry. I hate saying no to you."

"Fine," I spit out with aggravation—not at him, but at this entire situation.

"I'm sorry, Raquel. I'm not trying to be a dick, baby. I want to protect you."

"Yeah," I mumble, pushing myself away from him. "That's always everyone's excuse for telling me what I can or cannot do."

"That's not how it is with me." He clasps the back of my head, pulling me right back to him, his forehead landing over mine. "Forgive me. I promise, I'm not trying to hurt you."

His raw tone grasps at my heart, tugging at every part of it.

"I've never cared about any woman as much as I do you, sweetheart. That's God's honest truth. You're special to me. And if I let you do this and something happens to you…" He draws back, sighing harshly, his eyes locked to mine. "I'd kill every person who had a hand in hurting you. Do you understand what I am, baby? Do you understand I'd kill for you with no hesitation?"

My lips tremble at his solemn confession while my eyes sting with tears as they go downcast.

"It's okay if you're scared of me," he goes on, nudging my chin up with a finger. "But you should know who you're fucking."

"I…I'm not scared."

"Really?" His thumbs line my lower lashes, the corners of his mouth curling up with a mournful smile. "Your tears don't lie."

And he wipes them away.

"I'm not crying because I'm scared," I explain, my hand falling over his.

"Then why, baby?"

My heart pounds in my throat, afraid to tell him the truth. Nervous that it makes me depraved somehow.

Taking a deep breath, I just say it. "I never realized how much I wanted someone to care about me enough to commit murder."

He tilts his head back, looking at me like I have five heads. His hands move away, and then a boisterous laugh slips from his throat. He keeps laughing, unable to stop, and I join in, not even sure what I'm laughing at.

"Hey," I giggle, smacking him on the chest. "What the hell is so funny?"

"Babe, of all the things you could've said, I never expected you to say that." He runs a hand past his face, his chuckles slowing. "I thought you were about to tell me that you're not just scared; you're terrified. Shit, who knew you were just as crazy?"

"Hey!" I snicker, rolling my eyes. "Only on Sundays."

"It's not Sunday."

I shrug my shoulders as my lips wind sideways.

"You're so fucking beautiful." He rolls on top of me, grabbing my wrists and pinning them on each side of my head. "Who the hell knew you'd be this perfect for me?"

He groans with an arch of his hips, his mouth descending to my neck.

"I hope you know…" he adds in between soft kisses down to my shoulder. "I'm gonna fight like hell to keep you."

And with a hungry touch of his lips, he steals all the excuses from my mouth. All the reasons I can't stay. He kisses me with all the goodbyes we haven't yet had, convincing me to hold on even when it seems impossible.

# Eighteen

## DANTE

"**I** don't fucking understand how we can't find a bunch of old men!" Dom roars as he stands, his attention bouncing between each of our men in the basement of Vixen.

It's early, so none of the club employees are here. It's just my brothers and me, plus a few dozen of our men.

"It was a dead end, sir," Reach, a new guy we hired, explains. "They were there, we know that much, but they must've moved to another location before we arrived."

Reach came to us highly recommended by Damian, one of the owners of JDG Global Security, a company we use for safeguarding our events at the hotels we own. Like Damian and the other two owners of JDG, Reach is Delta Force. They all served together back then.

Four days ago, after Vincenzo told us that the Bianchis might be upstate at Faro's cabin, we sent some of our boys there, with Enzo leading the team. But all they found were discarded cigars and beer cans.

"How can they always be a step ahead?" Dom marches around the large, bare space that's dimly lit with ceiling lights. "Our priority is finding all the women and children, as well as that club. We will continue to take every one of their men, and I'll personally cut off their heads and send them to their wives if that's what it takes for one of them to talk. Those animals have crossed a line, and for that, they will all die."

"Yes, sir," the men swear in unison, their oath resonating with both Enzo and me.

We'll stop at nothing to free those children and anyone else they've held against their will. Fury consumes any shred of humanity I have left.

Will Raquel ever forgive me if I have to be the one to take her father's life? I don't think so.

A sudden flash of pain pounds in the center of my chest. My heart only beats for her. And once she's gone, there'll be nothing left of it. But what I told her was true: no matter what obstacles keep us apart, I'll fight like hell to keep her.

She's worth the war. Worth everything. She's the only bright light left in the darkness. Without it, the demons inside will take over for good.

# RAQUEL

For the past few days, since Dante wouldn't allow me to call my mother, I haven't been able to stop thinking about my parents, especially my dad.

We were always closer than my mother and I were. Sure, he has a very archaic view of the world for men and women, but I'm still his little girl. He loves me.

Growing up, we sometimes talked about mundane stuff like cars, which he loves. I think that's why I became so interested in them when I was twelve. I wanted more of his attention. I wanted him to be home with me more than he was out with my uncles. But it didn't work. Those other things were always more important. So I was stuck with my mother most of the time.

She was never sweet or kind, like one would imagine a mother to be. She was hard, her expectations as tall as she is. I guess I took my short height from my father's genes.

My mom not only expected perfect grades and a perfect appearance, but she always expected me to do as she wished in all aspects of my life. From the sort of job I should have to the type of man I should marry, my life was written for me the day I was born.

I guess it's a good thing that me being a doctor was part of her plan too. She would have preferred if I became a plastic surgeon though. It was months of fighting when I announced I wasn't doing what she wanted for once in her life. She flipped, cursing with every Italian word you can think of.

It was my father who was able to calm her. He reminded her it wasn't the end of the world, that general surgery was also a great career path. And she got over it.

Eventually.

If it wasn't for my father, I don't think she ever would have. She'd probably have stopped paying for my school tuition until I saw the light. *Her* light, that is.

Growing up this way was rough, but I kept reminding myself

that other people had it even harder. Chiara was a prime example. Everything her father put her through was unspeakable. Compared to my cousin, I'm lucky.

"Would you like some more?" Janet asks, already placing two strips of bacon on my plate, along with a cinnamon apple muffin.

I should feel an ounce of shame with the amount I've already eaten, but nope. I feel no such thing. Her cooking is the stuff of dreams.

"Thank you," I say, grabbing my fork and getting some of that bacon into my salivating mouth.

"I'm so glad you're enjoying it." She puts some on her plate, sitting beside me. "I see things with you and Mr. Cavaleri are better these days." She chews politely, glancing at her plate.

"They have been, yes. He's really wonderful." The grin falls off me easily.

"Well…" Her attention wanders to me. "I can tell you he's never brought a woman home in the years I've worked here. So I'd say he thinks you're pretty wonderful too."

My lips tighten with a smile. It's too bad we can't have more. That these next couple of months are all we'll have together.

We continue eating quietly for a few minutes, and then it hits me. There's something she can help me with. I know Dante will be upset, but he'll get over it. Letting my parents worry that I'm dead somewhere is wrong.

"Ugh," I groan, throwing my fingers up to my forehead, hoping I'm a better actress than I think I am.

"What's wrong?" Concern lines her eyes.

"I need to call my mom, and I realized I forgot to charge my very dead phone."

"So use mine." She places her fork down, getting up to retrieve her bag from the table across from us.

"Are you sure?"

"Absolutely!" She digs inside her handbag, her eyes on me. "Wouldn't want your poor mother worried about you, now, would we?"

"No, I guess we wouldn't."

Shame fills my cheeks as she strolls over, handing me the cell. Dante's house doesn't have a home phone, and I'd obviously never ask to use a phone belonging to one of the guards.

"Thank you." I take the cell and get to dialing my mom's number.

It takes a few rings before her voice comes through the line.

"Hello? Who's this?" A twinge of her famous attitude comes across.

My throat tightens. Getting off the chair, I tread over to a hallway outside the kitchen where I can talk privately.

"Um, hello?" she continues. "Who the hell is this? You'd better not be some telemarketer because, believe me, I'm going to find your ass and—"

"Mom. It's me."

Silence. The seconds trail by, each one like its own eternity. All I hear is her irregular breathing.

"It's Raq—"

"Oh my God!" she finally cries. "My poor baby! Where are you? Are you hurt?"

I hear her heavy pants, the worry etched in her exhales. Worry I've never heard before. And I don't quite believe it.

"You tell me where you are and I'll come get you," she continues. "I have your dad's rifle. You don't have to be scared."

Is this a plot to get me back?

I release a heavy sigh, realizing she thinks I was kidnapped. "I'm not coming back, Mom. I left on my own. I only wanted to call so you guys knew I was okay."

Stillness blankets her voice, as thick as I know her anger is.

"Of course you're coming back," she finally snaps. "Don't be ridiculous."

"I'm not, Mom. I've found someone to help me get what I always wanted, and that never included marrying Carlito."

"You ungrateful child! I don't understand how you could do this to me!" She sniffles, every bit the drama queen as usual.

But she's always been a better actress than I ever was.

"To you?" I snap. "This is *my* goddamn life!"

"How dare you…"

Her words are gone to the howling of her breaths, so sharp they could cut me. Then she clears her throat.

"You don't have to marry him," she throws in with desperation stealing her tone. "I promise. No more. If you really hate him that much, then we'll figure it out. Your father and I *love* you. We don't want this."

My eyes widen, doubt slithering into my head.

"I don't know if I believe you, Mom. You never cared how I felt before, so what's changed now?"

"Of course I care about you, sweetie," she huffs. "I'm your mother, and I love you. If you tell me who you're with and what his name is, I promise I'll get you out of there, no questions asked."

My heart clenches. She's never spoken to me so sweetly before. Why did she have to wait so long?

But I've made up my mind. I can't go back. I can't take the risk that she'll change her mind about Carlito.

"His name is Dante."

There. Not like I gave her his last name. There are a ton of Dantes in New York.

She's quiet again. Too quiet.

"Mom? You there? I can't be on the phone long. I have to go."

"Oh, my poor, innocent baby," she cries. "I knew it. I knew you were with one of them. Your father and I suspected it all along."

My body goes rigid, anxiety balling in my stomach. "What are you talking about? Do you know who I'm with?"

She can't possibly. How could she? Dante doesn't know my family.

She sighs before she says the words I never thought I'd hear. "Of course I do. You're with a Cavaleri."

Dread itches across my skin.

"Wha—" I gasp, my pulse thrashing uncontrollably in my ears, fogging over the sound of my mother's continuing voice.

"I bet he told you he'd help you run away. Is that it? He lied, honey. He doesn't want to help you. He hates us. His whole family does. He's just such an evil man, and he manipulated you. He never told you any of this, did he, sweetie?"

I can't seem to say a word. I'm caught in a trance.

"It's okay. Don't blame yourself. You don't realize how many bad people there are in this world. This is why I've always done everything I could to protect you."

My knees grow weak, practically giving out. He wouldn't lie to me like that after everything we shared.

"I don't believe you," I choke out.

"It's true. I'm sorry to be the one to tell you but you have to know who he really is." I hear her muffled footsteps as she shuffles around. "They're the family after your father. They're the reason why he can't come home."

Tears burn my eyes. So many of them I can barely see straight.

"You're lying."

"I swear, I'm not. He's only trying to trick you, to hurt you as a way to punish your father. What did he tell you? That he's going to keep you safe? It's all an act. He probably plans to kill you." She lets a breath fall sharply. "I can't lose my only daughter. Let me help you. Let me get you out of there."

I back against the wall, my body sliding down as the phone falls away from my ear, still gripped in my aching palm.

Kill me?

No, Dante wouldn't do that. I refuse to believe I have feelings for my own murderer. But could he really be the one at war with my family?

I met his brother, Dom, once when he cut his hand and needed my help. Are they all involved? Is that why Dante has so many bodyguards around? Is it to protect him against my family?

*Oh my God! How could I be this stupid?!*

My lower lip trembles.

I slept with him. I gave him pieces of myself I can never take back. The phone falls out of my hand, bouncing on the rug between my legs, and I shatter. My palms cover my face, sorrow shackling me like a web of invisible chains. My quiet sobs split through me like fresh slices across my body.

The passion we shared was all a lie. He doesn't care about me. He was merely using me. I'm nothing but a puppet.

"Raquel! Are you there?"

I pick the phone back up, wiping away under my eyes with the other hand. I try to steady my tremulous breaths and tearful gasps, but it's no use. I'm too far gone.

"Are you crying?" Mom asks. "What happened? Is he there?"

"N-no. I…oh, God, Mom. I married him." I cry quietly, so Janet doesn't hear.

"What?!" she bellows.

I pull the phone away from my ear, not wanting to hear her screaming.

"Raquel, what did you say?"

"I said I married him. It was part of our deal, okay? Three months of…of marriage for money and a passport."

"That son of a bitch. When your father and uncles find out…" Her voice hits an all-time high. "I didn't want to tell you this over the phone, but your uncle Faro was killed. Rumor is Dominic, one of the Cavaleris, took Chiara, and she…she did it. She killed Faro. Can you believe that? I just…I never saw that coming out of her. She was always such a sweet girl. I don't understand how she could murder her own father in cold blood."

"What? Wait. I'm sorry. I don't understand any of this." My fingers bite into the center of my chest, the heavy thud of my heart rattling with a deafening beat.

"I know. She's crazy like her mother."

Dante's brother took Chiara? When?

This can't be real. Dante can't be who she says he is. Chiara wasn't kidnapped. I just spoke to her. She would've told me.

Why didn't she tell me?

I can't breathe, though I desperately try. The room is spinning; my left arm is prickling from too much anxiety.

"Raquel, let me help you." There's sincerity in her tone I haven't ever heard from her. "I swear, no more Carlito. I just want you back. You tell me where they live, and I'll get you. I would've gotten you as soon as possible, but we couldn't find their addresses."

I don't know if I trust my mother, but right now, I trust Dante a lot less. Or more like not at all. I have to leave, and once I'm out of here, I'll figure out what to do. If that means moving away from my family, then I'll find a way. I have no choice.

The man I thought would be the answer to all of my prayers turned out to be nothing but a monster in disguise.

"He has guards everywhere," I explain. "You can't come alone. Maybe I can find a way to leave the house and meet you somewhere."

I massage my temple as the pounding inside it radiates down the back of my neck.

"Don't worry about any of them," she continues. "I'll get your father's men on it. I'll arrange everything. There'll be a van by the house in exactly one hour. All you have to do is come out the front, pretend you have a good reason, and then we'll get you."

I shake my head with disbelief.

He betrayed me. He lied to me. He never cared about me.

He was just another Carlito. Using me. Hurting me with his deception.

No more. I'm done allowing people to treat me like garbage. I deserve more than that. I owe that to myself. Letting my eyes slam to a close, I know I have no other choice but to leave.

"No guns, okay? And don't come with too many people, or they'll get suspicious. I don't want a fight. Promise me."

My mom might as well be a mobster herself. She's scarier than my father on most days. I guess that's because she's the daughter of a don. My grandfather died before I was born, but from everything she's told me about him, he was powerful and ran his family with an iron fist.

"I promise. No guns. Can I call you on this line?"

"No. It's not mine. I'll be out in exactly an hour. I'll text you the address now. Hurry."

"Okay. Everything will be okay. You'll see."

"Yeah. See you soon."

I hang up and send her the address, then erase the text before getting to my feet. Returning to the kitchen, I find Janet with a mug in her hands and the smell of coffee drifting in the air.

"Are you okay?" Her brows furrow as her pale blue eyes assess me. "You look like you were crying."

"I'm fine." I brush a hand over my face, leaving her cell on the counter. "My mother can be difficult."

"Ah," she laughs. "One of those, huh? Sounds like mine. She's still alive and driving me crazy any chance she gets."

"Sounds like they're related," I snicker as I head for the freshly brewed coffee, grab a mug from the cabinet overhead, and pour some.

"Maybe they could become friends and leave us alone."

"Ha. I wish." I roll my eyes at her playfully as I find the creamer and sugar.

"Me too, honey. Me too."

She gets off the chair, advancing toward the sink to wash her now-empty cup.

"I'll see you later for dinner, okay?" Her hand falls to my shoulder.

"Yeah." I return a smile. "Thanks again for letting me use your phone."

"Anytime." She moves over to the table and grabs her handbag, waving goodbye before she goes.

As soon as the door clicks to a close, that gnawing in the middle of my gut is back. The hurt Dante left inside pours into my heart. I weep silently into my hands, the tears like drops of acid, burning scars across my palms.

After long minutes of drowning in heartache, I force myself to finish my coffee in slow sips, knowing that in less than one hour, nothing will be the same.

# Nineteen

## RAQUEL

The hour arrives quickly, and the fear of my escape grows with every step I take toward the front door.

I've come up with a reason to go outside. I don't think Dante's men will refuse me. If they do, I'm screwed. Everyone will be. My mom will not let it stand. I can already hear her calling the family and arranging an army to come get me, no matter what she said.

If her foot soldiers don't see me up front when I'm supposed to be, they'll find a way to get me, even if it involves bullets. My mother might have promised to keep the guns at home, but I know her. She'll make sure every man is strapped. I have a feeling Dante's men won't let me go that easily, either.

*Dante.*

His name alone brings a lash of pain into my chest. I'm going to miss him. Miss what we had—or what we could've had. I really liked him, and if I'm being honest, it was starting to feel like a little more than that.

Tears sweep over my gaze as I exit the kitchen, but I rapidly brush them all away. He doesn't deserve them. Whoever he is, he isn't who I thought he was.

Dante was a fabricated illusion, tempting me with lies. I see it all now. If Mom is right—and I have every reason to believe she is—then the moment we met at the bar, he knew who I was and he knew what he was doing. Everything must've been part of his well-constructed deception.

But why? How could he do that to me? I'm not part of any of this. I don't deserve to be caught up in the war between my family and his. If I ever get the chance to look him in the eyes, I will demand to know how he could do this to me.

Despair and anger pulse within every one of my heartbeats, radiating down into my bones and lacing with my grief.

*I hate him.*

*I wish I'd never met him.*

*I'll make him pay for this. Somehow.*

I march toward the front door, with two guards on each side.

"Hi. I'm sorry I don't know your names, but do you mind?" I gesture toward the door with an outstretched hand. "I have a food delivery coming."

"I'm Elliot, ma'am. We can get it for you," says the tall one, who's probably in his late twenties.

The other is a little older, maybe early forties. I wonder if they're one of the ones who heard me come by the pool.

*Oh, God. I can't think about that now.*

Clearing my throat, I grin. "I'm sure you can." My eyes dart between them. "But I'll be two seconds. You can even watch…"

My face grows hot, eyes widening.

"Me. You can watch me…uh, get the food," I stammer, swallowing against the lump now wedged in my throat.

*Holy fuck. I can't even get it together before my damn help shows.*

The younger one lets out a bit of a chuckle. "All right. Go ahead. We'll try not watching too close."

He winks, and it takes some willpower to keep my mouth from dropping wide as he opens the door for me. Both of them walk out, their boots stomping over the concrete before they pause on the steps leading down onto the street.

*So they did hear me! Ugh! This is awful.*

I groan with utter humiliation, inhaling the scent of freshly cut grass. I should be glad I'll never see them again…but I'll never see Dante again either.

Why should I care? What's wrong with me that I can't help but miss him already?

Was it really all pretend? Even after he got to know me?

It didn't feel like that when I was wrapped in his arms. When he held me. I felt like I mattered. Like he cared.

Could he really have been doing all of that if he didn't have any feelings for me? Is he that much of a monster?

I don't have time to consider any of it, nor am I willing to stay to delve into the secrets he's so good at keeping. We're done.

Before I have time to contemplate any more, tires screech in the near distance, dragging closer until a white van lurches to a stop.

My heart pounds as the men behind me take steps forward, footfalls crunching over the gravel. I jog toward the van just as the door slides open, and a man with a black mask hops out, pistol raised at Dante's men.

I don't have a moment to scream or run back to safety. His hand stretches to my arm, grasping it roughly and pulling me up against him, my back to his front.

*Pop.*

*Pop.*

Bullets fly from his weapon toward Dante's men, the suppressor on. I try to duck as one whizzes past me toward the van, and fear begins to settle heavily over me.

Dante's guys rush toward us, continuing to shoot back, and more run from inside the house at full speed, but they're all too late. The masked man continues to fire, dragging me into the van and closing the door behind him before someone else guns the engine. Bullets strike at the vehicle, but it does nothing to stop us.

*This isn't what I wanted! I should never have agreed to get my mother's help.*

Once I focus on my surroundings, I notice four other masked men inside, taking up the bench seating. They all look up at me silently.

My muscles freeze as panic swells within me. Something isn't right.

The van speeds down the road at a dangerous pace. My body rattles from the force as I stand. The man who dragged me inside is still behind me, his arm curled around my front, his rough exhales swarming up my neck.

My pulse thrashes in my ears while terror like I've never felt causes me to break out in a sweat.

*Boom.*

I draw in a stuttered gasp from the loud noise.

The van must've hit something, but the driver continues rushing down whatever road we're on now. There are no windows back here. I'm blind.

I remember there being a security officer at the gate when I first arrived at the community Dante lives in. Why didn't he call for help? Did they hurt him?

"Who are you?" I ask the man.

He doesn't respond as his fingers dig deeper into my hip.

My skin crawls. Creepy, rotting dread enters the pit of my stomach.

"You don't recognize your own fiancé?"

My inhale freezes on a gasp as blood drains from my face, an icy shudder running up the length of me.

This can't be real.

This is a dream.

She wouldn't.

She couldn't betray me like this.

*Thud.*

*Thud.*

My heartbeats are no longer my own. They explode so quickly, I'm afraid my heart will rip right out my chest.

"Car-Carlito? Wha-what are you doing here?" My voice is broken. Small. It's pitiful that it even belongs to me.

"When your mother called and told me the happy news of having found you, I couldn't wait to come."

"She called you?"

The disbelief is etched so deeply in my tone, it's hard to hear it. My mother's betrayal hurts far more than I can ever forgive.

She never meant to let me go. Her control over me has no end. I should've killed myself when I had the chance.

A sob slips from my throat as tears well up within my eyes and stream down my face.

An evil chuckle breaks from his mouth. "My God, you're pathetic."

He moves forward, facing me now. His hand reaches for my jaw, fingers gripping harshly.

"You'll be crying a lot worse after what I do to you," he spits out crudely. "You better hope you didn't fuck that asshole—or anyone, for that matter. I'll fucking kill you if you did."

I pant, the gasping exhales leaving me in a frenzy. His hand falls away.

"When we get to where we're going, you're going to tell me everything you've been up to with him. I can't even say his fucking name!" he bellows.

"His name is Dante," I fire back, the angry waves of emotion rocking my very foundation.

"Shut up, you slut!" he screams so loudly that my head whirls back, but not before the handle of his gun slams into the back of my head.

Stars form before my eyes as my eyelids drift to a semi-close. I whimper in pain, inadvertently covering the burning ache in the spot he hit me.

Everyone I ever thought was on my side—or should've been— has betrayed me. My parents. Dante. Even Chiara didn't tell me the truth about everything she knew. All of them are liars.

My head wobbles back and forth as the darkness encroaches from all sides.

My eyes can't stay awake. Everything flickers in and out.

Is this death?

No. I can't die.

It can't all end this way.

*Dante…*

# DANTE

After the meeting with my brothers earlier this morning, Dom went home to be with Chiara while I decided to go shopping for Raquel. I wanted to buy her something nice. Something sparkly to match her eyes.

I spent almost an hour figuring out what sort of earrings to get her. She doesn't seem like the flashy type, so I settled on six-carat studs. That seemed like a good size. The other stuff looked too small.

I don't even know if she'll like them, but I want her to have something. It's not my way of apologizing for the lies I've been telling. I just want to give her something to show her she's special. We may have started untraditionally, but I hope she realizes that besides my brothers, she's the person I care most about.

As I drive home with the earrings in my pocket, I can't wait to see her face when I give them to her. I'm only a few minutes out when my cell buzzes in the cup holder, the head unit displaying Elliot's name.

Pressing a button, I let the Bluetooth take over. "What's up, man?"

"Boss," he utters, out of breath. "They took Raquel."

My heart stops beating.

"What the fuck did you just say? When?" My tires screech as I stomp on the gas pedal.

"Just now, sir. She told us she was waiting for a food order, and I fucking bought it. Then seconds later, a van came, guns blazing. We shot back. They grabbed her and—"

"Fuck!" I howl, pummeling my fist on the console over and over. "Was she hit?"

My words are framed with madness.

*What the hell did she do?!*

"I don't think so. It happened fa—"

"You don't fucking think so?!" The vein in my neck pulses angrily. "What the hell have you all done? Did anyone chase the van? Was it Carlito? Her father? Who came for her?"

"I don't know, sir. They were masked."

"So what the hell *do* you actually know?!"

"They shot the security guard up front and rolled in. We're tailing them," he adds. "We've got two cars after them. I'm sending you the van's location now."

I glance at the text he sent, my breaths razor sharp as I read the words.

"They're not far. I'm going after them." I drop the call, speeding over a hundred miles an hour and whizzing left in front of one car, who honks repeatedly.

Driving quicker, I zip past another vehicle in the middle lane, nearly hitting it.

She must've figured out the truth and called her mom. But how? They couldn't have found her on their own. My brothers and I bought our homes as an LLC. Our names are not listed. Our addresses aren't either. We've been very careful, avoiding phone lines and keeping burners.

*God damn it, baby. Why did you do this?*

If I don't get her back…

I slam a fist down over the console.

"Fuck!" I roar, stamping on the horn to make the car in front of me go faster.

The one on my right veers into the middle lane, letting me

pass. Finally exiting off the highway, I go down the less populated roads, knowing they're only a block away.

*Faster.*

*Faster.*

The tires burn through the concrete.

I need to get to her. I need to save her. If I can't…if she dies… it's on me. I won't forgive myself. She was mine to protect, and I failed. I let them take her. I did this.

I make a sharp left, finally seeing the van and recognizing the Audi behind it, which belongs to my guys. We supply all our men with one for work purposes.

I speed faster and loop around to the right of the van, driving parallel. My eyes go to the door, then the passenger side window. A man sits there; his face turns to mine, his dark eyes visible through the ski mask as his lips curve into a vicious smile.

My hand is on the gun, ready to use it. But I can't let the bullets fly if there's even a small chance she could get hurt.

The asshole stands, moving out of sight, and suddenly the door in the back glides open until I come face-to-face with someone I know. The one whose skin I'll enjoy peeling from his face. There's a nine-millimeter in his hand.

"Where is she, you son of a bitch?" I ask Carlito, who's unmasked.

"Oh, look. It's my long-lost best friend. Long time no see. How you been?"

I keep pace with the van, my eyes glued to his. Thankfully, the street here is quiet. Woods surround their side of the road, while mine is filled with grass, sloping downward on a small hill.

"Is she alive? You'd better fucking hope she is."

Grating laughter is his response. "You know, I had no idea who the hell you were until recently. You got me good. But lying to a man over drinks and a stripper should get your balls cut off."

"You're no man." My mouth curls cruelly.

"Yeah…" He moves his other hand behind him, and I keep my finger on the trigger. "We'll see about that."

As I'm about to shoot him right between the eyes, he drags a body forward.

Her body.

On the floor.

*Raquel?*

I elevate the pistol so the barrel meets his face, my pulse wild.

"Might not want to do that," he announces, his hand gripping her shirt at the front and lifting her up to a stand.

Something's wrong.

"What the fuck did you do to her, you piece of shit?!"

Her head hangs forward, eyes closed.

*No! She can't be gone.*

My heart drenches in the sin of my regrets.

*What have I done? Why did I involve her in our fight?*

"If you shoot me, I'll make sure the bullet lands in her. She's still alive, but barely." He laughs hard, and my hand itches to use my knives on him and make him scream.

"I'm gonna make you suffer. I promise," I tell him.

"All you are is a pussy with a bunch of threats. After I rip her to shreds, I'll let you have her rotting corpse." His hand clutches tighter around her shirt, raising her body off the floor and into the air. "She's *my* woman! She'll always be mine until she dies."

He ogles her like the depraved fuck he is. How the hell do I get her out of this?!

"I'm finally going to get a taste of this body." His weapon drifts down her breast to her stomach.

Anger spirals from my guts, and my teeth grind until my jaw

rattles. I veer the car closer to them.

"You have two choices, my friend," he continues. "You either let me go and allow me to have some fun, or…"

The gun coasts up her body, the barrel landing on her temple.

"I can shoot her right now and we end this."

*Fuck! What the hell do I do?*

Maybe I can fire at him and my men can take care of the ones in the front.

Damn it. No. Too risky. He could pull the trigger and kill her instantly.

The only good option is to let Raquel go and find her on my own before he can kill her. But he'll make it slow. He's going to hurt her, and I don't know how I can knowingly let it happen. But what fucking choice do I have? I have no doubt he'll kill her right in front of me.

With the deepest regret rattling through me, I decide to let her go, only to find her again.

"This isn't over. I'm coming for you."

"Good luck. May the best man win."

Then he speeds off down the vacant road while I slow, dialing Dom's and Enzo's numbers.

This war just got a little more personal.

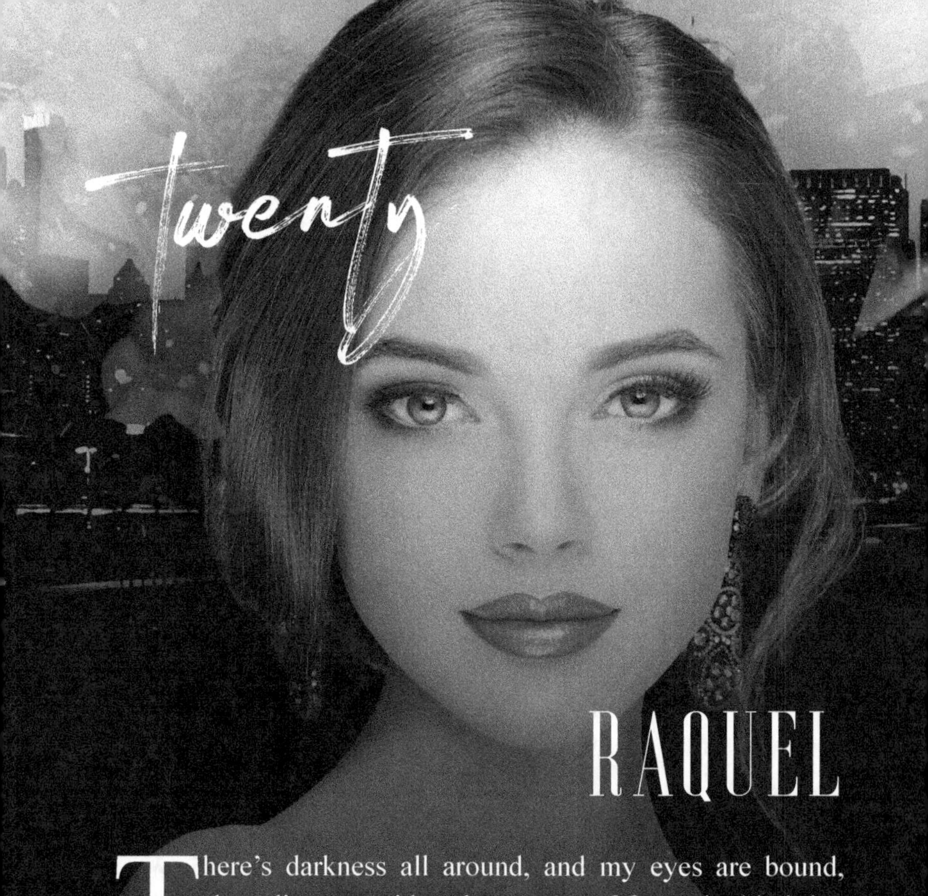

# Twenty

## RAQUEL

There's darkness all around, and my eyes are bound, shrouding me with a deep sense of fear. The kind that creeps up the back of your neck and has your body shivering from an icy chill that isn't there.

Carlito must've placed a blindfold around my eyes after he knocked me out. At least I'm not dead. At least there's a chance.

*A chance for what? For suffering?*

Who would possibly help me? Dante's the only person who can, and he doesn't even know where I am. I don't believe for a moment that he'd want anyone to hurt me. If he knew Carlito brought me here, he'd come. It's obvious that my so-called mother lied about trying to help me, so why would I believe her about Dante? He's been nothing but good to me, unlike my own family.

There's no way he'd want to kill me.

My wrists throb on my lap, and I feel something tight fastened around them.

*Dante. Help me.*

The cloth soaks up the silent drops of misery. I hear my breaths and the pounding of feet somewhere further away, taunting me. My lungs ache with heaviness, like bricks upon bricks piling over my fear.

Carlito's not immediately beside me. I can hear him speaking low with someone else, but I can't hear what they're saying.

*Who else is here? What do they plan to do to me?*

"I think she's finally awake." Carlito's voice buzzes through my mind like a swarm of hungry bees, itching to get a taste and leave some scars behind.

His footsteps crash against the floor, closer now. So close I can smell his rotting body odor, like sweat mixed with death. My pulse accelerates and my stomach fills with terror as I force myself to shrink deeper into the chair.

I don't have to wonder what he'll do. I know he'll hurt me. His viciousness can finally see the light of day, just as he's wanted it to for so long. I'm his now, and my mother allowed it to happen. My own flesh and blood.

He roughly yanks the blindfold off of me, and my eyes narrow as they adjust to the bright fluorescent lighting and find his irate glare.

I quickly scan the area, noticing the high ceilings and large open space. Thin boards of wood line up next to chainsaws. It looks like a carpentry factory. My insides wrench as I focus on the blades.

Is that what he'll do to me after he's had his fun? Cut me into pieces small enough not to ever be found? Did my parents sanction this for my defiance?

I refuse to believe they'd do that. Maybe this is merely Carlito's way of scaring the hell out of me. Because it's working quite well.

"Be easy on her, Carlito," says a voice behind him.

My brows burst up, and my eyes practically fall out of my head. *It can't be.*

My heart constricts so firmly in my chest that the air instantly evaporates.

"No, Sal, that's not what she needs. You've been too easy on her. This is why she ran off." He turns around, and that's when I meet the eyes of my father.

"Daddy?" I shudder as tears fill my eyes and cascade down my face.

But he doesn't even look at me. His gaze is on Carlito, as though I'm nothing but a ghost. And maybe soon, I will be.

"If you would've let me have her when she was sixteen like I wanted, we wouldn't have had this fucking problem!" he howls. "Now she's probably damaged goods. I'm sure she let that fucker Dante have her."

My father's thick gray brows slant with a frown as his head shakes with disgust.

Carlito clamps his shoulder. "Leave her with me, Sal. Let me teach her how to be a proper wife. It'll be a lesson she'll never forget."

I gasp, my insides curling with panic.

"Daddy, look at me, God damn it! You can't do this!" I wail with more heartache than I can bear, my chin trembling. "Please. Don't leave me with him."

His shoulders drop with a sigh, and he walks around Carlito as both of them look at me.

"I'm sorry, Raquel," Dad says. "But he's right. You've shamed this family with your reckless, childish behavior. And to marry that vile creature of a man? I can't forgive that."

I choke on a sob. His love for me is no longer in his eyes. I can see that now. It vanished long before his soul did.

"Carlito is your rightful husband." He continues with his ugliness. "It's his rightful place to punish you for the shame you brought him."

I can't believe he would allow this. My own father. I can barely look at him. I'm trying not to cry, but the tears of my torment continue to wreck my very existence.

"How could you?!" I scream. "You're my *father*! You're supposed to protect me, not send me into the arms of a savage!"

"You bitch!" Carlito roars, his palm striking my cheek and whipping my face to the side. "You don't talk about me that way!"

My face pulsates with white-hot pain. I inadvertently yank my hand up, wanting to ease the ache, but forget the rope binding my wrists.

"Go, Sal," he tells my father. "I've got this. I won't kill her, I promise." His eyes are on me with a hateful sneer. "But she'll *wish* she was dead."

"I'll be downstairs."

And with that, my father slips out of the room and leaves me alone with my abuser.

"Tell me, Raquel." Carlito treads around me slowly, garnishing my anxiety and fear. "You let him fuck you?"

His hand sneaks to the back of my head and clutches my hair, pulling so hard my scalp burns as he looks at me.

"Did you give that scum something that belongs to *me*? Did he take your virginity?"

A laugh bubbles out of me, small at first, until it collects more fury and begins spiraling into cackling too big to control.

"You thought I was a virgin?" I ask, tears running down my face. "You're a bigger idiot than I thought." My shoulders roll with another laugh. "I haven't been a virgin since I was seventeen, when Lenny fucked me in the back of his mother's van."

His other hand surrounds my neck, his fingers creeping deeper and suffocating me as his glare turns harsher.

"Dante, even with all his lies…" I huff. "…is a better man than you could ever be, and believe me, the orgasms he gave me were the best ones I'll ever have."

The punch to my cheek comes so fast, I don't even see it coming. Light flickers in and out of my right eye, and stars go off like fireworks on the Fourth of July. The taste of copper filters through my tongue as I try not to cry.

Carlito stands before me, removing a knife with a long, shiny blade from his waistband. The sheer level of anger on his face is scarier than the weapon in his hand.

"I didn't know who he was when he got all friendly with me at the club," he tells me. "Did you know about it?"

He bends, his face nearing mine, so close I can smell cigarettes on his breath.

"Did you know what he was doing, you bitch? Were you in on it?"

"No," I hiss with a tremor, not from fear anymore, but from pure, unadulterated rage. "He's going to find me. And whether I'm dead or not, he's gonna kill you. So painfully, so slowly, you'll wish you'd done it yourself."

He chuckles, running his knuckles down my face and pushing into where he hit me. "I'll gladly die knowing I took you from him."

"If you kill me, my father will kill you."

"Is that what you honestly think? He left you here with me,

didn't he? He'll forgive me if I take things a bit too far."

His words sting, pouring salt on a wound that already bleeds. His hand clamps around my jaw, but I fight the pain, refusing to let him see me crumble anymore.

"Do you think he really gives a shit about you?" he says too close to my face. "Your mother gave you up, and your father abandoned you when you begged for help. You're a stain on your family's name. They don't want you. Your death will be celebrated. And if you don't die, you'll be too ugly for anyone else to love you."

His fingers tighten, making my pulse fire faster.

"I'll take your fucking tits and slice open your cunt. Then I'll carve out your face."

I gasp for air, unable to hold back the terror crawling over me. The skin on my arms prickles and pinches.

"You'll be no good for anyone." The knife nears and slices down my black t-shirt until it comes apart, the pointy tip almost piercing my skin.

My entire body breaks into a tremor as my heartbeats race so quickly they nearly explode out of me.

Using his thumbs, he yanks the shirt completely open, exposing me to him.

"Mmm," he moans, walking back a step so he can take pieces of my soul I'll never get back. "I've been dying to see you naked for so long. It's a shame what I'll have to do to your body. But…" He takes a step up, the tip of the knife against my breast. "You've left me no choice."

"Ahh!" I scream as the first slice to my areola comes.

The cut is small, but deep enough for the blood to ooze, dripping down my breast and onto my jean-clad thighs.

"This is only the beginning, Raquel. Better get used to the pain."

Then I scream as the next slash comes.

# DANTE

"Where the fuck is she?" I ask Raquel's mother, Simona, while my brothers stand behind me in her kitchen.

"I don't know." She narrows her eyes, tipping her chin up.

"You're a liar." I press the barrel of my nine-mil under her jaw. "I know she spoke to you before the van came. I know whose phone she used to call you. You're the one who told Carlito to take her. I should kill you for it."

I crouch my face to hers, my teeth gritted like a caged animal.

"And if I wasn't falling in love with her, I wouldn't hesitate to slice your throat."

"Love?" Her cackle is as cold and vile as the heart she doesn't have. "Oh, God. You're as foolish as my daughter." She presses her lips tight, mocking me with a laugh, like I'm pathetic. "Love doesn't exist, my boy."

I back away, not wanting to be anywhere near this insane excuse for a woman.

"Love is a made-up feeling we experience, but it slowly dies until nothing is left. You'll see that if you ever get to find her." An ugly smile makes it to the corner of her mouth. "She knows who you are now. I made sure of it."

I really want to kill her, but I won't let her get to me. If Raquel knows about me, that's something we'll figure out together. But my focus right now is finding her.

"I'm not interested in a philosophy lesson from you." I lift the weapon, pushing it into her temple. "Let me make this crystal clear. I don't care that you're a woman. You hurt my wife. So you either tell me where she is in two seconds, or I beat it out of you. If you prove to be anything but useful, my men outside have been instructed to slit your throat and let you bleed out on your pretty white rug."

"My husband was right about you all," she hisses with a sneer. "You're animals."

Her bound legs jerk against the chair, making it rattle on the floor.

"He should know. He created us." I straighten myself as I continue. "I guess he should've thought better than to have a hand in the murder of my family."

"That's not *my* problem." She arches her chin, brows bending in indifference. "*I* had nothing to do with it."

"Maybe not." I shuffle a step, glaring into her hard, cruel eyes. "But you're no innocent. You sent her to him. You knew what he'd do to her, but you didn't give a fuck, did you? What sort of mother would do that? Not mine. She'd do anything for us. And your husband—your *family*—took her. They took everyone from us."

"I expect a certain level of respect from my only daughter," she continues, running a finger past the edge of the hair surrounding her face. "And she's failed. The consequences of that are entirely her fault."

"Wow! You're an evil bitch, aren't you? Maybe I should kill you and save Raquel from you."

I don't understand how any mother worth a damn would allow her own child to be hurt in any way. But it's like she really doesn't care what happens to her own kid. How someone like this gave birth to Raquel, a good fucking person, I will never comprehend. There's something not right with her.

She rolls her eyes. "Oh, please. You wouldn't hurt a woman."

"Bitch, you're not a woman. You're a monster, just like your husband."

*Pop.*

"Ahhh!" Her screams shatter through the walls, cracking like the bones in her foot.

I slant my body forward to whisper in her ear. "That was for Raquel."

She pants, her body trembling. There's no pity, just feral wrath.

"Whatever I do next will be for *me*, and believe me, it'll be a lot worse than that," I warn. "So, again, where is she?"

She weeps openly, no longer holding on to her bravado. Slanting my eyes to a close, I pull in a dramatic inhale, my gun pointing to her stomach.

"Wait," she snivels. "I…I'll tell you."

But she doesn't. She sobs instead.

"I don't have all fucking day!" I shout. "He could be killing her already!"

"There's a carpentry factory that Carlito's uncle owns. They're there."

She grumbles off an address, and Dom's already texting the men in one of our cars outside, so they can head there first and wait for us. If she's there, they're bound to find some vehicles outside, and if Carlito moved her, we'll need to know that too.

I give her my back, marching toward the door.

"Wait!" she calls. "Aren't you going to let me off this chair? I need a doctor. Please!"

"You'll stay right there until Raquel is in my custody. My men will cut the ropes when I text them, so this is your last chance to tell me if you're lying. And you'd better fucking hope she's alive, or I'll come back, and this time, the bullet won't be so kind."

Then I'm rushing out, hoping like hell that the woman I want to bare my soul to is still alive enough for me to do it.

# Twenty-One

## RAQUEL

I never realized how much trauma a person can withstand before they withdraw and crawl somewhere inside their mind like a child in fear, pulling into a corner of a darkened room.

The walls of my mind surround me from all around, closing in as I hide within them, even while knowing there's no safety there. Just fear.

My tears fall like pieces of my skin.

My worth.

My dignity.

It's all been ripped from me by a man my parents sent me to. By my father, who's merely standing by and allowing the cruelty to happen.

The knowledge of that is deafening, louder than my crying as I sit shackled on this chair. I hear my screams, but they're distant, like I'm being taunted by the noise. Like I'm being chased by it and keep glancing behind me, hoping the monsters are too far to catch me.

But that's one thing about monsters: they always find you in the end.

His blade lands against my collarbone. "Should I cut your face next? You think he'd still want you if I did? I doubt it."

His vile chuckle snakes up my stomach, venom seeping through the slices of my skin he left there. There are probably dozens on my body. I stopped counting after the first few.

Maybe I should just let him kill me. Eventually he'll cut an artery and I'll be done for. It's for the best. It's better than this torture. Better than this agonizing pain.

Does my father hear my screams, begging for his help? Is he listening to them in silence? Does he really not love me enough to help me?

The laceration on my arm burns, but the other cuts compete for my attention. I ache everywhere. My jeans are long gone; I sit in just my panties, waiting for him to cut them off too.

His knife started at my breasts, randomly tearing through my skin, but the gashes didn't end there. He moved on to my arms, then my stomach, then the sides of my thighs. I'm marred and bloody from head to toe.

"Did you go deaf or mute?" He slaps me hard.

I mutter, my lips trembling out Dante's name. I've been calling out for him for what feels like hours. His name is branded to my lips, but I don't say it out loud. The pain would be much worse if I did. But I can't stop thinking about him, needing him, and knowing he would come if he could.

He's the only thing I have left to cling to. My last dying wish is to see him one last time. No matter what my mother said, I know the truth is far more complicated than she claimed. Something far different than the treachery of her words.

I know he cared about me. I know the time we had wasn't pretend. She can't take that from me. No one can.

Dante and I were a complication worth exploring. But it's too late now. I'll never know if we could've been more than just our bodies wrapped in lies.

"I think I'll take your cheek now." Carlito's voice poisons my thoughts as the blade nears my skin.

My breaths climb while my gaze focuses on the black handle. My stomach rolls with a wave of nausea as the knife draws toward me for the cut I know is coming.

*I can't anymore. I want this to be over. Please let me die. Ple—*
*Boom.*

Something explodes from behind Carlito's back.

I gasp as my lungs go numb in fear and my pulse slams harder in my neck. I catch the widening of his eyes before the knife falls from his grip.

He turns, leaving me there as he takes a step away. There's a fog forcing itself through the hollowness of the open door, prowling among us like something else I should fear.

"Sal? You there?" Carlito asks as his boots crunch over the floor.

*Silence.*

If my father's back in the room, he isn't talking. Maybe he's finally come to his senses and wants to save me.

More footsteps come stomping in. Someone's definitely here. I can't see their faces, but I can hear multiple people marching inside.

I'm afraid to move, unsure if I'll be greeted by friend or foe. Who would come for me anyway?

But maybe I can run. Naked or not, I'd rather live and try to get help. Where would I even go, though? I don't know where I am. I could be across the country, for all I know.

Loud scuffling breaks out as multiple men begin shouting and fighting. I don't recognize any of their voices. The fog circles around me until the cloudiness is all I can see.

How the hell do I get out now?

"Raquel?! Where are you, sweetheart? Tell me you're here."

I gasp.

*Dante?*

Is he really here? Did he look for me?

It can't be. My mind must be playing a cruel trick.

"It's Dante. Scream out! Please, baby. I can't fucking lose you."

There's a pause; all the footsteps are now gone except his, crashing wildly like he's jogging.

This place is huge, and with the haze, it's impossible for him to see me. I try to speak, but my lips don't move.

"I'm sorry," he continues. "For all of it. I don't know if you can hear me, but I needed to say it anyway. I never thought I'd care about anyone the way I care about you. I promise to make everything up to you, starting now."

His voice cracks as it edges nearer, like he's walking toward me.

"Answer me. Tell me you're still alive."

He's even closer now.

My heart clenches. He came for me. He really came. A quiet sob pours out of me until I'm blinded by the tears.

"God damn it!"

I hear the anguish in his tone, the torture stemming from his heart and into mine.

"I haven't had the chance to tell you how much you mean to me. I can't lose another person I love. Fuck, you can't be gone."

*He loves me?*

I whimper. The tears come harder now, like chaotic waves of misery.

"Baby?" he says with so much tenderness, it nearly rips out my heart.

Thank God for the mist, because when he sees me, I don't know what he'll do. What he'll think.

Will I disgust him? Will he turn away from me like everyone else in my life has?

"Dante?" I whisper, as though still caught in disillusionment. "Is that really you?"

A strong, masculine hand is on my shoulder now as the fog begins to dissipate, and when his face starts to clear, I find the familiar eyes of a man I've come to know. The one who deceived me, but the one who saved me too.

Even with everything my mother said about him and even with the rest I still don't know, I know one thing: I can trust him. Not just because he's the only one I have, but because he's the only one who matters now.

"Baby…" His brows lower as his palm rests over my cheek, while his eyes fall to my naked body filled with the evidence of my cruel torture.

He pulls away, and my heart breaks. I feel even more exposed as I shiver from the lack of his warmth. I should've known he'd find me unappealing this way. I'll have too many scars for him to find attractive.

But the next thing I know, a knife is at my wrists, cutting off the rope. He drops it on the floor before removing his black hoodie and the black t-shirt underneath.

He secures his shirt around a wound on one of my thighs. This one is actively bleeding, while the others have visibly slowed.

"Let's put this on, okay, baby?"

His eyes swim with emotion while his gaze scatters over me, and his jaw twitches as he puts the hoodie on my body. It hits me at my upper thighs, thankfully keeping me concealed.

The people I heard with him are gone. Even Carlito isn't here. He must've sent them into another area.

Scooping me up into his arms, he starts walking toward the exit.

"What he did to you…" He sucks in an angry breath. "I'm gonna do far worse. Believe that. I'll make him know suffering. I'll make him wish he'd never laid a finger on you. And from now on, no one ever will."

I burrow my face into his shoulder, sniffling with a cry, wanting that more than anything. I want that son of a bitch to hurt. I want to take the knife he used on me and bury it in his neck over and over, until I no longer hear him taunting me.

I shiver. The depravity of my desire scares me, but I want it anyway.

"I have to see it," I confess.

"See what?" He stops, his eyes boring.

"See you hurt him." I swallow away the heavy throbbing in my throat. "I need it, Dante. I need the closure. Don't take it away from me."

"Baby, I need my men to take you to the hospital."

"No." My tone is harsh. "Please, Dante. I have—"

"Shh. Whatever you need, wife." He lowers his mouth to my forehead; his tender kiss whispers down my body.

*That word…*

I cry, unable to still the waves.

"Does that mean you still want to be married to me?" His gaze sweeps over my face, dripping with an ache.

"Of course I do, Dante." I lean into him, feeling accepted. Wanted. Loved.

"God," he breathes out. "I'm so damn happy to hear you say that."

I try to smile, but it comes out broken.

"If you want a hand in hurting him at any point…" he says. "If you need to do it yourself, I'll have a knife waiting for you. I know all too well about revenge, and I'm not about to take that away from the woman I love."

"There's that word again." I crack a hint of a grin through the tears dimming my vision.

"What word?" He smirks. "Woman? Revenge? There were just so many."

"Oh, Dante," I cry, my voice splitting into pieces. "I really thought I was gonna die. That I'd never see you again. Thank you. Thank you for finding me."

"I'll always find you. No matter the cost." He slants his forehead against mine while his arms form a protective shield, and I know with them around me, no one will harm me again.

We stay that way for seconds, or maybe minutes. It's hard to say when I feel so safe and cared for. He's the first to retreat, staring deep into my eyes.

"I'm falling in love with you, Raquel. The moment you were gone, that's when I was ready to admit it to myself." His lips kiss the corner of mine, and my eyelids flutter from the sensation. "I know we have a lot to talk about once this shit is taken care of, but you and me? This is real." His face contorts with painful regret. "You own me as much as I own you. And there's nothing more I want in life than that."

There's so much truth within those words, and the reality of it hits me.

"I want that too."

I may have a lot of questions that I need answers to, but he's the one who showed up for me when my own family turned away. That's enough.

His gaze holds mine in unbending passion as his mouth nears until it caresses my lips. Our breaths tangle for space, and where his end, mine begin. We fuel each other's bodies, like his love fuels my soul.

"Are you ready?" he asks, pulling back enough to see my eyes.

I know what he means: for Carlito to be brought back in. For him to die. Because I know he'll kill him. There's no doubt.

"Yes." The aches on my body burn under the fabric, reminding me what Carlito did.

"Raquel…" he says, our eyes connecting as he holds me to him. "You have to know, when I hurt—when I kill—I'm not the same man I am when I love you. I become someone else. Someone you might not want." He sucks in a long, hard breath. "And I don't know if I'm ready for that."

I place my hand on his cheek, letting the stubble graze my sensitive skin. "I don't know who you see when you look in the mirror, but you know who I see?"

When his eyes drift to a half close, I continue.

"I see a man who risked his own life to save the daughter of a man he clearly hates. Someone strong, brave, loyal, and with a heart big enough to chase all my villains away. That's who you are, Dante. You need to start seeing that man. Because I do."

"Baby…" He inhales sharply.

Then his lips are on mine, kissing me slowly, and in our

kiss, there's more than just love. There's forgiveness wrapped in redemption.

This kiss…it heals a part of me I didn't realize was this broken. The part that always needed someone to hold her hand, to love her, to tell her she wasn't alone and that the burden of the fight wasn't just hers to bear. That's what he's done for me. That's who he is.

He gently draws away, walking us to the corner where there's a brown leather sofa I didn't notice before.

"You gonna be okay here?"

"Yeah, I'll be fine. I promise."

"Okay."

He lowers me onto the couch, kissing my cheek, then my lips. His eyes remain on me as he treads back, as though leaving me here is too unbearable. He lets out a loud whistle, then footsteps hit the floor like an army marching toward their commander.

I recognize the first two who walk in as Dante's brothers. I don't know any of the others. There are six of them in total, not including my tormentor and the man who calls himself my father.

Dominic grips Carlito around his throat, dragging him inside. His face is already marred. One of his eyes is practically closed, and the other has a bloody gash under it.

My father is held by Enzo, whose expression is enraged.

"Drop him, Dom," Dante says.

His brother does as he's told, kicking Carlito in his back once he's down.

Dante squats, retrieving something from both his calves, and when he pulls them out, I realize they're knives. I'm close enough to see the shiny metal.

I'm instantly there, when it was just Carlito and me, when he was hurting me while I begged him to stop. My pulse races and my throat closes in as I recall every detail.

My hands ball into tight fists over the top of my thighs. I want to see that man dead. As for my father? I don't know. Because that little girl who loves him is still somewhere deep inside. I'm not ready to face his mortality, and I don't know if I can watch the man I love take his life.

"What was it you said to me when you held that gun to her head in the van?" Dante asks, creeping closer until his sneaker bumps Carlito's face.

*He did what?*

I don't remember any of that. It must've been when I was knocked out.

"Let me refresh your memory." He kicks him hard in the face. Carlito grumbles, blood spilling from his mouth. "I believe it was, let the best man win. I guess that's not gonna be you."

I get up, needing a better view. Wanting his blood. His pain. Wanting everything.

Dante rotates to the sound of me coming.

"You okay, baby?" Concern spirals with his darkness.

"I'm fine here. Do what you have to do."

My eyes find Carlito, glaring into the ugliness, but he doesn't try to lift his head.

*I love you,* Dante mouths before turning back around.

I want to say it back, but I want those words to come when my mind isn't polluted. When I can solely think about us and nothing else.

"There's one thing I don't forgive—what neither one of my brothers forgive—and that's when someone hurts the people we love. And that woman…" Dante gestures toward me with his head. "…was mine before she was ever handed to you like you bought her."

His foot lowers on Carlito's outstretched hand. Those groans would sadden me if they belonged to just about anyone else, but from him, they sound like victory.

Dante lifts his shoe in the air, and Carlito's hand crunches when the two meet. His screams color the walls in bright revenge, and all I want is more. I want the brutality. I want the savagery to slam over every part of Carlito's body like it did mine.

Dante meets my eyes, darkness clouding over tenderness. His breaths are harsh, but my exhales are harsher. An unspoken bond forms between us. His blood interlaced with mine. His vengeance entwined with my own.

A vow.

Unbroken.

Ours.

"Did he use a knife on you?" Disdain and compassion war for residency on his face.

I nod as my body folds into itself, protecting me from the memories.

His focus returns to his enemies, and I watch them from the side, able to see both.

"You allowed your daughter to be brutalized?" The knife in Dante's hand crawls to my father's throat, whose expression lacks emotion.

That's the way the Bianchi men operate. Emotions equal weakness.

But it's the opposite. Men who are afraid of expressing what they feel are cowards, and my father is the worst kind. I see that now.

"You had my family killed. My mother. My father. *My little brother*. All of them are gone because of you and your brothers, and you were about to have your daughter killed too?"

*He did what?*

A hand clasps over my mouth.

*No.*

Anguish for what Dante endured hurts more than my own pain. Losing that many people…

How could my family have been involved in that?

"Your mother wasn't my idea," my father adds. "I tried to tell him not to, but Faro—"

A menacing laugh is Dante's only response as he takes a step back, flipping the knife in the air before he catches it.

"Wow. What a hero. How about a round of applause. Hmm?" He starts to clap, and all the men around them join in.

Then, suddenly, he's on my father again. The blade tips up into his throat, making droplets of blood pool around the pointy edge. My heart thrashes in my rib cage.

"And my eight-year-old brother? My—"

I gasp. Dante glances back at me, but my eyes only know my dad.

*Eight? Who is this man I call a father?*

My pulse pumps wildly as tears leak from the edges of my eyes. I step forward, one foot after the other, until I'm right in front of him now. My hand whips out, striking his cheek as my lips curl with disgust.

"You killed a child?" My voice jitters with raw pain.

He swallows. "Not me…Raquel… Your uncle. He—"

"Stop!" I bellow, my palm in the air. "Were you there?! Did you watch it happen?!"

His silence tells me all I need to know.

"Did you try to stop it? Did you do anything at all?!" I scream.

He tightens his mouth and avoids my eyes, glancing down instead.

"Show me you're worth something! Show me you have some

humanity!"

But he continues to avoid my accusations.

"I don't know you." I shake my head. "This isn't my father."

I fail to keep the ache out of my voice. It's broken, just like my family.

"Hurting children. Women. *Your own daughter*. You disgust me."

He's far worse than I had suspected. His crimes are unforgivable.

A protective arm curls around my front as Dante draws me close so I don't have to see my father anymore.

"I'm sorry," he whispers with a tremor. "I'm so sorry you're hurting."

I meet his gaze. "You're not the one who should be apologizing. Not to me."

My palms cup his cheeks, the adoration spilling from every pore. I hate that our beginning is plagued by malice. But from ruins, beauty rises, stronger and harder to tarnish. No one will break us. Not anymore.

I lift up my feet just as he lowers, and our lips meet in a brief, soft kiss.

"I have to end this, baby," he gently says. "I need you to see a doctor."

"Okay." I return to where I originally stood, letting him finish what they began.

Dante strides over to Dominic, who reaches into his pocket and hands Dante what appears to be a torch, taking one of the knives in exchange.

"She's too good of a person to have parents like you," Dante tells my father.

The torch roars to life.

"Stand him up," he says of Carlito, who's uncharacteristically silent.

"Before you die—before I take that from you—you're going to know what real pain is like. And once she's satisfied that I've taken enough, only *then* will I allow you the mercy of death."

Carlito's chest widens, his face showing fear now. It's in the way he breathes. The way he stands. I don't need to see it up close to know it's creeping into his blood, the way mine was.

Dante flips the knife in his palm, eyeing it with concentration. He wields the weapon with expertise, and that alone should have me cowering, but it doesn't.

He doesn't scare me.

He never did.

Nothing about him ever will.

The knife strikes so quickly, I almost miss the first cut. He slices Carlito straight across his shoulder. Blood oozes out, absorbed by the white fabric of his shirt.

Dante doesn't stop there. The screams of the man who ignored mine fill the room. Cut after cut, Dante doesn't leave an inch unmutilated. Carlito's cheek leaks like a steady fountain, and the blood from his forehead drips into his eyes as he cries.

He flips the torch on, nearing it toward Carlito's face, and then a scream like no other drowns the space. A shiver runs down my arms and nausea swirls in my throat from the stench of incinerated flesh.

My father's mouth falls, even his fear on full display.

Dante growls like a beast as the torch runs over every wound on what's left of Carlito's body.

The smell.

The torture.

It's finally too much.

"Stop," I say, my inhales and exhales rivaling. "Enough. It's enough."

Dante stares at me through someone else's eyes, his unblinking gaze possessed. Rapid, short breaths fly out of his mouth. He removes a gun from his waistband as Dominic drops Carlito back onto the floor, and without parting his eyes from mine, he points the weapon and shoots.

My eyelids drift down as the bullet rips into the man I once thought I'd be forced to marry. Now he lies dead before me.

Even with my bruises and scars, both on the outside and in, I've won. I've made it. I'm alive, and I no longer have anything to fear. Not when Dante is with me.

Will my father meet the same fate?

I don't think I can watch him die. It'll be too much for my heart to withstand, especially with Dante being the one to do it.

Dante rushes to me, dropping the weapons on the floor. His hand clasps the side of my neck, those eyes spilling with ferocious adoration. He's both rays of sunlight and blackened smoke. One can't exist without the other.

"You know I love you," he says. "But what I have to do next, I don't want you to see."

It's as though he's read my mind, or maybe it wasn't that difficult to assume that I shouldn't witness my own father's death.

"I need you to still want me after this is over," he whispers, slanting his forehead over mine, his lips trembling as they brush over my mouth.

The way he just said those words…their emotional grip tethers to my heart. My palm slants over his cheek, moving a fraction, while my gaze searches his with depthless fervor.

"I'll always want you, Dante. Always," I murmur softly, just for him. "I've never been surer of how much I'm falling crazy in love with you. Saying it here with all this ugliness isn't perfect, but

I think it's time you realize that I'm not going anywhere. You're not the villain, no matter how much you've made yourself out to be."

He sighs sharply. "Thank you."

His breath fans over my lips, and as he kisses me, a gunshot rips through the air, rocking the very core of me. We both whirl to the sound, finding my father on the floor and Dominic holding the weapon.

I begin to sob and shake once I realize my father is gone forever.

"I'm sorry, Raquel. It had to be done," Dominic says, his expression hard, yet sympathetic.

"I…I know," I cry.

Dante's arms come around my lower back, holding me in a soft, supportive grip. I bury my face into him, and his hand begins stroking my back as I let the tears fall.

The end is just as painful as the beginning.

# RAQUEL

After Dante took me away from that place, I came straight to the hospital, even though by that point, it was the last place I wanted to be. I tried to insist on treating my own wounds, but Dante wasn't having it. He gave me no choice.

I knew I was being foolish, but I didn't want to be poked and prodded, even when it might have been for my own good. I had him promise not to take me to the same hospital I work for, so he drove a little farther to the next best one.

The day has turned to night. I tried to get the doctors to allow me to go home after they tended to my wounds, but the on-call doctor wanted me to stay for observations and promised I can leave tomorrow morning.

Every single time I close my eyes, I see that blade Carlito held in his hand. I feel the agonizing pain, as though I'm being slashed all over again. I try not to sleep, afraid the memories will follow into my nightmares.

The police have also come by for a chat. That was one interesting conversation, considering I couldn't exactly tell them the truth. It's not as though I could have said, "Sorry, officer, but what really happened was that I got kidnapped by a psycho, who my mafia parents allowed to hurt me, only to be saved by my husband, who doesn't exactly have a clean record either."

Instead, I told them I was leaving our house when a van came out of nowhere and a single masked man took me inside and hurt me while I was barely conscious before tossing me on the street a block from our home. There are no cameras in that vicinity, so the police will have a difficult time corroborating my story.

It'll remain unsolved. Indefinitely. They just don't know it yet.

I'm sure they recognized my last name, and I'm sure they're very aware of my family's reputation. I bet they assume what happened to me was some sort of payback for something my father did. I doubt they'll spend too much time trying to solve my case.

My mind jumps to my father's dead body. Those eyes staring blankly at me.

A knot aches in my throat. I miss him, yet I hate him at the same time for what he did to Dante's family.

Earlier, I begged Dante to tell me everything, and he did so reluctantly. He wanted to wait until I was home with him, but I insisted, and he doesn't stand a chance when I beg.

Not only did he tell me about his past, but he's given me a glimpse into the awfulness my family has caused. Children and women being trafficked and hurt.

I know he's going to find them and get them the safety they so desperately deserve.

He hasn't left my side for a second. He's only gone now because I pleaded with him to run home and take a damn shower and put on clothes not splattered in blood. His brothers are here, and Dominic said Chiara was on her way too.

I can't wait to see her. Even knowing she never told me the truth about any of this when she knew it all, I don't care. None of that matters anymore.

She's the only family I have left, and I know she didn't keep secrets without a good reason, or at least one she thought was good at the time. Chiara's always had my back. She'd never hurt me intentionally.

I stare at the cheerful lavender walls, feeling anything but. I can't stop thinking about the call I should probably make. My cell phone is beside me on the nightstand. Still no missed calls from my mother. She really doesn't care.

Dante told me what he did to her.

*No secrets*, he'd said as he spilled every dirty detail, describing how he had no hesitation when he shot her.

But the way he said it…it's like he wants to find the one thing that'll make me turn and run. But I'm not running. He did what he had to do to find me, and if he hadn't hurt her, she'd never have told him. I don't feel sorry for her. If anything, I wish he'd hurt her more. I'm sure she knew what Carlito would do and welcomed the torture. She'd have deemed it a proper punishment for my disloyalty to my fiancé and the family.

But Carlito was never anything but a virus she attached to me. I owed him nothing, and I owe her even less. Picking up the phone, my fingers tremble as I dial her number. The call rings twice before she answers.

"What the hell do you want?"

"I never wanted anything from you except my freedom and your love. But now, your love is the last thing I want." There's malice in my voice, but I no longer care. I'm done.

"Good. Now you have your freedom. I don't want anything to do with you, either. You're dead to me as much as your father is."

I close my eyes and pull in a breath so soft she can't possibly hear it, saying goodbye to the mother I never had.

"I'm glad that we're in agreement for once," I say. "One day, when I'm a mom, I hope like hell I don't turn out like you."

She snickers, all high and mighty. "When you're a mother, if you ever get to be one, I hope your daughter doesn't turn out to be a slut. That's what you are. Spreading your legs for that disgusting man. You know what he did to me?"

"I sure do. I'm only sad he didn't do worse. You deserved it."

"You little bitch!"

I'm the one laughing now. "You think you're so much better than him, don't you? You've always thought you were better than everyone. But you never were, *Mother*."

I know this conversation is the last one we'll ever share. It's a relief. I've finally shed her. She's been forever ripped from my roots.

"I wish I'd never had you," she huffs.

I can picture her face as she says that. The tension spiraling over her muscles.

"Someday, when you're old and alone, you might realize what a horrible mother you were," I remind her. "But by then, it'll be too late."

Her rough breaths cut through the line, and I can practically feel their teeth puncturing my skin.

"Go to hell," she finally spits out.

"You'd better pray I never see you again. Because if I do, you'll get a lot more from me than a bullet to your foot."

She gasps.

"I am my father's daughter, after all."

"You're nothing."

Then the line goes dead. I got to her, and not a damn thing has ever felt better.

I clutch the phone to me, saying goodbye to that part of my life and knowing I'm better for it.

There's a light knock on my hospital door.

"Come in," I say, knowing who it is already.

Chiara peeks through the door, concern swimming in her round, brown eyes.

"Just get in here," I laugh. "Give me a damn hug already."

A big sigh sways her shoulders before she comes in and shuts the door.

"So does this mean you don't totally hate me for being an awful cousin?" She tugs the corner of her lower lip, her brows creasing.

"No, I don't hate you." I roll my eyes.

She rushes to my side and takes a seat on the single black armchair next to my bed.

"Fine, maybe a little," I tease. "How could you not tell me about any of this when we spoke on the phone? Who Dominic and Dante were? Killing your damn father?" My eyes widen as I remember what she did. "How much have you actually been hiding?"

Pressing a button, I lift up the top half of my bed, which allows me to sit up.

I can see pure exhaustion in her eyes. See it plaguing her body. That's one thing about us: we're as close as sisters. I know every one of her expressions, even when they're as simple as an eye twitch, which usually means she's mad as hell but trying not to show it. You don't want to mess with her when she's that pissed.

"I'm sorry, Raquel. I only wanted what was best for you." Her eyes plead for understanding as her head slants, lips set in a deep frown. "When I called you that day we spoke, Dante begged me not to say anything, and just hearing how he talked about you, then listening to how happy you finally were…" She exhales harshly. "I didn't want to rip it away, even if it meant you being mad at me in the end."

Her palm lands on my knee, squeezing gently.

"But I knew I'd win you over eventually. I'm very hard to resist."

A bubble of her laughter blends with mine as my eyes meet hers.

"Now I kind of want to stay mad at you," I throw in. "Just to prove a point."

"Well, it worked out anyway, right?" Her face winds with a grimace. "Kind of. You know, minus you being here and all. But Carlito is dead."

She grins mirthlessly, like someone pointing out the positive in a crappy situation.

"Yeah, we seem to have a row of dead bodies following us, don't we?" I shake my head, hating the way our life has been.

She shrugs, but I can tell how much it bothers her too. She's always been the strong one between us. The one keeping people up when all she wants is to hide where no one can find her. I don't know Dominic at all, but I hope he's the man who can finally hold *her* up for a change.

"How come you never told me about Dominic when we were kids?" I've been wanting to ask her that as soon as I found out about them from Dante.

"I was afraid you'd blab to your parents, bigmouth."

"Hey!" I swat her on the chest. "I was good at keeping secrets. Maybe. Sometimes." I roll my lips side to side. "Okay, fine, I was awful."

"Yeah." She giggles. "Remember that time I told you I had a crush on that neighbor of yours, and you told your mom, who told your dad, who ended up telling mine? Yeah. Mm-hmm. I wasn't telling you shit about Dom, especially not with how much my father hated him."

"Dante filled me in on all that. I'm sorry your life was such hell, Chiara. I know I've said that over the years, but I don't think I truly grasped how much you had to live through, especially being so young."

"It's okay, cuz. What doesn't kill you makes you one tough-ass bitch."

"Well, you are that." There's genuine awe in my voice.

"Oh, I know." She tosses her hair back while her eyebrows flip upward. "So, when are we busting you out of here? Dante told me all your wounds should heal well. I'm so glad you're not dead." She grins.

"Well, thanks. It was a close call there."

She balls her hand. "Every time I think about it, I want to raise Carlito from the dead and kill him all over again. Dante said he suffered. Did he really?"

"Yeah, Chiara. He suffered. Dante doesn't play games."

She leans back in the chair, her eyes to the ceiling for a mere second. "My man."

We spend a few minutes discussing our corrupted family, the people our fathers are involved in trafficking, and our uncles, who are still out there, probably wanting Chiara dead for killing her father. Probably wanting to take me out too. It's risky for her to even be at the hospital, but I know nothing would've stopped Chiara from being here. Not me, and sure as hell not Dominic.

"I talked to my mom right before you got here," I throw in. "We're done."

"Well, I'm happy for you. Cut the toxicity, and that woman was toxic. We both know it."

"I know. It just hurts. I'd do anything to have the kind of mom you—" My pulse slams into my ears and my eyes bug out at my own stupidity as I look away.

"The kind I had? It's okay. You can say it."

Her face lights up at the mention of her mother, and my own turns with disgrace.

"She died," Chiara adds. "But I had her. I loved her. And the time we had, was our time. So it's okay. Don't feel bad. She *was* amazing." Her hand is back on my knee, holding me reassuringly.

I lift my head, finding kindness in every facet of her expression.

"I wish you'd had a mom like that too," she says.

Tears well in my eyes. My heart is surrounded by a bout of emotion, squeezing at me from all sides.

"I'm so lucky I have you."

"I'm lucky too." She smiles softly. "As people, we tend to see the world in all its negativity, but I've learned to see all the good instead. And you're one of the good things."

She gently circles her arms around my neck, and mine come around her, clutching tight. My cousin. My sister. My friend.

"Ow, shit," I mutter as one of the wounds on my upper arm burns.

"Damn it. I'm sorry." Her face contorts with horror as she practically jumps off of me.

"It's okay." I brush it off. "I'll be fine. I can't wait to go home tomorrow."

"With Dante?" She sits back down on the chair, wagging her brows.

"Duh. I don't think he'd let me get my own place in my condition, even if I wanted to." I pause, staring absently and missing him. "And I don't want to. I mean, we *are* married."

"Wow, someone's got it bad."

"Speaking of, how are you and Dominic? Or Dom, I should say?"

"Hot. Amazing." She stares dreamily at me. "God, that man… who knew? And those ties…."

She bites into her lower lip as her head falls to the back of the chair.

"Umm…okay. So when are you planning on telling me what happens with said ties?"

She peers back up at me. "Probably when you're well enough not to bust your stitches?"

"I don't have *that* many."

Her shoulders reel with a laugh, and then she fills me in on all the ways he likes to…uh, enhance their sexual experience with his work ties. She tells me everything, going back to how it all began from the time they were little.

We spend a while talking, and it's nice to have her back with me after thinking I'd never see her again. But here we are, forgetting about our past, at least for now, and focusing on the present.

The past will always be there, and the future is buried in the unknown, but the present is what we live for. And I'm here. Living, fighting for every moment and every breath, and never taking it for granted.

# Twenty-Three

## DANTE

“**I** love that you want to take care of me,” Raquel murmurs, her breath wafting against my neck. “But I can walk, you know.”

She nuzzles closer with a yawn. Her arms are wrapped around my neck as the tip of her nose rubs up and down right below my ear.

My cock hardens while my eyes drift closed. I want inside her so badly, I almost forget she only got home from the hospital earlier today.

“I know you can walk all by yourself,” I groan hoarsely. “But this is a lot more fun.”

“You’re not wrong.” She sighs with contentment. “Where are you taking me?”

"Upstairs. To sleep," I clarify.

My savagery has bounds, and that includes not getting anywhere near that pussy until her stitches dissolve.

"Okay." She yawns again. "Will you stay with me?"

Her eyes lift to mine, and this fierce sense of love and protection clasps to my very being. My pulse doubles, triples, speeding to an unruly pace as she gazes deeply.

"I'd never want to be anywhere else, sweetheart."

She smiles so sweetly, it makes me want to spend every second of every day making love to every piece of her heart and every inch of her soul. I never thought the man who only knew bloodshed— whose demons were louder than his humanity—would find someone to quiet the monsters and send them back to hell.

Leaning her head on my shoulder, she tightens her arms around me as I take us up the stairs. She got discharged a few hours ago, and we just had lunch. But all throughout, I could tell she needed a nap. I want her strong. Healthy. I want everything with her: a future, a family someday. She's my girl, and I won't let her forget it.

Once we're upstairs, I flip the covers and lower her onto the bed, moving in beside her. She lies on her back, finding a comfortable position.

Propping myself up on my elbow, I look down at her. "Does anything hurt, baby? Do you need more meds?"

She shakes her head. "I'm okay. Don't worry."

But her broken smile betrays her.

I run my thumb across the angle of her jaw. "You don't have to be brave for me, baby. You know that, right? Nothing would hurt me more than knowing you were hurting and I could've done something about it."

Her eyes glaze over. "I love you. You know that, right?"

My hand drifts to her cheek, cupping her softly in a firm grasp, and the amount of love I feel for her makes my heart fucking jump like it's about to explode.

"God, Raquel…" I lower my forehead to hers, pulling my eyes to a close while the tips of our noses brush over one another.

"I know," she whispers.

We don't need to say it to feel it. The words don't have to be profound. Love is in everything we do.

We stay that way for mere seconds that might as well fill lifetimes in between. And for the first time, when I close my eyes, I'm not afraid of what I'll find on the other side.

# RAQUEL

A week passes in the blink of an eye, and every day, I've spent in Dante's arms. He's cared for me. Looked out for my well-being more than my family ever did. With him, I've finally found another person besides Chiara that I can count on.

I slip into a long, rose-colored spring dress, running my palms over the material at my thighs while getting ready for the barbecue at Dom and Chiara's as I stare at myself in the full-length mirror. She wanted to do something for all of us. To have a day where we don't have to think about the awfulness that has been thrown our way.

Enzo and Joelle will be there too. I met Joelle a few days ago when Dante and I stopped by Dom's. We didn't really get to talk, but I know she worked at the club with Chiara, and her son was one of the kids taken by my family. I still don't know her story, nor will I ask. The last thing I want is to dig at her grief. I can't imagine having a child and then having him ripped away from me and never seeing him beyond once a month.

My finger crawls over the bandaged gash on my arm, barely resisting the urge to scratch. The wounds have gotten better, and I'm no longer in too much pain, but they're still there, reminding me of what happened.

But the real trauma is the one inside my head, when no one's here to see it, hear it, or feel me gasping for air. It's not nightmares. It happens when I'm awake. When I'm alone. When Carlito finds a way to infiltrate my reality and bring my worst fears to the surface.

Like right before, when Dante went into the shower and I began getting ready for today. It's as though I'm back there every time. Like I'm still on that chair with his knife to my neck, but this time the blood is dripping from my throat, and in my living nightmares, I die.

I know I should mention it to Dante, that I should see someone about it, but who can I tell? I can't speak honestly to a counselor. I guess I could lie and continue the charade about being attacked by someone I don't know. The cops still buy the story, so a therapist would too. But what's the point of talking if I can't tell the person trying to help me the truth?

Dante's shower abruptly stops, whisking me from my thoughts. I place them back in the box of things I'd rather forget.

The door creeps open, and he strolls out, a white towel draped around his hips. The sculpted muscles of his abs, that V dipping lower to that part of him that's already visibly hard, has me wondering why I didn't shower with him.

His hair's damp, falling over his forehead in the sexiest way. He grins at me while I continue to stare, and it's like I'm seeing him for the very first time. It might as well be, considering he's refused to touch me since the incident. He's worried he'll hurt me, but I'm more than capable of knowing what I can and cannot handle. And right now, the only thing I can't handle is the thought of those large hands anywhere else but on me.

He saunters closer, and my gaze runs over his chest and to those eyes I could fall right into without ever wanting to climb out. His arm curls around my lower back, tenderly moving his body into mine, while his lips fall to my neck, peppering soft kisses before they find the shell of my ear. His warm breath brushes over my skin, and I groan from the sensation, from the growing need between my thighs.

"I'm not against you objectifying me," he growls hoarsely, the desire evident in his tone as he repeats the same words from the night we met.

My hand tangles with the soft, wet strands of his hair.

"Dante," I rasp with a desperate cry, needing him, missing him.

I'm craving that connection between us, wanting it to ground me, to make me forget everything else but us.

The water falls from the tips of his hair, seeping in between my breasts, and the chill hardens my nipples.

"We shouldn't," he mutters gruffly.

But his hands don't accept the denial spilling from his mouth as they find my ass, squeezing and massaging, while the fingers of his other hand grip my hip possessively.

"We should," I retort, arching myself further into his touch. "I'm fine. Stop denying what we both want."

He lets out a deep-chested growl as his lips run up my throat, his teeth nipping and raking over my jaw like he wants inside everywhere.

His heavy-lidded gaze flashes to mine. "What did the doctor say yesterday?"

I suck in a breath as he glides the hand on my hip lower, his fingers gathering up my dress and teasing the edge of my panties.

"Sorry," I gasp. "But I didn't ask him whether I was allowed to fuck my husband."

"You should've." His index finger hooks into the lace, sliding it left. "Your husband *really* needs to know these things."

"Tell him it doesn't matter what the doctor says," I moan, grasping his hand and pressing it into my wet center. "It only matters what I want. And I want you, Dante. Now. Right here."

I push his touch further into my core, and he swears through gritted teeth.

"We can be careful," I breathe.

His finger finally dips in between the lips of my pussy while his eyes look up to mine as he reaches my achy clit, rubbing it with slow, agonizing circles.

"I've missed you," I confess on a gasping sigh. "I need this."

He steels his jaw while his other hand rides up my spine until his palm is around the base of my neck, gripping it like a tight vise. "So do I, baby. I need you bad."

Then his lips slam to mine, his hungry groans pervading through the silence and latching on to my ravenous moans.

His hands go to my hips, and our mouths refuse to part as he walks us up against the wall. My nails claw up and down his back as he lifts the dress up with a fist, all the way to my stomach, the towel still somehow covering him. He's careful to avoid where I've been hurt as he buries his hand in my hair while he kisses me roughly, urgently, like he never wants this to end.

My core tightens, needing him to fill the emptiness. I'm hollow everywhere, wanting his love and the passion between us to quench my dying thirst.

He places a hand right where I'm aching for him, moving my panties to the side again. Two fingers slowly slip into my most intimate place. Inch by inch, he enters me, stealing my gasps with his lips. His fingers curl into my G-spot, his thrusts matching the tempo of his tongue in my mouth as he slams into me harshly. My orgasm builds as my whimpers tremble out, and he sucks my lower lip, groaning in the most delicious way while curving his fingers deeper.

This feels too good. It's all I want. This undying desire when we're together, reaching the point of madness.

"Fuck, you're so damn tight," he growls, biting and sucking along my jaw before falling back to my lips, his tongue fighting its way inside.

He fingers me with a barbaric tempo as I cry out unashamedly. His teeth nip my lower lip before his mouth is back on mine. The savagery of his kiss has me delirious.

I'm close, teetering on a tightrope, ready to fall. To surrender.

His thumb brushes harder over me, and before I can come, he stops. He kneels, those eyes looking up at me as I cry in protest from being denied…until his tongue finds my core and two fingers slide back inside me. And when the tip of his tongue flicks around my clit this time, I crash wildly into the eye of the storm, and I welcome its fury.

"Yes! Oh, God, Dante." His name is a stammered breath.

My hand buries in his hair as I pull while the release hits me with its full force.

He doesn't give me a second to come down from the high before he's back, that mouth hungrily on mine, sucking onto my bottom lip.

"Face the wall."

That commanding tone has my pussy aching for another round as I place my palms there and bend, angling my head toward him. He bunches the dress over my ass and lines the crown of his cock with my entrance, then slams home.

He grabs my neck, pulling me back and kissing me with savage devotion, fucking me harder while swallowing my gasping moans. Another orgasm swells within me, and I swear out his name as our lips part. His gaze remains fixed to mine, the connection unbreakable.

Ours.

Everything else disappears. It's only us here.

There's something to be said about looking into the eyes of the one you love while he's inside you. It's unnerving, yet unparallel. It's another level of intimacy and a high like no other.

"I love you," he rasps as our mouths brush softly, our breaths falling faster.

His hips slam into me with roughened strokes, stretching me to the point where pain mingles with pleasure.

I try to say it back, I really do, but I can't seem to find the words. I'm devoured by our untamed hunger and the sensations fluttering over my entire body.

He keeps the tempo of his hips hard and deep while his mouth finds my neck. The sound of flesh to flesh, skin to skin…it's undoing every scar, every bad memory. I'm lost to the lust. To the melody of us. I'm lost to the way he loves my body and my heart. Like no one has before.

Dante Cavaleri.

My husband.

I've finally found someone to keep me safe, but he's so much more than my protector. He's the one I was waiting for when I believed all hope was lost. But he was merely waiting to find me.

"I wanna hear you come," he groans.

His cock grows even thicker as his release draws closer, right along with my own. And when he hits my G-spot this time, I fall, screaming out his name as the orgasm tingles through me, curling over my toes.

The warmth. The buzz. It's everything. Just like he is.

My name is on his lips too as he finds his own release. Feeling him come undone inside me with no barrier between us makes the experience even better. He knew I had an IUD placed, and knew how much I wanted it this way.

Our breaths battle for space as his face falls against my back, and he curls an arm around my stomach as I straighten.

"How late are we to the barbecue?" I try to calm the racing of my heart.

"Late enough that they'll know why," he chuckles, kissing the back of my head. "Especially with how messy your hair is."

"Ugh!" I face him, throwing my arms over his shoulders. "You should probably get dressed while I fix myself up."

"Probably." His voice is hoarse and husky against my ear, sending a shiver down my body and throwing me into the fire once more.

My need grows again as his hand finds my inner thigh, slinking upward until two fingers rest over my pussy.

"Or we can be really late."

# Twenty-Four

# RAQUEL

After another two mind-blowing orgasms, we finally get up and ready ourselves to go. Strapping on my ivory flat sandals, I slip my hand into Dante's as he locks up before we head over to Dom's home. Well, I should say Dom and Chiara's, since she now lives with him.

I glance over at a very put-together Dante as we walk hand in hand.

"How come you don't look like a man who just gave his wife four orgasms? That's so unfair." I shake my head as a knowing grin cracks his face.

"You're always beautiful," he tells me, kissing my temple. "I like the way you look right now. All messy, cheeks flushed."

"Messy? Oh my God. I look messy? Maybe I should go back

home and put my hair up."

I tried to get my strands to cooperate after what we did, but it was no use. My straightened hair now appears to be a wavy mop.

He curls his arm around my hip, pulling me to his side. His bicep is rock hard, flexing beneath his long-sleeved cobalt t-shirt. He looks so casual, yet insanely sexy. Dante is the type of man who can pull off any look flawlessly, like he's always meant to wear it.

We're almost to Dom's—only a few feet away—when he stops, turning me so we face one another.

His thumb tips up my chin. "You need to stop doubting yourself, baby. You're flawless. Not just to me. To everyone." He places a hand against the side of my neck, his thumb gliding past as he leans over and kisses me tenderly, dousing me in the power of his words. "And I like you messy. Dirty. Knowing it's me who made you that way."

Heat slithers up my body, bolting right into my core. My pulse quickens, caught up in his smooth gaze.

"Now let's go and eat," he continues, his voice turning hushed and gravelly. "So we can get back home. I'm going to double the number of orgasms you had earlier."

"Impossible." My eyes widen as we continue on our way and make it to the front of Dom's house. "There's no way I can do that."

He knocks, flashing me a lopsided grin. "I can't wait to show you just how wrong you are."

The door flies open, and Chiara's annoyed expression greets us.

"What the fuck, guys?" She plants a hand on her hip, her brows raised. "You couldn't let us know you'd be late?"

"I'm sorry," I say, closing my arms around her in a tight hug, and she returns it.

Her eyes dart from me to Dante as we separate. Dom walks over from behind her, tipping his chin up in greeting.

"You know…" Chiara announces, closing the door. "We need to let each other know when we don't show up on time. We kinda have people that wanna kill us, in case anyone forgot." She fakes a smile. "So maybe the next time you two wanna fuck each other's brains out, send your girl a text, 'kay?"

My face instantly flushes.

"I didn't say we—" I try to finish, but she holds out a hand.

"Girlfriend, please. Your hair and those cheeks gave you away."

"See?!" I turn to Dante. "I told you I should've gone back and fixed my hair!"

"We all fuck, cuz," Chiara throws in. "I'm just glad he's doing it so well."

My cheeks burn. "Can we stop talking about my sex life? Please?"

Dom shakes his head with a deep smirk, and I grow even redder.

"Oh, hey. *Now* it's a party!" Enzo bellows with a beer in one hand and Joelle curled around his other.

She's almost as tall as him with her high-heeled strappy shoes and a tight, knee-length black dress. Her eyes are as blue as the clear sky on a summer day. She runs a hand through the front of her long, wavy strawberry-blonde hair as she separates from Enzo and comes over to me.

"Hey, Raquel." She reaches for a hug, one I willingly give her. "I'm so glad to see you again."

"You too." I smile warmly.

She's on a whole other level of beautiful. I feel inadequate in her presence, but she seems nice and down-to-earth, so it's hard to hate her, even if I wanted to.

"Come on, guys. Let's eat," Dom says, making his way to Chiara and tightening an arm around her hips. "I'm fucking starving."

The way he said that as he gazed at her has me thinking he wasn't simply talking about the food.

Dante is back beside me, kissing my temple.

"I've missed you," he says over the shell of my ear, his breath skirting up my neck and making a hum of desire channel through me.

"You were gone for two seconds," I whisper as we tread behind the two other couples, heading for the yard.

"Two of the longest seconds of my life."

Staring up at him with a giggle, I find a huge grin spreading over his face, the kindness seeping through his eyes. The devotion there tethers to my heart, making it heavy with all the things it carries for this man, forever my husband.

Divorcing would've been pointless, even after he told me the whole truth. Because in time, I would've wanted to marry him all over again. I understand why he did what he did. My forgiveness was easily given.

I sway my body into him, my head finding his shoulder. This is so nice. I can't believe it's my life.

We might still have a lot of hurdles to get through, both from my family and from our own inner battles, but like Chiara said to me at the hospital, if we don't stop to appreciate the things we do have, we'll let the beautiful moments pass us by. I don't want to lose sight of that.

Chiara opens the double doors, and we step out. The air is rich with the scent of barbecue, making my mouth water. We head down toward the pool, where a large rectangular table with ten chairs waits for us, along with someone in front of a grill. I can only make out the back of his head with his short black hair peeking out from under a white chef's hat.

"Who's that?" I ask Chiara, who takes a seat beside me while Dante pulls out the chair on my other side.

"We hired a caterer," she whispers, leaning her head toward me. "I didn't want Dom to be occupied with cooking. I wanted him to have a good time with his brothers." She purses her lips. "He's been so on edge with everything going on. This was my way of trying to relax him a bit."

I glance over at Dom across from us. His foot is bouncing on his knee as he sits next to Enzo, taking a swig of his beer while his eyes dart over each corner of his property. Dante and Enzo talk, laughing away, not noticing their brother's state.

"I see what you mean."

"That's how he is all the time. It worries me, but at the same time, I get it. You know?" She sighs, a line etching between her brows.

My hand lands over hers on her lap, squeezing in reassurance. "Yeah, it's understandable. I still can't believe what our fathers did. I don't think I'll ever come to grips with them killing a child. Trafficking. I'm disgusted."

She bows her head. "I know. I wish you had met Matteo. He was the cutest little thing."

"I wish I had too."

We pause in silence for a few seconds, as though saying goodbye to the little boy she once knew.

Our men rise and head to pick up our plates, already filled with food. The utensils are already on the table, along with two bottles of wine, both red and white.

Once the guys return, everyone digs in. The clinking of knives and forks is a welcomed sound. Normalcy is something I need badly to help me forget the horror I lived through when Carlito captured me.

Reaching over, I pick up a bottle of the red wine, using the opener to uncork it. Chiara and I are both fans of red, so I pour her a glass, then some for myself.

"Would you like any?" I ask Joelle, who's been quiet beside Enzo.

"Yes, please." Her mouth tugs up at the corners as she holds up her glass from across, allowing me to pour some into it.

"A toast, guys," I say to them all, lifting up my drink. "To family, and to the friends who became family."

"I'll drink to that." Enzo raises his beer bottle, clinking it to my glass, and everyone else starts to do the same, repeating my sentiments.

I take a long sip of the semi-sweet wine. The taste of blackberry infused with a hint of cocoa adds a nice touch.

Chiara's glass remains untouched as she cuts into her steak, slipping a piece into her mouth. I tilt my head, staring at her with razor focus, finding it a little odd that she hasn't even tasted a drop.

"Aren't you drinking?"

My question hangs in the air while Chiara's flitting gaze avoids an answer, drifting between her food and me. I take a bite of my burger, picking up my drink.

"What? Are you pregnant or something?" I casually throw in with a laugh as I take another mouthful.

But instead of laughing with me, her face grows serious.

Too serious.

The table suddenly goes quiet.

"Babe?" Dom's eyes swell.

But Chiara avoids him too.

"Oh my God!" I blurt out. "You're really pregnant?"

"Ugh!" she grunts, throwing her palm over her face. "Yes."

"What?!" I practically jump off my seat.

Everyone else is silent, their faces clouded with disbelief—including Dom, whose mouth is set to a tight line, his awestruck eyes still glued to her.

"Chiara, you serious?" he finally asks.

Her fingers drift slowly down her face as she turns toward him.

"Are you mad?" Her face knits into a frown. "I'm sorry, I just found ou—"

He gets off his seat so fast, circling his arms around her and lifting her off the chair and into his arms.

"Mad? You thought I'd be mad, baby girl?" His lips meet hers in a quick, deep kiss as her thighs come around his middle. "Do I look mad?"

He grins, kissing her again and pulling her closer while her palms rest on his shoulders.

"God, Chiara," he whispers as they pull apart an inch. "You know how much I love you?"

"I have some idea." A wide smile tugs at her lips.

"A little you and me. Can you imagine that?"

The way he says those words, there's so much endearment in his voice. It's touching to see how much he loves her so obviously. It spills from his eyes. I'm happy for her, insanely happy that she found him. Again. He lifts her up in the air, kissing her stomach as his eyes flutter to a close.

We all needed this. Something good. Something positive to cling to.

"Shit, should I be picking you up like this?" he flusters as he pulls back, sliding her down onto the ground.

"What do I know?" She shrugs with a laugh.

"You're really going to be a mom," I add.

I'm still in shock. She's pregnant. I'm going to be an aunt. Happiness interlaces with disbelief.

She tries to sit back down on her chair, but Dom whips out his hand.

"Where you think you're going?" he asks, gently pulling her onto his lap as he takes his seat.

He nuzzles her neck as she leans into his embrace, kissing the top of his head.

"This is wonderful, Chiara," Joelle adds.

A smile is on her face, but it carries a hint of sadness. I can only guess why.

She was robbed of the experience of being a mother. She never got to see her son grow up. Dante said he's around eight now.

My uncles, my father…they're all animals. How could they do this?

I guess I shouldn't be surprised at what they're all capable of after finding out they had Matteo killed. Who knows what else they've done?

"Congrats, brother!" Dante stands and steps over to Dom, clasping his shoulder.

"I've got dibs on the cool uncle," Enzo adds as he also gets to his feet to congratulate his brother.

Then they both give Chiara a warm hug.

"I'm only like four weeks, guys," Chiara explains as everyone sits back down. "I found out this morning when I took a test."

"What made you take one?" I ask, completely curious.

"I don't know. My sense of smell was really strong all day yesterday and I felt a little nauseous, so I asked Sonia to pick me up a test. I really didn't think I was."

Dom's hand is on her jaw, cupping it, as he reverts her gaze to him.

"Sonia knew before me?" He lifts a curious brow.

"Kind of?" She grimaces. "I mean, I didn't confirm it once I found out, but she was excited at the possibility."

"I bet she was." He chuckles as his hand drops.

We spend the next half hour or so talking, excited for the soon-to-be parents, before the ladies and I stand up and head to the loungers by the pool while the guys have their own time. Chiara clutches her cup filled with seltzer water, her eyes drifting over to Joelle, who's drinking her wine. She's sitting on a lounger beside Chiara, mind seemingly preoccupied as she stares into her glass.

"So how is being with Enzo?" I prod as I lean over, trying to break up the awkwardness.

"He's not so bad." Her lips tip upward as her face slants sideways.

"Is that right?" Chiara adds, wagging her brows. "So, have we forgotten about that MMA trainer from your gym? The one I never texted?"

"Who is that again?" Joelle laughs teasingly.

"Wow. I guess you really do like him," Chiara says.

"Yeah, he's pretty good to me, considering the start we had." She momentarily glances down onto her lap. "We know each other from the club. I don't know if you knew that. He was one of my customers."

"No. I don't remember him." My cousin shakes her head. "You know how it was. I really didn't associate with the men, unless it was with my fist."

"She's a badass," Joelle says to me. "I've seen her in action, and let's just say, I pitied the person at the end of her fist. One time, she broke this guy's two front teeth when he tried to touch me."

"Oh, damn. I remember that," Chiara bursts with a laugh.

We continue drinking as they exchange stories from the club, while I soak it all up.

Finally, Chiara pulls in a sharp inhale. "Look, Joelle. I have to say this, so please let me get this out."

The mood shifts, and Chiara, who's sitting in the middle, swings her body toward Joelle.

"I'm sorry for what my family did to you and your son. I'm sorry you didn't feel like you could come to me for help. It breaks my heart to know how badly you were suffering while I thought you were working there willingly." Her eyes surge with unshed tears as she clenches her jaw before continuing. "You don't have to forgive me, but I need you to know that I knew nothing about any of this. Neither of us did."

Joelle sniffles, swiping under her eyes as she nods.

"I was afraid to tell you. Afraid to tell anyone, really, in case they…" Her chin trembles. "In case they killed my son."

Her face falls into her palms as she quietly sobs into them.

"Oh, Joelle. I'm so sorry," Chiara cries, gently gliding her hand up and down her back.

Standing up, I go to sit beside Joelle too, placing an arm around her and giving her the comfort she probably needs.

"He's so beautiful." Joelle sighs mournfully. "I'm so grateful he looks exactly like me and not his—"

Her face turns hard.

"Not his father?" Chiara finishes, eyeing her curiously.

She nods.

"Who's his father, Joelle?" I ask.

A sinking feeling hits the pit of my stomach. Like when you know something dreadful is about to happen before it actually does.

Her hazy gaze tosses from Chiara to me.

A cold shudder breaks over both of my arms and my skin tingles.

She sucks in a breath, her features drowning in pain. "I never wanted to speak of this ugliness before, but I think it's time. Anything to help find my son."

"Time for what?" Enzo appears from behind us, the other guys with him. "What's wrong, baby? Why are you crying?"

He walks over to her, clasping her cheek in his palm with his brows pinched.

"They asked me who Robby's father is." Her hand falls over his as she stares up at him, getting to her feet. "I think it's time I tell you. All of you."

Enzo only stares, unable to move, probably clutched in the same trepidation that's coursing through me. She gives him a sad smile before edging his hand off of her, then turns her attention to everyone as he now lowers to where she sat.

"Enzo already knows some of this, but not everything." She briefly darts her eyes to him, then scans each of our faces. "When I was nineteen, I was traveling with some friends across the country. It was just the three of us in my Jeep. Elsie, Kayla, and I all went to high school together and decided to take time off from college, wanting to experience the world before becoming doctors. That was always our plan. I was going to be a pediatrician, Elsie wanted to be a heart surgeon, and Kayla's dream was to become an oncologist."

A trembling hand runs up to her mouth.

"We had no idea that two days into our adventure, we'd never see each other again." She walks over to Enzo, sitting on his lap while his large hand rests over her knee protectively. "After getting dinner at one of the restaurants where this man, probably in his thirties, wouldn't leave us alone, we hopped back on the road. But once we were on a long stretch on an empty highway, the engine died. We tried to call for help, but there was no reception. We thought we'd be stranded there. We waited for what felt like an hour until we saw a single car."

She runs a hand past her face, dropping a sharp exhale.

"The three of us were so excited. We jumped onto the road, waving our hands, until the large, white SUV stopped. We thought we were finally safe. How wrong we were." Her eyes brim with tears. "The man who stepped out was none other than the one from the restaurant. I didn't think anything of it at first, until two others stepped out with him."

Her breaths come faster now, and her knee shakes as she tries to find the rest of her words.

"Here," Dom says, handing her a bottle of water.

Enzo grabs it and opens it for her before she drinks almost half the bottle.

"I…I'm sorry," she stammers, her eyes glazed. "This is really hard to relive, even after all this time."

"You don't ever have to apologize to us." Enzo wraps her in his arms, tucking her into his body.

"Yeah, don't be sorry, Joelle," Chiara adds. "You don't have to do this if you can't."

"I want to."

She nods before telling us the rest of what I know will be a horror.

"I never saw those other two men before. But they looked older than the other man. They approached us, asking what happened, and when we told them, they pretended to help at first, and one of them even examined my car. But suddenly, the other older man grabbed Kayla, knocking her on the side of the head with a gun. Elsie and I screamed for help and started to run away, but we had nowhere to go. As Elsie ran, the man from the restaurant shot her leg and dragged her back while she cried. I stopped running then. I knew they'd take me anyway, dead or alive."

Tears are running down her face now, and mine. My heart clenches, feeling her agony.

"They knocked me out too, and the next thing I knew, I woke up in a dark cage with voices whimpering all around me. I called for my friends, but they weren't there."

She uncaps the bottle and drinks some more, then hands the rest to Enzo, whose face is hard as the fist on his thigh rattles with the force of his anger.

"The day I met my son's father, he took me out of the cage and put a black woven bag over my head as he led me up the stairs. When he took the cloth off my face, we were in a bedroom, and, um…"

"Fuck!" Enzo growls, his hand jumping to the back of her head and turning her to him. "Tell me who he is. I'll fucking tear his body apart limb by limb."

"You can't put yourself in danger for me. I just need you to find my boy." Her chin trembles with a sob. "The rest doesn't matter."

"Like hell, it doesn't. I'll kill that motherfucker if he isn't dead already. I'll make him suffer for days, and that won't even be enough."

His breathing grows harsher with every second he stares into her shattered gaze. I can see how much she means to him, how much he means to her.

"Tell me who it is, God damn it. I need to know, baby."

We all wait in bathed silence for her to say something.

"I didn't know his name at first, or who he even was, but later I found out he was in charge of all the women and children they held in cages. He was the one that the men who watched us answered to."

Dante places his hands on my shoulders from behind, his fingers biting into my skin.

"One night, when he did what you can only imagine, he asked me to call him by his name. He—he said his name was…" She looks at Chiara and then at me as she swallows heavily. "It was your uncle Agnelo. He raped me repeatedly. All the others used a condom. My son is his."

"I'll fucking kill him!" Enzo roars.

My body grows ice cold. It's like I'm numbed in place. Just when I think my family couldn't stoop any lower, there's something else that shocks my system.

"He's gonna fucking die painfully for this," Enzo swears, the back of his hand under her jaw as he lifts her eyes to his. "I'm so damn sorry, baby."

His arms clasp around her, holding her tight.

"He's mine, you hear me?" he tells his brothers. "I'm going to be the one to kill him."

Chiara runs off the chair, and when I turn back to see where she went, I find her grabbing a garbage pail from beside the table we ate at and hurling into it. Dom runs after her, helping her, while I don't know what to do or say.

Dante takes a seat beside me.

"I can't believe how evil my family is." Tears leak out of the corners of my eyes. "What they did to her, and to the other women and children. It's unimaginable."

"I know, sweetheart." His arms come around me, scooping me onto his lap. "You're not at fault for who your family is." His thumb moves along the base of my jaw while his eyes delve into mine. "It's not on you or Chiara. You hear me?"

I nod, leaning into his hold, just as Chiara walks back over.

"I'm sorry," she says to Joelle. "I'm sorry for all of it. If he were here, I'd kill him."

Joelle stands, stepping toward her and gently taking her hand.

"I don't blame you or Raquel." Her eyes dash to me for a moment. "You're not responsible for their actions. Don't be so hard on yourselves."

"Yeah." Chiara slips out of her embrace, pacing, as though she can't come to grips with any of this.

But neither can I. It'll take a while to digest the level of evil my family has enacted on their victims.

"Sir?" One of Dominic's guards marches over to him. "One of the cameras on the other side of the fence malfunctioned," he says quietly. "The men are looking at it."

"I'll go check it out."

Dom gets to his feet, and as he does, my eyes land on the man behind them.

The chef.

Now that I'm really paying attention, there's something about him. I tilt my head curiously as our eyes meet, and I find familiarity there. I can't place him, but I know we've met before.

*But where?*

I force myself to dig through my memories, but I'm still unable to figure out where I could've seen him.

He stares at me, his almost-black eyes cutting into mine, as though recognizing me. And when he rotates toward the grill, I gasp as I find the tattoo of a sparrow on his neck.

# Twenty-Five

# RAQUEL

"Babe? Are you okay?" Dante questions, but his voice might as well be miles away.

I can't pull my attention off the man. I'm frozen in shock.

My mind spins with questions.

*Why is he here? Is it for me?*

And before I can find my voice to warn them, he spins toward us with a gun in his grip, his aim on Chiara.

And then he shoots.

*Pop.*

The bullet roars to life before everyone realizes what's happening, and it punctures Chiara from the side of her stomach.

Her eyes grow wide as she glances down to where the bullet

hit.

"Chiara!" Dom screams, running to her.

She starts to fall backward into the pool while blood trickles down her hip, her fingers coated in red. She hits the water, and a deafening splash paints the air.

The man who shot her, the one pretending to be a chef, is a man I now realize is Carlito's cousin. Before he has a chance to strike another person, the weapon still raised, Enzo draws his gun and fires a deadly bullet between his eyes. Joelle cries as he pulls her into hiding behind a tree.

I hear my own screams as I run toward the pool to jump in with Chiara.

She can't be dead.

*And the baby! No!*

The sobs crash over me. Heavy. Shattered.

They did this to her. Our family. They hurt her.

"Chiara!" I wail.

A hand slams around my stomach from behind, dragging me as I shriek in protest, and places me behind a bush as more men run out from the other side of the yard. My family's men.

*The camera. It must've been them.*

The shouting. The gunfire. The chaos.

It all ensues quickly around us.

"Stay here, God damn it," Dante warns.

But my eyes are on my cousin, who I can see from where I am.

Dom's men shoot back, forming a protective line, while water drips from his clothes as he checks her pulse, then lifts her up in his arms, shielding her with his body while running into the house.

"Do you want to be next?!" Dante snaps.

*She has to be okay. Please. She has to survive.*

I tremble with a heavy ache in the middle of my chest, my

entire body riddled with shock as my eyes finally look to Dante.

"I know you're worried," he says. "But don't you move for anything! I'm not losing you, okay? I love you. Do you fucking hear me?"

He grips my jaw with the rough pads of his fingers and pulls his mouth to mine, grazing his lips over my damp ones and leaving me with a kiss before he rights himself.

"I'll be back." His jaw pulses before he pulls a gun from his ankle and reaches out his hand. "Take this."

I nod frantically as tears stream down my cheeks. I can't seem to make my mouth move as my trembling hand extends toward the weapon and I grip it in my unsteady palm.

"You're everything to me. Remember that."

Then he's gone. I lose him to the fight, unable to see him now from the angle I'm at.

A silent scream slices through the fog in my brain, clouding over the sound of bullets whizzing past me. My stomach curls with fear. There's so much of it.

Fear for Chiara. For Dante. For all of us.

I rock back and forth, hugging my knees with the gun hanging from my hand, waiting for this horror to be all over so I can get to Chiara. So I can see that the people we both love are all okay.

I want them all to be all right. We can't lose anyone.

When will enough be enough? When will my family stop hurting people?

Agonizingly slow minutes trickle by, and the gunfire doesn't seem to have slowed. If anything, it's grown.

Someone falls to my left with a loud thump, and I jolt my head with startled panic before finding a man in a black t-shirt with blood dripping out of his mouth, his unblinking gaze staring at me lifelessly.

Is this what my life with Dante will always be like? Never-ending wars?

We can't sustain a relationship this way, or have a future. Look what happened to Chiara. She might lose not only her baby, but her damn life. And for what?

My uncle Faro deserved what she did. He deserved it years ago. As for my father? He made his bed. He knew what his brother did to Dante's family and didn't care.

The bullets are less frequent now, but the fighting isn't over yet. I wonder if Joelle is okay where she is with Enzo gone. She has a son to live for. That poor woman.

"Give us Chiara and Raquel. That's all we want," says a voice I know quite well.

It belongs to my uncle Benvolio, the new don.

*He's here? The bastard came for us personally?*

My hand stiffens around the gun, wanting to kill them all.

"I want that whore, Joelle, too. Where is she, huh?" my uncle Agnelo chuckles, sending a chill running down my spine.

They're both here. I can only hope this is where they die.

Enzo's demonic laugh breaks from his chest. "I'm gonna rip your damn head off just like I did to your men, who are lying dead, where you'll soon be. Both of you. I'm gonna enjoy gutting you like a pig."

"You fuckin' jackass motherfuckers," Agnelo says. "Who do you think you are, huh? You're all about to join your mommy and daddy. My nieces, Joelle…they'll all be following you there too."

Dante growls like an animal possessed before a single gunshot cuts through the conversation. I jerk back as my body shudders from gripping fear, not knowing whose weapon it came from. My heart is heavy in my rib cage, like I'm trapped under pounds of boulders, unable to move or breathe.

"Nice try," Agnelo taunts.

Suddenly, madness ensues all over again. The sound of gunfire, the grunts, things cracking and breaking from the fighting.

The weapon in my hand rattles as I pull air into my lungs, steadying the fear and swallowing it away as the tears fall. Unending misery that I no longer want to feel.

*Leave us alone!* I shout within my head as my exhales huff out, fear replaced with rage.

Before I realize what I'm doing, I stand up, my body soaked in fury as I come out of hiding, no longer worried about dying. I just want to hurt my uncles. I want them dead, once and for all.

I draw my pistol up inch by inch as my feet move. I see Uncle Benvolio first, fighting with one of Dom's men. Dante is on the far right, his weapon pointing at someone. He doesn't see me yet. A heap of dead bodies lies on the ground.

No one notices me as I slowly creep toward my uncle.

No one sees my gun as it points at him.

No one pays attention.

Not until I pull the trigger.

Not until my uncle falls, the back of his head marred with a bullet hole I put there.

Everyone around me stops fighting, as though caught in a trance.

"Raquel?" Dante calls. "Give me the gun, baby."

He walks toward me slowly as I stare at my dead uncle.

The one I killed.

*I killed someone.*

*Oh my God.*

I realize I'm the one in a trance now. The gun is still extended as I blink rapidly and my mind comes to focus. Finally turning toward Dante, I find the worry in his eyes as he gently grabs my wrist, lowering it to the ground before taking the gun from me.

"Come on. I'm taking you inside." He places an arm under my thighs and lifts me up, cradling me close against his body.

I peer over my shoulder at the death I caused. My heartbeats quicken to a wayward pace.

"I…I'm sorry. I was so angry, and—"

"Hey. It's okay, baby." His arms tighten around me. "You did nothing wrong."

Tears fall from my eyes as the hurt, the realization of what I did, crashes into me. I'm a doctor. I save people. I don't kill them.

We make it inside Dom's home, which is filled with more men. Too many to count.

"You're going to stay here with them while I help clean up the yard, okay?"

"Yeah, fine." My voice shudders right along with my hands as he lowers me to the ground.

"Take care of her," he tells his men before his eyes are level to mine and a hand clasps around the side of my face. "Everything's going to be okay. Chiara will be fine. This will be over soon. I swear."

He leaves a quick kiss on my lips.

"You don't know that," I cry. "I need to see her. Did Dom take her to the hospital?"

"Yeah. I'll take you as soon as I'm done here. I'm not letting you out of my sight."

"Please don't get hurt," I beg.

Both his arms are around me now, wrapping me snugly. "Shh. Don't cry. I love you, Raquel."

I pull back. "I love you too. So don't leave me, okay?"

"Not if I can help it." His palm fits over my cheek. "The devil himself would have to drag me away from you before I would ever go willingly." He drops his lips to my forehead, pulling in a harsh breath. "But I have to finish this if we ever want a life together."

"I know." My brows furrow with both understanding and anguish.

None of us should ever know this much pain. We didn't ask for it. My family shoved it down our throats, and until we rip it out, we'll never know peace.

With a final look into my eyes, he mouths *I love you* before running off into the fight. Something he's been doing his entire life.

# Twenty-Six

## DANTE

At the first sign of death, Agnelo ran. He's too afraid of what we'll do to him, and he should be. His death will be slow, unlike that of his brother, who's currently lying on the concrete, too dead to tell us what we need to know. But we have a few of their men still alive, tied up on the chairs.

Enzo and I are too overcome with rage to let them die humanely. With Chiara in the hospital and our women being caught in the midst of danger, we're going to make this as brutal as possible.

"If my brother Dom were here, it'd be a lot worse for you," I tell a nameless man who's bleeding from the top of his cheek, the thick gash seeping crimson thanks to my blade.

I clutch the blue handle of my knife, pacing around him slowly. The tip of the weapon edges to the side of his throat, licking upward.

"Tell me where they keep the kids, and I *might* consider being a little nicer." I push the blade in deeper and pierce through the skin, making drops of blood drip down his neck. "Not that nice, but still a lot better than torching your body while you're still breathing. I'd tell you to ask some of your friends how much fun that was, but…"

I glide the knife down slowly, curving the angle of the blade around his Adam's apple.

"Listen…" He coughs harshly before catching his breath. "I have no fucking clue about no kids. I swear it."

I blow out an exaggerated breath, pacing over to Enzo, who has another man on a chair in front of him.

"I'm really disappointed, Ricky. I had high hopes for you."

"My name isn't Ricky."

"Well, today, it is." I glare, my eyes seeped in violent vengeance. He shuts his mouth quickly.

Enzo hands me a torch while I place the blade down, picking up the red gasoline canister from behind him, where another two are waiting for us. Holding the container in my hand, I tread back to Ricky, placing it between his stretched legs.

"I have no patience, so you either tell me something valuable, or I burn you alive." I switch the torch on as he pants, his eyes glued to the blaze of the flame: calm, yet dangerous.

"Please, man, I don't kn—ahhh!" He screams as the fire incinerates through his shoulder, making the air reek in burning flesh.

I'm almost immune to it, that stench I can only describe as burning leather with a pinch of garlic. Sweet. Sickening. The unpleasant smell took a little time to get used to. It's funny what a human mind can embrace when not given a chance to know otherwise.

"I know you know," I warn as the torch lowers to his bicep, almost searing him there too. "Speak."

"They…" he cries. "They told me nothing."

"That's too bad." I lower the spark back to his body and let the fire tearing through his muscle speak for me.

His wailing and groaning only irritates me. I lift the canister and twist the cap off.

"Mmm, smell that?" I ask, inhaling the odor of gasoline. "I hope you love it."

Then I flip the can and let the liquid pour down his body as my men move back.

"Please, don't do this," Ricky—or whatever the fuck his real name is—begs.

But I ignore him. They came for our women. They were going to kill them. For that alone, they will know death more painful than they've ever imagined.

Closing the canister, I drop it on the floor, along with the torch. Removing the matches from my pocket, I light one up, staring at the dancing flame and respecting its power before I toss it onto Ricky's lap.

His screams are trapped within the roaring glory of orange flames, caught in his regret. He should've spoken. He knew. I know he did. But he was afraid of what the Bianchis would do to him or his family if he were to tell us.

I have no sympathy. We all make our own choices in this life, and his was to be a Palermo. *This* is his fate.

He stops screaming as death claims him, and I let the water hose wash away the rest of the blaze and find the charred flesh of the man who once sat there.

Moving to the other sack of shit next to Enzo, I get the torch and hand it to my brother.

"Do you see that?" I ask the man, turning his face sharply with my fist toward where his friend once sat. "That's about to be you if you don't give us the location."

He wails as he glances at the destruction I enacted on good old Ricky.

"Okay. I'll tell you." He gulps. "I'll tell you where the kids are kept. But once I do, promise you'll just shoot me, man. I don't want that to be me. Please!"

"You'd better not fucking lie to us," Enzo warns, grabbing the front of his shirt and balling it roughly before coming face-to-face with him, his teeth gritted and bared. "I'll personally come after every member of your fucking family if you do. Your mother. Your grandmother. Her fucking mother too, if she's alive. We understand each other, pal?"

"I swear, man. I won't bullshit you." He shakes his head violently as Enzo backs away a couple of feet. "They're sick. What they did—what they're doing—is sick. I wanted no part of any of it. I never did. The kids. The club. None of it."

"What club?" I pretend we have yet to hear about it.

His eyes widen, his lip bleeding from the kick Enzo gave him earlier.

"Speak!" I bellow, my punch flying out and hitting him square in his jaw. "You'd better not skip a fucking detail."

It takes him a minute to catch his breath, and he mutters in pain before he opens his mouth again. "They've been taking kids and women for their sick sex club."

My hand unintentionally balls into a fist as my muscles tighten. Every time I hear about that place, it makes me fucking insane.

"I swear I don't know where it is. Only the members with a gold card and a spade on top of it know that info. It has a phone number on it. They call it, and someone comes to pick them up and blindfolds them. If anyone speaks about it, they're automatically killed. I heard about one guy who was offed and tossed into the river when he told his buddy about the place."

Enzo rushes toward the guy, removing a nine-mil from his holster and pointing it at the man's temple. "What else?"

"Please don't shoot me!" he cries. "I'm telling you everything, okay?"

Enzo backs away only a fraction.

"They've got this lawyer. Jo-Joey Russo," he stammers. "He knows where it is. He's a member. He knows everything. I'm telling you. You find him, you find all the answers."

That's what Joelle told Enzo too. But we can't find that motherfucker anywhere.

"You said you knew where they're keeping the kids. Spit it out."

We need to find those children and women. To find Joelle's boy. We need to save them all. Something we couldn't do for our own brother or our parents.

"There's a two-story building downtown where Joey has his office. The whole building is his. The kids and women are in the basement, kept in cages. It's soundproof. Concrete walls and roof." He sucks in a quick exhale. "There's a door that leads to the basement from the building lobby, but there's also a cellar door on the corner in the parking complex."

"You knew all this and never reported it? Not even anonymously?" Disgust settles in my gut as my face turns with a snarl.

"You gotta understand, I didn't want it to come back to me. They would kill my kids. Faro and his brothers will kill anyone who stands in their way. That club brings them a lot of money."

"Who owns it?" I bark.

It sure as hell isn't under the Bianchi name, because we would've found something registered to them besides the legit businesses we destroyed.

"I don't know. I really don't. I'm guessing Joey, but I can't be sure."

Enzo plants the gun between his eyes, and the man rattles with a cry.

"Shit. Can I just call my kids and tell them I love them? Please? Let me say goodbye."

Tears drip from his eyes, and for once, I feel sorry for him.

Enzo looks at me. Both of us are gripped in the past. I know he's thinking what I am: how we never got to say goodbye to our father or our mother. How they were ripped away from us by a ruthless killer. How our brother never got to grow up.

But we can be better than that. We might not spare his life, but we can give him something we never got. I nod once at Enzo, and he returns the gesture.

"Where's your phone?" I ask.

"Left pocket."

I reach inside to retrieve it.

"I've got my wife's number under 'Sweetheart,'" he sniffles, crying harder.

The cell requires a fingerprint, so I place the screen on the index finger of his right hand at his back, and the phone unlocks.

I dial her number, putting the call on speaker. After three rings, she picks up.

"Hey, Anthony," she says with exhaustion as the sound of screaming kids echoes in the background. "I'm making dinner. You gonna be home to eat?"

"I…uh, I don't think so. Not tonight. I've got too much to do.

I'm sorry." His voice breaks in a silent sob as he takes a pause, sucking in a cry.

"What's wrong? You sound weird."

"Nah, all good." He lets out a chuckle. "Just missed you. That's all."

"Okay?" Her response is marked by skepticism. "I miss you too. You sure you're okay? Do I gotta beat anyone up?"

"Nah, baby. I'm all right. I love you."

"I love you too, Ant. You come home soon."

"I'll do my best, babe. Can I say hi to the kids?"

"Yeah. Sure. Georgia! Runo! Get your butts off the damn couch!" she shouts. "Are you two crazy, jumping like that? You trying to break your neck?"

He laughs, tears streaming down his face.

"Your kids are driving me crazy, Ant."

"Why do they have to be my kids when they act like that?" he laughs.

Fucking hell. I shouldn't have let him call them. Killing a man when you hear the voices of his family is torture. But I know I had to give him this for what he gave us.

"Daddy! Hi! I miss you." A little girl's spunkiness comes on the line.

"Hey, princess. I miss you too. Stop giving Mommy a hard time, okay? She works too hard."

"Okay, Daddy. I promise to be good."

"That's my girl." He grins, the love for his kids evident in the glint of his eyes. "I love you so much. You have no idea."

"I do know, Daddy. You always give me the tightest hugs and the best kisses."

His eyelids glide shut as his features twist in pain. "Your brother there?"

"Yep. Here, Runo."

"Hey, Dad." The boy sounds maybe a few years older than his sister.

"Hey, buddy. I want you two to behave, okay? When I'm not there, you're the man of the house, and you've gotta act like it. Help your mom and your sister. Make me proud like you always do."

"Okay. I will. By the way, can we get burgers and fries after my baseball game tomorrow night?"

His tears quietly fall past his face and onto his lap.

"Yeah, sure, kid. Whatever you want. I love you so much. You and your sister have been the best thing me and your mother ever did."

"I love you too, Dad. I'll see you tonight. Georgia wants to draw with me, so I have to go."

"Yeah, uh…okay." He swallows hard, trying to keep his voice level. "Love you all."

"Bye, Dad."

Then the line cuts off and his sobbing comes louder as his head bows.

Enzo lifts his gun, aiming it at Anthony's head, but my brother's eyes are on mine and mine are on his.

"How old are your kids?" I ask.

"Georgia is four and Runo is almost eight." He pulls his face up to me. "They're good kids. Nothing like me. I don't want them caught up in this life. We've done what we can to get them away from it."

I glance at Enzo again, my mind fighting with what we should do and what I want to do. My brother can easily read my mind with just a look.

"You serious?" Enzo implores.

"I don't know." I shrug, completely warped with indecision.

"What?" Anthony's focus darts from me to Enzo. "Please, don't hurt my family!"

"We don't hurt innocent kids." My glare lands at him. "That's what you and your people do."

"I swear I wasn't involved. I'm a piece of shit for not helping them. I know that. But if it meant protecting my own kids, then I had to do what I needed to. I'm sorry if you can't understand that. But if it wasn't for my babies, I'd get those kids out myself. I have my limits."

There was a time when I'd never have considered letting a member of our enemy go, but fuck, I'm getting soft. Maybe it's loving Raquel. Maybe it's remembering the bond we had as a family. But the next thing I know, I'm using the knife in my hand and cutting off the binds at his wrists.

"What are you doin'?" His brows hunch over as his lips flutter in confusion.

"We're giving you a second chance. Don't make us regret it."

"You…you're letting me go?" he cries, falling onto the ground with his palms connected in prayer. "Thank you. Oh, God, thank you."

"You have to get your family and get the hell out of New York. I don't care where you go, but if I were you, I'd run and hope they can't find you."

I have a feeling that if they suspect we let him live, they'll know he talked, and it'll be lights out for everyone in his family.

"I swear. I'll be gone. I'll call my wife now, and we'll leave immediately."

He rises to his feet, wiping at the tears on his cheeks, interlaced with the blood from the cut on his face.

"Thank you for this. You're honorable men. If there's anything you ever need, I will help you."

"We don't need your help," I say, handing him his cell. "Go. Now. Before we change our minds."

He clasps his hands together again. "Thank you."

Then he runs out of there like hell.

Enzo comes to stand beside me. "You think we did the right thing?"

I shrug. "I hope so."

# Twenty-Seven

# RAQUEL

It's much different being inside the walls of a hospital as a visitor. I never realized what my patients' families went through until this very moment. Waiting for news on Chiara's status is the worst kind of torture.

I sit slumped in the brown chair while Dom paces. The grim look on his face speaks to my heart. Dante and Enzo are here too, all of us just hoping she's okay and clinging to the hope that she'll make it.

The last thing I heard from Dom was that she needed immediate surgery. We don't know where the bullet hit or how bad it is. It could have entered her intestines from that angle, or any major organ. It's so hard to say from where I stood and how fast it all happened.

Minutes tick by until almost an hour passes.

I stand up and march over toward the nurse's station, needing an update.

Just as I'm about to ask, a tall woman in blue scrubs walks out of the double doors, scanning the large waiting area. "I'm looking for the family of Chiara Bianchi."

Dominic rushes to her. "Yeah. Here."

His eyes widen as I quickly follow.

She removes her blue cap and grips it in her palm as her attention darts from Dominic to me.

"Ms. Bianchi is in stable condition. The bullet went right through from one side of her stomach to the other, missing her intestines. She's very lucky. She'll make a full recovery in about two weeks and should be able to go home in a couple of days."

I exhale a sigh of relief as my body breaks out in tingles from the anxiety I was holding on to, while Dominic runs a hand down his face.

"Thank you," he whispers, his voice cracking. "How's our baby?"

With that question, the doctor's face contorts with a fragment of a scowl. I know that look. I've worn it myself when I had to deliver awful news. Like the news I know is coming now.

*The baby is gone.*

"I'm so sorry, Mr. Cavaleri, but—"

"Fuck!" he cries with a roar, stomping to the corner of the room.

His brothers quickly follow him.

"I'm really sorry," the doctor tells me. "This is my least favorite part of the job."

"I know." And I do, more than she realizes.

She nods once, her features solemn. "You'll be able to see her once she wakes up."

Then she leaves me.

Chiara looked so happy about the baby, and once she realizes what she's lost—what our family took from her—she'll be in far more pain than I can imagine.

# DANTE

Dom stayed back at the hospital. Not that we'd expect him to come with us while we went after the children and women. Not while Chiara lies in the hospital. Not after they lost their baby.

My stomach curls with rage. *They* did that. The Bianchis. Those fucking bastards kill everything. I can't fucking wait until every one of them is dead. Gone. Where they can no longer destroy innocents ever again.

We'd better find those kids and women at Russo's building, or I'll personally go after Anthony for lying.

It's the weekend, and the timing couldn't be more perfect. There's only a small office building across the street from Joey— the bastard—Russo's office, but they're closed today. So is Russo's law practice. We killed all the cameras in the area too, not wanting to be caught if anything goes south. We can't have our names tainted.

My brother and I step out of our SUV, parking it in the empty lot where Anthony told us we could find the cellar doors. I don't know what's waiting for us on the other side, but there's only one way to find out.

Our men shuffle out of the van parked adjacent to our vehicle, following us to where I can already spot the silver cellar doors. I quickly reach them.

"All right, listen, everyone," I tell them as they circle around me. "Enzo and I will go in first, and you all will follow. Keep the bullets to a minimum. Only if we need to. We don't want to hurt anyone innocent. Got it?"

"Got it, boss," some of them say, while others nod in agreement.

With that, I remove my torch, the same one I used on Ricky, and light the padlock on fire. Silently, it melts away until it's deformed and splits in half, allowing us entry.

Grabbing the doors, I pull them apart, and they creak open. Darkness shrouds the inside, not an indication of life within the walls. I slip the torch into my pocket, removing a mini flashlight and a nine-mil, holding them at my left thigh.

I move down with slow steps, flicking the flashlight on and illuminating our path. One more step, and I'm the first to reach the bottom, not finding anything besides crates of files.

Blue. Green. Yellow. There are bins of every color, but nothing else.

My nostrils flare, teeth clenching. Every inhale and exhale is harsher than the last.

I flip the light over every corner, but I can look as much as I want. There's no one here at all. No one here but us.

"That motherfucker lied! There are no kids here!" I explode with my heart hammering in my ears and practically ripping out of me. "We should've killed him! Why the fuck was I so stupid?!"

My brother wanders further inside, knocking down the files with a roar.

With one more look I'm ready to go, and as I do, my arm hits a crate, and the gun falls to the floor with a loud clank.

"Shit," I mutter, lowering down to retrieve it.

And when I do, I hear a distant clattering sound, like someone banging a pipe or some kind of metal.

"Anyone hear that?"

"Wha—"

Holding out a hand, I stop Enzo. "Shh. There it is again."

"Hello?" I yell out. "Anyone here?"

The clattering is louder now, as though multiple pipes are being pounded on from a distance.

Enzo and I stare at one another as I point a finger to the floor.

"It's coming from down there," I whisper.

"Shit. You think that's where they're hiding them?"

"Only one way to find out."

Enzo grabs a flashlight from his pocket, and the six men with us do the same, all of us looking for some kind of door. We scatter every inch of the place but find nothing.

"Fuck!" I shout, kicking over a crate as my hand squeezes the back of my neck.

"Boss," one of our men calls out.

"What?" I raise my eyes to him as my chest erupts with unruly breaths.

"Look." He points down at my feet, and I follow his movement until—

My eyes flash to a square trap door, camouflaged with the tiles, with a small brown handle protruding.

I crouch down, whistling for Enzo and the other men. Wasting no time, I lift up the door, not giving a shit if there are five, ten, or a hundred of their men down there. I'll take on every one of them singlehandedly. I'll rip apart their bodies, piece by piece, and scatter them across this goddamn place before I let them stop us from saving every single person they've locked away.

This will be over tonight.

I let my flashlight lead the way as I cross down, my footsteps pounding over the metal. The stench of piss attacks my senses, and

I gag, fighting through it.

"What the fuck is that smell?" Enzo mutters behind me.

"What the hell do you think it is? Shut up a minute."

"Hello?" I call out. "Anyone down here?"

I see nothing at first—just a concrete wall in front of me—and my hope is almost zapped away. But as soon as I make a right turn, I see them.

A shudder crawls up my back.

Cages. So many fucking cages.

Women. Children.

Their faces are painted with dirt and blood and their bodies are barely clothed as they crouch down in what look like large dog crates, some with two people at a time. There are over twenty crates here, at least.

"Please," comes a woman's supplicant voice from directly in front of me.

Her blonde hair is caked up around her gaunt face. Her cheekbones are protruding, and her arms are thin enough to crack.

"They need to eat," she begs, her brows cowering as she huddles over her knees. "We're hungry, sir. Just feed the kids. Give them something. Don't just leave them here. They'll die."

"We'll need more men and more vans." My voice climbs to make sure all of my guys hear.

Roger radios for backup.

When my flashlight whips in the direction of the ceiling, I find a single lightbulb there. I yank the string, providing enough light so that we can all turn off our flashlights.

"Hey…" I approach the woman's cage with my hands raised.

She shudders, her entire body waking with violent tremors.

"I'm not going to hurt you." I keep my tone even and soft. "I'm not one of them. I'm not one of the people who put you here.

We're here to save you. To get you all out of here."

Whispers erupt from the other crates.

"Why should we believe you?" she asks, swiping a piece of hair that's stuck to her forehead away. "The only people who come down here are the ones who hurt us. How do we know you're different?"

"I don't know how I can prove it to you, but I hope that as you look into my eyes, you can see I'm telling the truth." I take another few steps closer. "We've been looking for you all. We just wanna help you guys."

She sits up a little higher, looking slightly less terrified. These poor people, living worse than animals.

"The men who are involved in this killed my parents and my baby brother a long time ago, when he was only eight," I explain. "So, believe me, I want to kill them all. Painfully."

Her hazel eyes fall to the floor for a moment before she looks back up.

"I'm sorry," she sighs. "They killed mine too. My parents owed the Palermos a debt they couldn't pay, so they took me when I was sixteen, along with my twelve-year-old sister."

Her voice drops as she peers down onto her knees.

"Is she here too?"

She shakes her head. "She's dead now. Murdered during one of their…um, parties."

*Fuck.*

I can see from her expression that she doesn't want to say more without knowing how much I know.

"The club?" I ask.

She nods again, her eyelids falling half-closed and her face bending in grief.

"Do you know where it is?"

"No. None of us do. When they need us, they clean us up, blindfold us, and take us there. I wouldn't even know how to get there. I'm sorry."

"Don't apologize. We'll find it." I move closer. "So, how about we get you all out of here and somewhere clean?"

"As long as there's a shower." She cracks a small smile.

That's our cue to break open every cell and release the children, mostly young kids under ten, and women no older than twenty.

My pulse thunders louder at seeing those tiny, tattered faces looking so terrified. Alone. I've seen a lot and I've done a lot, but finding them, knowing my brother was the same fucking age…it kills me.

"What's your name?" the woman asks as I help her climb out of the cage.

"I'm Dante. My brother Enzo is the one on my left." I gesture with a tip of my head.

"I'm Serena."

"Nice to meet you, Serena. I'm glad we found you."

Tears shine brightly in her eyes, sloping down her cheeks. "I am too."

"Don't worry about anything. We'll make sure you all have a safe place to stay for as long as you need."

"Thank you," she trembles out.

"I'm sorry for what happened to you."

Her lashes flutter, her lips set to a scowl. "Yeah."

It's a good thing we own hotels. Finding them a place to stay while we figure out what to do with them won't be an issue.

"You think you can help me find someone?" She wipes under her eyes.

"Of course. We'll do our best. Who you looking for?"

"While I've been down here, there were these two women, a

few years older than me, but I haven't seen them for a long time. I just wanted to know if they made it out somehow or if they were—"

The words cut roughly, and she's unable to finish them, but I know what she wants to say. If they were killed.

"What are their names?"

"Uh…" Her gaze darts away, like she still isn't sure she can trust me.

"I promise, I wouldn't hurt your friends."

She licks her cracked lips.

"Elsie and Kayla," she finally answers.

My brows shoot up.

*Oh, damn. Joelle's friends.*

"I'll help you," I reassure her. "We'll find them."

"Thanks."

"We need help over here!" one of our guys shouts.

"I'll be right back," I tell her as I jog all the way to the end to see what's going on, with Enzo following me.

I find two of my men huddled on the floor with a woman who appears just as disheveled and scared as Serena kneeling beside them. All of them have their attention on someone on the floor, who I don't yet see.

As I near, my man, Trevor, turns and shakes his head, and I finally notice the little boy with blond hair coated to his forehead.

"Boss, he's in bad shape. Hardly breathing. We've gotta get him in the van right the fuck now."

"All right. Take him!"

Trevor lifts up the emaciated child, who looks barely seven.

"Do we know his name?" I ask.

"Yeah," the woman says, getting to her feet. "His name is Robby. He's been sick, and they haven't com—"

"What did you say?" Enzo walks up to her as Trevor starts for the stairs. "Did you say Robby?"

"Yeah." She nods. "Why? Do you know him?"

It's then that Enzo stares hard at me.

"Go," I tell him.

He's already on his way, taking the boy from Trevor. But suddenly, he stops short.

"Fuck!"

The way he shouts, I know something bad is coming.

"There's no pulse, Dante. He's not breathing!"

# Playlist

- "And So It Begins" by Klergy
- "The Hunter" by Sam Tinnesz
- "Chosen" by Generdyn feat. SVRCINA
- "Gallows" by Katie Garfield
- "No Mercy" by Unsecret feat. Icetope
- "Six Feet Under" by Oshins feat. Leslie Powell
- "Afraid of the Dark" by EZI
- "Legend" by The Score
- "Him & I" by G-Easy feat. Halsey
- "Devil Inside" by CRMNL
- "Dancing Under Red Skies" by Dermot Kennedy
- "Big Bad Wolf" by Roses & Revolutions
- "Ignite" by Unsecret feat. Neoni
- "Empires" by Ruelle
- "Middle of the Night" by Elley Duhé
- "Trampoline" by Shaed feat. Zayn
- "Landmines" by Bellsaint
- "Take" by Wens
- "Moonrise" by Wildwood
- "Sacrifice" by Black Atlass feat. Jessie Reyez
- "Worship" by Laces
- "Body Say" by Demi Lovato
- "Chlorine" by XYLØ
- "I Can't Get Enough" by Benny Blanco, Selena Gomez, J

Balvin, & Tainy

- "The Devil Is a Gentleman" by Merci Raines
- "Ready For the Mayhem" by Unsecret feat. Alaina Cross
- "Darkside" by Oshins feat. Hael
- "Infinity" by Jaymes Young
- "Devilish" by The Phantoms
- "When I Look at You" by Miley Cyrus
- "No Good" by Unsecret feat. Ruelle
- "Fade to Blue" by Roniit

## *Savage Kings* Series

1.  *Ruthless Savage* (Devlin & Eriu)
2.  *Brutal Savage* (Tynan & Elara - September 6th, 2024)
3.  *Wicked Savage* (Fionn - January 6th, 2025)
4.  *Filthy Savage* (Cillian - May 5th, 2025)

## Standalone

1.  *Shattered Secrets* (Husdon & Hadleigh)

For Lilian, a love of writing began with a love of books. From *Goosebumps* to romance novels with sexy men on the cover, she loved them all. It's no surprise that at the age of eight she started writing poetry and lyrics and hasn't stopped writing since.

She was born in Azerbaijan, and currently resides in Long Island, N.Y. with her husband, three kids, and a dog named Gatorade. Even though she has a law degree, she isn't currently practicing. When she isn't writing or reading, Lilian is baking or cooking up a storm. And once the kids are in bed, there's usually a glass of red in her hand. Can't just survive on coffee alone!

Lilian would love to connect with you!
**Email:** lilanharrisauthor@gmail.com
**Website:** www.lilanharris.com
**Newsletter:** https://bit.ly/LilianHarrisNewsletter
**Signed Paperbacks:** https://bit.ly/LHSignedPB
**Facebook:** www.facebook.com/LilianHarrisBooks
**Reader Group:** www.facebook.com/groups/lilianslovlies
**Instagram:** www.instagram.com/lilianharrisauthor
**TikTok:** www.tiktok.com/@lilianharrisauthor
**Twitter:** www.twitter.com/authorlilian
**Goodreads:** https://bit.ly/LilianHarrisGR
**Amazon:** www.amazon.com/author/lilianharris

www.ingramcontent.com/pod-product-compliance
Lightning Source LLC
Chambersburg PA
CBHW060431310726
48977CB00001B/136